HE ARRIVED AT ␣

R. C. (RUBY CONSTANCE) ASHBY ␣ ␣ ␣ Yorkshire in 1899. She was e␣ ␣ ␣ ␣ ␣ ␣ ␣ ord,
and matriculated at St ␣ ␣ ␣ ␣ ␣ :ed
in 1922 with a degree in ␣.
   Before she began her l␣ ␣n a variety of
jobs, including secretary, tea ␣ ␣viewer, and publisher's reader. Her first novel was ␣26 and she went on to write
a total of eight novels under ti ␣ie R. C. Ashby between 1926 and
1934, the best-known of which are *He Arrived at Dusk* (1933) and *Out Went
the Taper* (1934). All of these books are quite scarce today.
   After her marriage to Samuel Ferguson in 1934, she published exclu-
sively under her married name, and her works underwent a complete
change of style. Her next book, *Lady Rose and Mrs. Memmary* (1937),
a romantic novel, was popular and well-received and was said to be a
favourite of the Queen Mother. She continued to publish a number of
romantic novels but was best known for her series of "Jill" books for children, which have remained almost continuously in print since the first
"Jill" book appeared in 1949.
   Later in life, Ferguson and her husband moved to Jersey, where she
died in 1966.

MARK VALENTINE is the author of several collections of short fiction and
has published biographies of Arthur Machen and Sarban. He is the editor
of *Wormwood*, a journal of the literature of the fantastic, supernatural,
and decadent, and has previously written the introductions to editions
of Walter de la Mare, Robert Louis Stevenson, L. P. Hartley, and others,
and has introduced John Davidson's novel *Earl Lavender* (1895), Claude
Houghton's *This Was Ivor Trent* (1935), and Oliver Onions's *The Hand of
Kornelius Voyt* (1939) for Valancourt Books.

Cover: The cover reproduces the extremely scarce jacket art of the first
British edition published by Hodder and Stoughton in 1933.

HE ARRIVED AT DUSK

by

R. C. ASHBY

With a new introduction by
MARK VALENTINE

𝕶𝖆𝖓𝖘𝖆𝖘 𝕮𝖎𝖙𝖞:
VALANCOURT BOOKS
2013

He Arrived at Dusk by R. C. Ashby (Ruby Ferguson)
First published London: Hodder and Stoughton, 1933
First Valancourt Books edition 2013

Copyright © 1933 by R. C. Ashby (Ruby Ferguson)
Introduction © 2013 by Mark Valentine

The Publisher is grateful to Mark Terry of Facsimile Dust Jackets, LLC
for providing the reproduction of the original dust jacket art used for the
cover of this edition.

Published by Valancourt Books, Kansas City, Missouri
Publisher & Editor: JAMES D. JENKINS
20th Century Series Editor: SIMON STERN, University of Toronto
http://www.valancourtbooks.com

Library of Congress Cataloging-in-Publication Data

Ferguson, Ruby, 1899-1966.
He arrived at dusk / by R.C. Ashby ; with a new introduction
by Mark Valentine. – First Valancourt Books edition.
pages cm
ISBN 978-1-939140-44-9 (alk. paper)
1. Detective and mystery stories, English. I. Title.
PR6011.E715H4 2013
823'.914–dc23
2013009651

Set in Dante MT 11/13.5

INTRODUCTION

THERE are perhaps few parts of England, unlike the other nations of Britain, that are truly lonely and remote: major roads and significant towns are seldom far away. But the least populated is probably the region of great moors in the most northerly part, the land around and beyond the Roman Wall, in furthest Northumberland. It is also one of the coldest areas, with frost that seldom leaves the hills in winter, and biting winds. It has historically been a 'debateable land', with more castles than any other county in England, its borders for centuries contested with Scotland, or between rival clans and families. As late as the 1745 uprising, much of Northumberland declared for Bonnie Prince Charlie and was the scene of skirmish, plotting, torn allegiances and betrayals. Aside from the grand sweep of history, it was also riven by local disputes, cattle-raiding, plundering, and outlawry. Feuds of blood are soaked into the desolate hills and fortified houses of the land. Yet there is also a fine beauty in the long horizons, dawns of pale gold and purple sunsets, and a latent mystery in the brooding hills and haggard stone.

An ideal place, then, for a chilling story of apparitions, uncanny incidents, and dark legends, and the apt choice made by R. C. Ashby for her sixth novel, *He Arrived at Dusk* (1933). And what a shrewd title she chose, prompting questions at once in the curious reader's thoughts. Who arrived? Why at dusk? Where did he arrive? What does he want? What happens after he arrives? We suspect at once some enigma, some cause for trepidation, some pall of gloom.

In this bleak, bare landscape, very evocatively described, there is a remote country house, where one evening the traveller arrives. It is true that this is the beginning of many strange tales: but Ashby makes it her own, depicting the journey from the station, the steadfastness of her chief character, and yet the impact the wilderness of the moors has upon him, with a terse precision. And why do travellers arrive at old houses at dusk? Usually because they must: circumstances compel them.

Her character Mertoun has responded to a commission from, it seems, Colonel Barr, the owner of The Broch, a house named after a nearby ancient stone tower, which looms beyond. The reclusive Colonel is seeking a scholar and specialist to catalogue his antiques and books. Again, the arrival of a young, learned but impoverished figure (often a governess or tutor or companion or secretary) in a lonely house is a device found in many forms of fiction. The ambiguous status of such genteel employees, neither part of the family nor part of the domestic staff, is often a cause of at least social tension.

But that is the least of Mertoun's worries. For he soon finds himself faced with a sequence of eerie incidents, involving the shadow of the broch, the living presence of the Roman past, and tense incidents in the house itself. Moreover, the fate of his employer, a mysterious invalid he does not see, begins to concern him. There are tales of a centurion's ghost, of a lost brother, of a sinister inscribed slab. There are rattlings and apparitions in the house. It is not too long before we begin to suspect something is amiss with these terrifying phenomena: but we are never quite sure, and if ever a book justified the term "page-turner" it is this one. Throughout, Ashby sets out a strong plot, full of uncanny incident, never letting up, and briskly hurtling the reader through the trials and perils of her likeable and credible protagonist.

All the way through, until almost the very end, the reader is kept in suspense about the cause of the strange and haunting events affecting the house. Are ancient evil spirits abroad, or is a macabre, but mortal, villain to blame? *He Arrived at Dusk* is the very epitome of a rattling good yarn, written with great gusto, with strong characters and with that splendidly bleak evocation of the stark and treeless Northern moorlands. Perhaps the only comparable dark tale from the period is Jessie Douglas Kerruish's rather better-known werewolf story *The Undying Monster* (1936). Although there are important differences between them, both books make the fullest use of the classic motifs of the haunted house and ancient curse story, brought up to date in a contemporary setting. This leads to a new sort of dread. Their characters are uneasy not just about what confronts them, but because there really shouldn't be

such hoary old things in their electric-lit world at all: it makes them
feel quaint. They are among the first to reflect with irony upon
the anachronism of ghosts and portents in this new age. There is a
double intrusion in play: not only the traditional incursion of the
unearthly into the human sphere, but an assault on the materialist
assumptions of a more sceptical and sophisticated society.

R.C. Ashby (the initials stood for Ruby Constance), was the
maiden name of a writer who later became better known under
her married name of Ruby Ferguson (1899-1966). As Ashby, she
published eight novels, some with strong supernatural implications, and most making use of family legends or folklore. The
first, *The Moorland Man*, was published in 1926, and the last,
Out Went the Taper, in 1934. She was clearly determined to be a
professional writer, alive to the demands of the market, with an over-
brimming imagination, and bringing a great zest to the telling of
her tales. Her trademark, somewhat akin to some of the crime-and-
witchery novels of Gladys Mitchell, was a blending of Gothic elements (lonely houses, stormy weather, legends, pagan remains)
with the antics and inventive vigour of modern young men and
women. *Death on Tiptoe* (1931), for example, is a deft, clever tale,
about what goes wrong when the lively new owners play hide and
seek in an old castle. There's something Wodehousian about these
bright young things, reckless and bold in their between-the-wars
ways, who scamper around and shout "Bungho" at each other, and
there's a touch of the world of Lord Peter Wimsey too.

He Arrived at Dusk was among her most successful thrillers.
Announced in February 1933, it went rapidly into a second edition the following month, and was for a while the talk of the book
papers, heralded (rather too boldly) as "the return of the ghost
story". The influential critic E.B. Osborn of the *Morning Post* was
particularly enthusiastic. "In reading it I had several splendid shud-
ders. The descriptions of scenery are admirable – you live in the
real Northumberland from beginning to end. The characterisa-
tion is also excellent. . . ." He praised also "the deepening sense of
evil in the atmosphere," and concluded: "Miss Ashby's mysteries
have always intrigued me, but her latest story transcends all her
previous successes and surely entitles her to the chieftainship of

the Clan Macabre. It is a piece of living literature, not merely an evening's entertainment." Nor was he alone. The *Saturday Review*, in a brief notice, called it "a well nigh perfect admixture of eerie horror, romance and good detecting."

But yet the book more or less vanished from view from the Forties onwards. It is only in recent years that there has been a renewal of interest in it. One keen champion is J. F. Norris, who in *Mystery File* acclaimed *He Arrived at Dusk* as: "Truly a little masterpiece of a book. Reminiscent of Christie at the height of her powers in its brilliant use of misdirection. . . . Really a classic of its kind. One of the best blending of [the] supernatural and detective novel genres written in the 1930s. Interestingly, this pre-dates Du Maurier's *Rebecca* by several years and yet has quite a bit of similarity [to] that book's use of a frightened narrator whose interpretation of events may or may not always be perfect." *He Arrived at Dusk* has become one of those titles that savants recommend avidly to each other, being careful not to give too much away. It has become very hard to find in the original edition.

Her last thriller, probably second only to *He Arrived at Dusk* for strength of incident and relentless pace, was *Out Went the Taper* (1934). It is possible that she was hoping for Hollywood interest in her work, because here the characters seem to be selected with an eye to the silver screen, including a fairly implausible young American, a Rhodes scholar, visiting friends in a Welsh mansion. E. F. Bleiler, in his *Guide to Supernatural Fiction* (1983) was appreciative, praising "a tangled complex of crime and the supernatural" which includes visionary experience and poltergeist activity, and concluding "the supernaturalism is strong . . . a good mystery".

After her marriage to Samuel Ferguson in 1934, Ashby used his surname for her books. Her first book under her married name was *Lady Rose and Mrs. Memmary* (1937), a complete change of style from her thrillers. This is a romantic novel described in a *Guardian* review of a recent reprint as "a curious, affecting confection of high Scots romance and social realism", but which "does not deny the inequalities of Victorian mores or the shattering of illusions that the 20th century will bring." The book was said to be a favourite of the then Queen consort (later Queen Mother), Elizabeth Bowes-Lyon, herself the daughter of a Scottish estate such as that depicted in the book. But Ruby Ferguson later won huge popularity as the author of the "Jill" series of pony club books for girls, which began in 1949 and concluded in 1962. They were composed for the delight of her step-grandchildren (her husband had sons from an earlier marriage). She also wrote over a dozen other books under this name.

For a while, even the basic details of her life were somewhat misty, and she rather mischievously could also be creative about some of them. But pioneering and careful work by Alison Haymonds has established a more reliable picture. She has established that "Ruby Constance Annie Ashby was born at home in Birchcliffe Road, Hebden Bridge, Yorkshire, on July 28, 1899. Her father David Ashby was a Wesleyan Minister and her mother was Ann Elizabeth, formerly Spencer. She was educated at the Girls' Grammar School, Bradford, and matriculated at St Hilda's, [Oxford] in 1919 when her father was a minister in Farnworth, near Bolton. Ruby gained a third class in English Language and Literature in June 1922." Ruby's grand-daughter recalls that she knew she ought to have got a better degree, but spent too much time playing bridge.

. Before she began her writing career, R.C. Ashby trained as a secretary and seems to have held a number of jobs in that field: she was apparently also variously a teacher, journalist, book reviewer and publisher's reader. The impression we get is of a busy, versatile and determined young woman, taking any work that would pay, but with a definite preference for those with some sort of literary element.

However, as Alison Haymonds notes, "Ruby's marriage transformed her life. The independent working woman became the wife of a wealthy, autocratic man, 13 years her senior, who was a considerable figure both in the business and Methodist worlds." Her husband was "a remarkable, self-made man, an electrical engineer who became one of the great Methodist philanthropists." The couple lived in a large house in Wilmslow, Cheshire, on the outer edges of Manchester. Here, Ashby listed her recreations as "travel, country life, hotel keeping"; and her interests as "English

History & Literature, Country Home Management". The last may have meant her professional work on behalf of her husband, but could also be a teasing reference to the country houses in her novels whose spectral "attractions" require robust management. The couple later moved to the Channel Island of Jersey, where Haymonds notes that she "continued to write, play the piano, paint, play bridge, write for the local amateur dramatic society . . . and enjoy getting involved in her husband's hotels."

Ruby Ferguson's creative autobiography of growing up, *Children at the Shop* (1967), seems in fact to have included much that was a romantic recasting of her actual life, inventing different backgrounds for her parents, and adding siblings that do not seem to have existed in reality. It was a last flourish of her fictional genius and exuberance of imagination. She died of cancer on November 11, 1966, and her grave is at St Brelade's on Jersey.

It is perhaps possible to see something of her character in Miss Goff, the spirited, resourceful, determined and independent young woman who devotes herself to looking after Colonel Barr in *He Arrived at Dusk*, defying all the terrors and travails of the house. The author's grand-daughter Sarah Ferguson has explained that "she was a delightful down to earth Yorkshire woman with a fabulous imagination and a keen sense of humour" and such qualities are strongly in evidence in all her early books. Powerful and inventive, lively and richly descriptive, with high ingenuity and a strong sense of drama, they are certainly ready for a new readership.

MARK VALENTINE

April 25, 2013

HE ARRIVED AT DUSK

CONTENTS

PART I

MERTOUN'S STORY

ENTR'ACTE

AMONG those who took part as eye-witnesses or more intimately as actors in the strange affair which came to light in Northumberland in the spring of 1931, that dramatic—I was going to say melodramatic—business was tersely spoken of afterwards as The Gladius Case.

The label has a cut-and-dried sound, scarcely appropriate to the title-page of this manuscript in which is written down for the first time an edited account of what actually occurred. "The Gladius Case" admits of no deviation from concrete fact; *He Arrived at Dusk*, I venture to suggest, will allow some amplification of detail and include the more human aspects of what was actually a grimly practical business. Hence the inclusion of Mr. Mertoun's romance which properly had very little to do with the main theme, and also his irritating insistence upon the accompanying state of the weather, the purpose of which is to prove that at least a few rays of sunlight did fall upon that winter-blackened northern heath.

The story as here presented is in three parts; three stories in one, three points of view; in fact, murder through the eyes of three men of widely differing mentality and outlook.

With regard to the construction: in accordance with the excellent ruling of Father Ronald Knox for a story of this *genre*, the action has taken place before the narration begins, and the opening chapter which introduces you to a London Club on a February evening in 1931 is entitled Entr'acte for the foregoing reason.

In the smoke-room of the National Progress Club, though the

noise of voices boomed like the surge of an inland sea, a super-human voice dominated all, a voice unhurried, supreme, slightly distorted; the voice of the radio.

It was not apparent that anyone was attending to that strident message. There was a certain pathos, thought one man whose name was Ahrman, in the unregarded voice so patiently telling its interminable tale. What was it all about, anyway? And who cared one whit, in any case? The B.B.C. had decided that here was something good for the nation to know, and about ninety-nine per cent of the nation thought otherwise.

"Turn it off!" muttered Ahrman's companion, suddenly savage; "Stop the thing, man. It's too much."

Ahrman looked round. Within a few feet of the radio three elderly members were sitting with rapt faces, drinking it in. Interference would be unwarranted.

"Sorry, Mertoun. Those old fellows. . . ."

Ahrman listened with pained curiosity.

". . . On May 14th we began our excavations at the broch of Durnigh. A single doorway four feet high admitted us to a circular court thirty feet in diameter. The dry-built walls, rising to a height of forty feet, shut out the morning sun. In the spot of which I have previously spoken, at a depth of only four feet, we discovered a hoard of relics; ornaments, bracelets, and pins, of brass, silver, jet, and lignite. It was a week later before the underground chamber was discovered, revealing the weapons, the querns, the bowls and lamps of serpentine and marble. Our greatest surprise was yet to follow . . ."

And so was the greatest surprise of the evening for the occupants of the smoke-room; for though the Club, being a political one, had a large and democratic membership, it was not usual to see a gentleman seize a tall glass of lager from someone else's table and fling it at the loud-speaker with such force and precision that splintered fragments cascaded in all directions, and streams of liquid dripped from the fretwork face of the instrument.

That was what Mertoun did. Then he turned on his heel and bolted through the swing-doors to the terrace.

Ahrman followed unobtrusively. His friend was standing, back to the River Thames, with one tight fist at his forehead, staring up at the lighted windows and rococo balconies of the Club.

"Nerves!" thought Ahrman. "These business men. Is he ruined?"

He crossed over to the parapet, eyed the dark river through a screen of trees wintry-bare, and approved the chain of lights spangling the rim of the Embankment.

Mertoun spun round and released his pent-up breath.

The sky above was black, and peppered with silver stars.

"The noise . . ." muttered Ahrman, vaguely sympathetic. "It's better here."

"Yes." Mertoun leaned on the parapet and dislodged a small piece of mortar which his fingers seized eagerly. "You see," he went on, "I've been looking at one of those things . . . from my bedroom window for weeks. Three weeks. There it was; that round, dark Thing, humped on the mound. Half the time there was rain, snow, sleet. I got to hate it. As that fellow said, it seemed to kill the morning sun."

"Quite!" said Ahrman. It seemed to him a case for a doctor. Absolute quiet, and firm yet kindly hands.

"I want you to tell me what to do," said Mertoun suddenly; "I'm—I'm haunted."

This to the other man seemed more normal. Many men were haunted. Remorse, maybe; or regret; or just a sharp, unhappy memory. He had to say something since Mertoun was so silent, and he said by way of encouraging and at the same time lightening the burden of the conversation: "I conclude you don't mean me to take that literally?"

"Why, yes!" Mertoun stared, without smiling. "Yes. I mean that." He turned sideways to the parapet and added: "Three weeks ago I wouldn't have believed it either. And yet——" He stopped and fumbled for cigarette and match-box, waiting with uplifted flame as though listening for sounds from the river. His hand was not unsteady. "What was that? A motor-launch, I think . . . I suppose you'll admit, Ahrman—as I was once prepared to admit with reservations—that bricks and mortar, wood and stone, can hold a certain psychic quality, derived from association with human personality. Conversely, that human personality, greatly enhanced by temporary emotion, can pass on a living and indestructible quality to surrounding objects, the influence of which may be apparent in various ways. It's a theory which doesn't affect the average man, because so far from his probable experience. I never gave it serious thought, and I can't say that I was ever sensitive to atmosphere . . . at least, not to that degree, until——" He blew out the creeping flame of the match.

"There's something in it," admitted Ahrman; "though I fancy it's apt to be greatly exaggerated."

He was sorry he had spoken, Mertoun took him up so eagerly.

"You grant so much? That makes it easier. Now can you go further and admit the survival of personality, apart from its impress on surrounding objects?"

"I don't know what you're getting at!" said Ahrman bluntly.

"Do you believe," persisted his friend, "that human personality is blotted out by death; or that it is capable of survival, on earth, among the surroundings of its lifetime? This is important to me."

"Possibly." Truth to tell, Ahrman was uninterested.

"Then do you believe," Mertoun pursued, "that a human personality of unusual power and vitality, belonging to a body cut off in its prime by death, could survive for years, or for centuries, and even manifest itself in unmistakable form to practical men who were incapable of being deluded?"

"No," said Ahrman.

"Any grounds?"

"Yes. Ghosts. Poppycock."

"In other words, 'We're in twentieth-century London, my dear young friend, and we don't believe in anything that hasn't got the price marked on it in plain figures.'"

"I'm sorry," his friend conceded; "but I'm a practical man. My profession demands it."

"So am I," said Mertoun, somewhat nettled. "Do you think I'm a spook-hunter?"

"Then why——"

Mertoun laughed curtly. He poised his little pebble of mortar and aimed at the shining coil of the river. The pebble fell short, and its fall was noiseless. A tram went clanging below, lighted and empty, and surprisingly dived into a subway like a salamander going to earth.

"I know what I've seen," said Mertoun.

"What have you seen?"

"Murder."

"Oh!"

"I thought that would jolt you."

"How long ago was this?"

"About five days."

"And where?"

"A few—comparatively few—miles from where we stand."

"What happened?"

"There was an inquest, and a perfectly sane, hard-headed coroner's jury brought in a verdict of—well, presumably suicide, though the poor fellow was stabbed in the back and everybody for miles around knew who'd done it. I saw the murderer."

"But that's a travesty of justice! I——"

"You can't ask a magistrate for a warrant against a man who died sixteen hundred years ago."

"Who died sixteen hundred years ago?"

"The murderer."

"Oh, come off it, laddie! You've had one too many."

"That's the easiest explanation," Mertoun said, frankly serious, and twisting the butt of his bitten cigarette; "I wish it were true. You say you'll believe that walls have ears, and voices too. That walls can speak and make you shiver to their message; that a house can hold an atmosphere of gloomy warning which nothing can remove or explain away. But it's too much to accept that unseen figure, the man himself without the flesh and trappings of his body—until one day you see him, as I did, in a whorl of light, and you know you'll never blot out that sight from your memory until your dying day. It was the same night that they found his victim . . . not the first."

"You don't mean to say that the creature had committed murder before?"

"And may again."

"Mertoun! Mertoun!"

"Thanks!" said Mertoun dryly; "I recognize the tone. My nurse used to check my flights of imagination in the same way." He turned his back on the river and made a gesture which included all the roofs of London. "In the face of all *that* it seems fantastic. I can hardly believe that I'm not suffering from the effects of a bad dream, but suffering I am. I couldn't be mistaken in my own mental reactions. And yet, London! My own office, crowded and undusted, as I left it three weeks before. And to-night the Club, a roomful of materially-minded dodderers betting on the prospects of a General Election before the autumn. It makes it all . . . so unreal."

"I grant you," said Ahrman, "that a psychic experience—presuming that you have had a psychic experience, which I very much doubt—would be apt to wilt in the smoke-room of a London club. These things usually require a lonely house and several leagues of moorland."

"Ah!" Mertoun frowned. "If you want me to tell you, you're making it impossibly difficult."

"Not intentionally," said Ahrman promptly. "I hope you are going to tell me the tale, and I shan't interrupt, however improbable it seems. Why did you try to smash the wireless?"

Mertoun shrugged his shoulders. "Coincidence. A fellow was describing the excavation of a circular castle, built by the Celtic tribes of Britain as a defence against the Romans. There are scores of them in Scotland, and one at least in northern England. I've stared at it every morning for three weeks, and every night the great black beast was still there. It . . . was a symbol."

"Was it really?" said Ahrman, not without irony. "And how long will this story take?"

"All the evening, I'm afraid. It may even be a little incoherent. I haven't tried before to put it into words."

Ahrman nodded. "We'll go inside. There's a little writing-room with a good fire. With luck, no one will be using it now."

"A LONELY house, you said, and a few leagues of moorland," began Mertoun. "That stung me. Because they're a condition that I shall have to induce you to accept. But the people involved were no ignorant rustics, but intelligent modern humans like myself, Charlie Barr, Miss Goff, Doctor Ingram. I needn't apologize for them. However, to begin from three weeks ago last Tuesday, which was the very day. In the morning I had a letter at my office asking me if I'd go up and value the contents of a house somewhere in Northumberland; furniture, pictures, books, that kind of thing. The writer, a Colonel Barr, had had my name recommended by an acquaintance who had done business with me; in fact, it was a client—an artist—for whom I'd furnished a period room. Business was bad just then and Barr's offer was attractive. Of course I accepted by return of post, packed a bag, and departed next morning from King's Cross. I had better say here and now that there were two unusual points about the letter, though at the time I didn't give them a minute's thought. One doesn't look for mysteries in normal business life. The letter was dated December 11 and written in a man's hand. I didn't receive it until January 17, and the envelope was directed in an entirely different, and apparently feminine hand.

Very well then. I arrived after dark at an appalling little station called Heaviburgh—empty milkcans and peeling advertisements of cocoa—and asked if there was a car from The Broch to meet me. There wasn't a car, but one of the two porters said he was going off duty in half an hour and would drive me over. The distance was seven miles, and it would be five shillings. The car was a fairly new Ford with an all-weather hood. It was raining and there was a swirling wind, so the shower-bath effect was constant. Also it was extremely dark and the roads were bad, so we never exceeded twelve miles an hour. Once there was a positive cloud-burst and the rain came at us like a wall of water. We had to stop for at least ten minutes. After that it grew a little lighter, and I could see scudding clouds and a greenish-white crescent moon lying on its back. The road was like a river. It ran between dry-stone walls, and beyond the walls were ragged fields, and beyond the fields rough hills, very black and bristling against the sky. It wasn't an attractive landscape, but I was interested because it was new country to me. I hadn't been in that part of England before.

My driver was a dour chappie, a Scot from Glasgow, with very little to say—until we suddenly punctured, when he became voluble. Of course I got out and helped him to change the wheel and by the time we were both soaked to the skin we had become quite brotherly. He told me he had been at Heaviburgh six years and his only pleasure in life was reading about Clydeside politics in the Glasgow paper which his sister sent him.

Off we went again, and soon we topped a rise and came out on a stretch of moorland; just miles of dead heather, black and rolling like a frozen sea. The desolation of it got me by the throat in the most curious way; it had the stark, bleak fascination of a Doré infernal landscape, and I can't imagine any worse punishment for sin than to be compelled to wander alone at night over such a wilderness.

However, nothing was wandering there, not even a sheep, and I was glad when we left it and found ourselves in broken country, hilly and cold, with very few and stunted trees. That is a practically treeless region. I was some time before I discovered what I missed in the landscape. Trees.

'You're from London?' my friend the porter asked me.

I can't attempt to reproduce his dialect, particularly as the local one was superimposed upon his Glasgow Scots, but it was not unmusical and every sentence ended on a high note.

I told him I was from London, and he then asked me if I were a doctor and if Colonel Barr were worse.

'I didn't know that Colonel Barr was ill,' I confessed; and he said yes, the Colonel had been ill for some time, in fact ever since his brother's accident; and there was a nurse in attendance, though some people said she was only the housekeeper.

This was just gossip and not very exciting, but I asked idly whether the brother's accident were serious, and he stared and said, 'Why, of course. He was killed. He fell over the cliffs.'

I mention that because it was the first I had heard of any cliffs. I hadn't realized that the house I was going to was practically on the coast, half a mile from the sea. Driving there in the dark I knew nothing of it; and it wasn't until the middle of my first night that the long moaning surge woke me and I jumped out of bed thinking I was dreaming, and saw across the sky that creeping shaft of weird luminosity, the beam from the lighthouse. It was a coast of rocks and turbulent seas. There was barely harbour for a fishing smack, much less a trawler.

But where was I? . . . Oh, yes, we came to the house in the dark and the pouring rain; and there it was, quite a large house with an east wing like a pointing finger, rather Gothic and stony-looking, and in keeping with its surroundings.

A manservant let me in and took my bags. Yes, they were expecting me; would I come upstairs. There was a stone hall with a lot of pewter and benches of rough-hewn oak that looked about seven hundred years old.

My bedroom was quite comfortable, though there wasn't a fire. Victorian, with a pompous-looking bed, scarlet rep curtains, a good carpet, skin rugs, and a winged chair. On the end of the mantelpiece was an anachronism, a very modern ash-tray in the form of a Bonzo dog holding a plate in its mouth. It made me grin and I was glad to see that there were no rules against smoking in my bedroom.

A jug of hot water came up in the hands of a particularly rustic young housemaid, and then a great silence descended and I was left to my own devices. It was eight o'clock and I was frightfully hungry. Nobody had suggested tea or told me the time of dinner or supper—if any. I wondered if I were expected to go quietly to bed. However at eight-thirty a cracked gong sounded and I found my way down.

There was supper laid for two in a rather dismal dining-room. The northern cold was beginning to get into my bones. I waited, and presently the retainer appeared and suggested that I should begin, as Mr. Barr had not returned yet. So I had my supper, which meant tackling a huge meat-pie, steaming hot and of positively medieval proportions, very roughly served in an earthenware dish, and associated with strong coffee and Stilton cheese. Then I sat back, lit a pipe, and the retainer left me.

The next bit is going to be difficult. I know I shall describe it crudely, and I'm afraid you'll completely miss the point. I felt something. There was a coldness that went from the tips of my fingers and shivered into my shoulders—that began it—and then, as though something had struck me, all the nerves of my brain gave a tortured leap and my hand flew up to my throat. I swallowed hard, twice, and it was all over. It lasted thirty seconds, and I never felt anything like it either before or after. It was like an electric shock from an unearthly battery. A hideous feeling.

In a few minutes I was quite normal again, but I felt restless and rather gloomy. I lit my dead pipe, and looked about me. If this were one of the rooms I had to value, the prospect for the owner wasn't remarkable. The fireplace was spurious Adam; there was a fairly good dresser worth perhaps twenty pounds; but the rest of the furniture was rough, farmhouse stuff, of no value apart from its obvious antiquity, and that value of course would be fluctuating. I mean, I was prepared to swear that the bench along the far side of the table from where I sat was no later than thirteenth century, and some people might be prepared to pay a good price for it if it came into the market, but in these days the demand is for named period furniture and not for isolated fragments, the flotsam of the Middle Ages.

And suddenly the most ridiculous idea came into my mind . . . I wonder if this place is haunted? I grinned rather, because it was such a schoolboy surmise; and then I stopped grinning and wondered why it was I was feeling so hideously uncomfortable, ill at ease. I know what you're going to say. That it was the pie, the Stilton, and the coffee on top of a particularly cold and miserable journey. I offered myself that explanation too.

I strolled over to the window and pulled aside the blind, one of those heavy green linen ones with a roller at the bottom. There wasn't much to see in the darkness and rain; only dripping bushes and the distant shoulder of a humpy hill, crowned with a heap of rocks. And beside the rocks was something that looked like a watch-tower. I remember thinking that I should hate to have to live long in that house or that neighbourhood. Two days, I guessed, would see my business through and myself back in London with an agreeable fee to compensate me. I don't mean to sound mercenary, but jobs and money do count in these days.

I stood against the window until I shivered. A cold wind was stealing through the chinks and it had a salty flavour I couldn't account for, not knowing how near I was to the sea. And yet that salty sniff made me think of the sea, and I thought of the cold seas of Eternity and, unaccountably, of the man who had fallen from the cliffs to his death. Morbid of me. I'm not like that as a rule.

It was half-past nine now, and I thought it was time that my client or some representative of his put in an appearance. If Colonel Barr were ill there was presumably another member of the family prepared to do business with me.

Presently I heard a door slam far away; then footsteps, and in came a man of my own age, and very glad I was to see him. He was a good-looking fellow, dark, a bit scholarly, and spoke with a slight American accent. It was so slight that it wasn't until he told me he had lived in the States that I placed his accent at all. However, he came in quite calmly, nodded to me, asked me if I'd had supper, and sat down himself to the cold remains.

'How long is it going to take you to do your job?' he asked conversationally.

'Probably about two days,' I said. 'Are you Colonel Barr?'

Of course I knew he wasn't, only nobody had told me anything since I entered that house, and I wasn't supposed to know.

'No, no,' he said brightly; 'I'm Charlie Barr. My uncle's ill. Been ill for a long time. I don't really know why he sent for you. I suppose you know what you have to do?'

I told him that of course I had the general idea, but I should like more definite instructions.

'Hasn't the nurse told you?' he asked, eating pie.

'I haven't seen any nurse,' I said; 'I haven't seen anyone except a man and a maidservant.'

He nodded. 'Oh, she'll be seeing you. She's probably busy. If I were you I should be inspecting the library. There are pictures and books.'

'Thanks,' I said; 'I may as well begin.'

I stood, looking awkward.

'Oh, don't you know the way?' he cried. 'I'm sorry. I'll show you.'

He jumped up and led the way down a passage to a long and lofty room, and began snapping on lights. Of course the house had its own electric plant.

'M'Coul!' he shouted. 'Come along here and put a fire in the library for Mr. ——'

'Mertoun,' I supplied.

He nodded. 'All right. I don't understand your requirements, but you can have a look around here. If you want paper and pens there are plenty on the writing-table.'

He smiled, and left me to it; and presently the man arrived with a shovelful of burning coals which he heaped into the empty grate and added logs. The room was swirling in smoke by now, but when it cleared I saw shelves from floor to ceiling, and—literally—thousands of books. Thousands of books, not only on the shelves but piled in great heaps on the floor.

'Ah!' I thought. 'A virgin gold-mine. Here's the wealth of the house. Unique editions.'

I wandered across and picked out a volume at random. It was Volume I of the *Transactions of the Society of Antiquaries of Scotland*. Next to it was a German book on criminology, called, I believe, *Grundzüge der Kriminal-Psychologie*. Next to that was a cheap modern edition of the works of Alexander Pope; next again, a handbook on Botany; then *The Elements of Political Economy*—I forget the author—published in Edinburgh, 1887. Then came, if I remember rightly, a reprint of Gordon's *Itinerarium Septentrionale*, originally published in 1720; and an Italian book about gypsies called *Gli Zingari*, back cover missing.

Believe me, in twenty minutes I was a sadder and a wiser man. That first random selection of mine was representative of the whole collection; there was no order, no coherence, no value; just thousands of miscellaneous volumes dumped together in one place, the possessions of a man, it was easy to see, who had never been able to pass a second-hand bookstall without filling his pockets with any rubbish that momentarily caught his fancy. And when read the volumes were flung upon a shelf or on the floor, without arrangement or plan. There could not have been in England such an appalling medley. I made a mental note; twenty thousand volumes at a penny each; roughly, eighty pounds. And I wondered whether a dealer would give ten pounds for the lot.

I spent at least two hours in the library over that first inspection, and I guessed that if there had been any treasures I should have unearthed one or two of them. But by then I was dog-tired. I switched off the lights and left the library. Only one light was burning, on the stairs. Mr. Barr and the servants had gone unceremoniously to bed. However, that didn't worry me, and I soon found my room and turned in myself.

I had a wretched night, tossing in those vague, unpleasant dreams whose horror you can't put a name to; and in the middle of the night the surging tide woke me and I saw the ocean horizon and the lighthouse.

I was glad when morning came, though it was still raining and the air was bitter. From my window, which evidently looked the same way as the dining-room, I saw the humpy hill and the watchtower I had noticed the night before. It was a circular tower and seemed to be roofless. It looked like a squat beast, crouching to eye the house.

I cut myself in shaving, said a few words, and went down to breakfast."

II

"Charlie was already at breakfast, and there were newspapers. He greeted me quite cheerfully with a smile. There was something likeable about the man when he smiled. His smile had an almost feminine charm; not that he was in the least effeminate. I expect I shall give you a host of wrong impressions before I finish this story.

Well, he smiled, and pushed across a dish of very well-cooked fish. 'Hope you didn't make a night of it,' he said.

I assured him that I was in bed before midnight.

'Sleep well?'

'No,' I said frankly.

I thought he raised his eyebrows a shade too quickly, but he casually picked up a newspaper, looked over the headlines, snapped his fingers, and put it down.

'That watch-tower we can see from here,' I said. 'What is it? I can see it from my room too.'

'Watch-tower?' He looked blank. 'Oh—you mean the broch? Well, that's just the broch, you know, that the house takes its name from.'

'Oh, yes?'

'Of course,'—he gave a short laugh—'the broch was here before the house.'

'What's it for?' I asked.

'Oh, it's prehistoric. At least seventeen hundred years old. It was the fortress of some old Celtic tribe.'

'Is there anything to see?' I asked.

'*Au contraire.* The thing looks infinitely better at a distance,' he replied. 'It's really a mass of crumbling masonry and not too safe. I don't care about that kind of thing—ruins, I mean.'

'Aren't there Roman antiquities here?' I asked casually, reviving some ancient memory.

He hesitated a fraction of a second, and then answered:

'Farther south. You mean the Roman Wall. It's quite worth seeing, if you ever happen to go that way. Hexham's an interesting place—though I expect you're really longing to get back to London. I don't blame you. There's nothing here.'

'One gets attached to one's own county,' I suggested.

He stared at me. 'Oh, I'm not a native; I've only lived here for twelve months. As a matter of fact, I was brought up in the United States. I'm almost an American; not quite, thank Heaven. I shall settle in England now. And if anything happens to my uncle— which I devoutly hope it will not—I shall have this place.'

'How old is the house?' I asked.

'It was built in 1817,' he said. 'As a family we're rather attached to it. It was my father's old home, and Americans think a lot of that kind of thing. You see, I can't help being rather American in my outlook.'

He read his newspaper for a few minutes, and then asked: 'What did you think of the books?'

I thought it best to be frank, and answered: 'I'm afraid they're not of any marketable value. I was rather disappointed. Did you think they were valuable?'

'Why, no!' he exclaimed at once. 'Personally I don't think there's anything in the house of much value. It was only a fad of my uncle's to have you come. You have to humour ill people, and Nurse said he'd got this idea on his mind, so I let her send for you. I let her do pretty well what she likes. I have to.' He smiled again, engagingly.

Of course, that explained the feminine hand on the envelope, and a very simple explanation it was. I was in the mood for accepting simple explanations just then. It was different later. I didn't say anything about the letter having been dated more than a month previously.

'I suppose I have access to the various parts of the house?' I said.

'Go where you like,' he replied promptly. 'Nurse will see to it that you don't disturb my uncle. Nobody's allowed to see him; not even I.'

I put on the appropriate face of condolence, and asked if Colonel Barr were seriously ill.

Charlie shrugged his shoulders. 'I'm afraid he's in a critical condition, poor old fellow. Not so old, either; he isn't seventy, and I should have said quite strong. It came on him suddenly, after . . . but, look here, I'll have to go. Can you manage? I suppose you'll finish to-day?'

'Probably,' I said.

'Don't think I'm hurrying you!' he said, with a quick smile. 'I'm really quite glad of your company; but there's a local farmer going to Heaviburgh with his car to-morrow morning, and if you're ready he can take you along. Otherwise the station car has to fetch you, and it can't be relied upon to turn up.'

'I shall probably be ready to leave in the morning,' I told
him.

'It's a miserable day,' he said. 'I shall spend the day in my study,
and they'll bring me a tray at lunch-time. You don't mind lunching
alone? Good. I'm working pretty hard.'

'Studying?' I said.

'Well, writing. I'm writing a book.' He said it in the shamed
way that writers always say it, as though it were a form of vice like
secret drugging.

'A novel?' I asked.

He shook his head. 'No. It's just a handbook on psychology.
Quite elementary, but there's a big demand for it in the States. It's
an arrangement I have with a publisher.'

'You must be an expert?' I suggested.

He laughed outright. 'Oh no. But I've lectured in New York
on the simple principles of mind-control. People there think it
miraculous. It's nothing but common sense. Psychology is one
of New York's steady crazes, especially among women. American
women are nearly all unhappily married and they've got to have an
outlet for their neuroses.'

It was my turn to laugh. 'You're no Yankee,' I said. 'You've got a
sense of humour.' It struck me that his handsome looks had probably done the New York women as much good as his psychology;
in the same way that a good-looking doctor can cure any feminine
patient on sight.

'Oh, but I'm quite serious in my intentions,' he said. 'I can't help
the kind of fools who come and listen to me.'

I rather liked him by now, and I was enjoying myself better
than on the previous evening. Everything was perfectly normal,
and I'd practically forgotten those half-impressions that had disturbed me. I gave myself a quarter of an hour to read the *Daily
Mail*, and then went up to my room to get pencil and notebook. I
don't know whether I opened the door too suddenly, but the next
minute there was a crash, and there stood the young housemaid in
the ruins of the water-jug.

She gave a slight scream. 'Oh, mercy!' she said; 'I thought you
was him.'

'Sorry,' I said. 'You'd better mop that water up with a towel or it'll soak through.'

She grabbed my towel from the rail. 'I'm all of a tremble,' she said. 'Mrs. M'Coul didn't ought to have told me.'

She began to scrub the carpet, and then replaced the dirty towel innocently upon the rail.

'Did you sleep all right? Bed comfortable?' she asked.

'Quite,' I said.

'We don't get many visitors,' she went on; 'it's nice to have somebody new to do for. How long are you stopping?'

Not being accustomed to the affable familiarity of north-country servants I murmured some sort of non-committal reply, and she said that she hoped it would stop raining for me. Clumsily preparing to depart, she said suddenly: 'I hates it. The nasty thing. Ought to pull it down, they did.'

I gave surprised attention and saw that she was looking straight out of the window at the broch, or watch-tower, or whatever you like to call the Celtic fortress.

'Oh, that!' I said.

'Uh-huh,' she grunted fiercely. 'It's unlucky.' And with that she clattered away.

It was just as I thought. The tower was popularly supposed to be haunted, just like every other unusual or empty building in a credulous countryside. Superstitious country people must have something to talk about. I laughed, and went downstairs with my notebook.

I spent that morning round about the house, and incidentally discovered the only two things in it that were of any importance to me. One of those I couldn't quite believe in, though I gave my client the benefit of the doubt. They were both in the drawing-room; one a spinet with painted panels in a neglected condition. I lifted the lid and thrilled pleasantly. It was a Ruckers, Antwerp, 1594. The doubtful object was a faded mezzotint upon the wall; it was signed Valentine Green, 1782, and, as I say, may or may not have been the goods.

To go back a little; half-way through the morning I returned to the appalling library which was my base for something or other, and in came rather a charming little person. Very trim little figure, fresh face, blue eyes; tawny hair under a full, spotless coif; no uniform, a sort of blue tweed dress. General effect rather nice, so I thought, 'Ha-ha. The nurse.'

She said right away: 'You're Mr. Mertoun, aren't you? I should have known you from your photograph.'

I opened my eyes very wide, and said: 'Now where on earth have you seen my photograph?'

'On a battalion group,' she said. 'My brother used to talk about you. He thought the world of you. He was in your company—Douglas Goff.'

I remembered him; nice boy, killed just towards the end, about August, 1918. So we began talking, about the War and so on, and about post-War jobs and all the rest of it. She'd trained in Edinburgh, and I told her how I'd gone into this antique business, and one thing and another. All this time we were standing, so I said casually, 'Aren't you going to sit down?'—and at once I was sorry, because she froze and became business-like after that. I gathered that she'd remembered she was on duty, and she didn't forget it again, which was a pity.

'I hope they've made you comfortable,' she said conventionally. 'I'm really acting as housekeeper, but I was busy with the invalid last night.'

'Quite,' said I. 'I hope Colonel Barr is better this morning.'

'I'm afraid you won't be able to see him,' she said. 'He never sees anyone, except myself.'

'And the doctor,' I murmured. Don't ask me why. I wasn't really interested, and I was actually thinking about something else. I suppose it was a subconscious connection of ideas spoken out loud. However, she took me up at once.

'Why do you say that?'

I shook my head frankly, and said, 'I don't know. It was rather obvious, wasn't it, seeing that Colonel Barr is so ill?' And I laughed.

She frowned. 'As a matter of fact,' she said, 'things are difficult. The doctor has been incapacitated for weeks with a fractured leg and concussion. He was thrown by his horse one night in the dark.

The locum is very young, and I didn't care for him when he called, so I'm carrying on alone.'

I said, 'Oh, I see.' But it did strike me that a really sick man who could send to London for an antique dealer might have sent as far as the nearest town for a doctor.

'I suppose you're finding your way about the house,' she said. 'Please ask me if you want anything. Have you been upstairs yet?'

I told her that I'd had quite a good general survey, and I hoped to finish the job with luck before bedtime. Now tell me, what was there sinister or shocking in that simple statement? I shall never forget her face. For a moment the fresh, bright colour left it and her eyes went dark. Then she pulled herself together and said: 'But there are fourteen bedrooms.'

'Yes,' I said carelessly, 'and it's quite enough to open the doors of most of them. Mid-Victorian furniture has no value within the terms of my commission from Colonel Barr. You understand?'

'Yes,' she said slowly. 'You'll be leaving then?'

'In the morning,' I told her.

'Aren't all these books important?' she said, making a gesture towards the shelves. 'I don't know anything about them, but Colonel Barr thinks a tremendous lot of his books.'

'I dare say,' I said, 'but it's a sentimental value only. He'd agree with me.'

'A lot of them are quite old,' she persisted; 'I thought old books were valuable.'

I explained to her rapidly and sketchily about rarity and first editions, and that these books were all quite common reprints. She suddenly remembered, I suppose, that she ought to be back with her patient, so she curtly nodded and went away. I was left with a queer impression that she was disappointed. But why?

I went on until half-past twelve and then took a half-hour walk before lunch. The rain had stopped, but everything was bleak and dripping. I never remember seeing a countryside which reminded me so much of the primeval slime; what I mean is, once out of sight of a dwelling, hundreds of years of civilization had left no impression whatever. It was all rough, tangled, wild. Heather, and rock, and sea; that hungry, grey North Sea which always seems to me so wolfish. Half a mile from the house the waves beat into a little cove at the foot of the blackened cliffs. Mud cliffs. I hadn't any inclination to go down to the shore. I leant up against the wind, which was strong and biting, and stared across at the lighthouse, which I could hardly see for mist. It was a dismal thought; three men imprisoned there for three months in utter isolation. I learnt later that the lighthouse had no local connection; it was staffed from distant Thorlwick.

As I stood there, looking back at the rounded, savage hills and out to the tumbling sea, I began to feel too much like stout Cortez for my comfort; I felt it was one of those places where in an encounter with man the wilderness would always have the best of it. So I went back to The Broch—the house, I mean; not the ruin.

I ate my lunch alone, and the girl—not the manservant—came to clear away. She said her name was Gwennie.

'Look here, Gwennie,' I said, 'is this house haunted?'

'I should have thought you'd have known that!' she said, looking stubborn. She had a fish-face, and fish-faces are naturally stubborn.

'And when I came in suddenly and frightened you this morning, you thought it was the ghost, didn't you?'

She bobbed her head up and down, picking at her apron. 'Not in the ordinary way I wouldn't have done,' she said, 'but it was Mrs. M'Coul saying she thought she'd catched a glimpse of him yesterday evening.'

'Have you ever seen him?' I asked idly.

She scratched her ear. Most unfeminine. ''Tisn't so much him as what he does,' she said.

'What does he do?'

'Well, once he threw all the breakfast things off on to the floor, the tablecloth and all,' she said. 'There was a thunderstorm that night, and I reckon it must have excited him. Mrs. M'Coul and I had laid the table for breakfast overnight; it was the very first night I came here, and the Colonel and Mr. Ian and Mr. Charlie had asked for breakfast at seven. But when we came down in the morning, what a mess!'

I laughed. 'My good girl,' I said. 'A storm! It was the wind down the chimney.'

'Was it?' she retorted. 'And does the wind down the chimney lay six plates in a row before the hearth and put a dollop of marmalade in the middle of each one? Because it was done. Mr. Ian and Mr. Charlie were that furious we nearly got our notices; in the end they had to believe it was *him* what done it. The Colonel laughed; but he laughed the other side of his face when Mr. Ian——' She snatched up a plate and clattered it upon the tray. 'It's Mrs. M'Coul,' she muttered; and I saw someone pass the door and glance in, presumably the cook. At any rate, the girl whisked herself away. I wondered why I'd taken the trouble to tease her.''

III

''The rest of the day was quite dull and uneventful. I went on with my job, smoked a lot of cigarettes, and planned what I should do with myself when I got back to town. Business was slack, and I owed myself the holiday I hadn't had at Christmas, so I decided I'd take a fortnight and go down to Cornwall to some pals of mine who have a jolly house with an ever-open door. I examined some oil-paintings which were copies, none of them any good; but there was one of a cottage interior that was rather attractive and I went to the trouble of cleaning it. I hoped Colonel Barr—whom apparently I was not to meet in the flesh—would appreciate the efforts of the unknown friend. I didn't think very much about my surroundings or the people I had suddenly come amongst. They and their affairs were really nothing to me; though if I had been of a curious disposition I might have rooted out a lot of interesting details. Most people of intelligence are interesting; so are most families. But I wasn't a novelist, or a detective, and it wasn't my job to value the personnel of the Barr residence. I didn't like the house, and I was glad I hadn't to live in it; that was all there was to it so far as I was concerned.

Darkness fell at about four-thirty, and once more it rained steadily. I could hear the rain sluicing against the shrouded windows. The man M'Coul brought me a cup of tea and told me that Mr. Barr had finished work and would like supper early if I were agreeable. I said I was ready for anything, so when I went down there was Charlie Barr, and I was quite glad to have somebody to talk to.

'Nearly finished,' I told him. 'It's fearfully desolate here. What does one do when not working?'

'I don't know,' he said, with a laugh; 'I've written reams in the last twelve months. In the summer I did a bit of shooting and riding; fished; went to Scotland for a month. It's a change from New York life.'

'I'll say it is!' I said. 'Aren't you ever going back?'

'Not while my uncle lives—and I hope he'll live for years. It's hardly fair to him. I'm the last of the family.'

'Decent of you,' I said.

'Oh no.' He shook his head. 'Being brought up an American I suppose most people would think I had no sense of tradition. That's where they're wrong. If my Uncle Bourdon hadn't died fifteen months ago I don't suppose it would have occurred to me ever to set foot in England. But I heard about his death over there, and I thought, well, there's only two of them left now and then me to carry on the name and the place. I hated leaving town, really; but I knew what my father would have wanted me to do. So I came over inside three months. It wasn't easy either, at first. Uncle Ian and Uncle Germain were rather grim old bachelors, and though I think they were glad to see me they didn't make allowances for a young man, used to a wider world. However, when the spring and summer came it was pleasanter, and I was out of doors nearly all the time. And, in the end, of course I was glad that I'd tried to humour the old fellows, when Uncle Ian died. And Uncle Germain has never been the same since. I'm afraid . . .'

I nodded in sympathy. It looked to me as though Charlie would inherit fairly soon, and it wasn't much of an inheritance, apart from the family feeling about it.

'Are you going back upstairs?' he asked.

'No,' I said. 'It's largely a case of making a fair copy of my findings. I'd better do it in the library. I've been using that as a base.'

'Good!' he said. 'I'll come in for a smoke if I won't be in the way.'

So we went to the library, where there was a fire, and we didn't speak for about an hour. By then I'd practically finished. So I said, rather ragging him: 'Look here . . . why don't you get your spook investigated? It would be something for you to do.'

For a few minutes he looked at me with a perfectly blank face, not uncomprehending—if you understand—just considering.

Then he said slowly, 'Spook? Has it touched your room? It shouldn't have done.'

I laughed. 'Sorry!' I said. 'You call my bluff.'

He stubbed the stone fender with the toe of his shoe.

'Something must have happened,' he said. 'I apologize on behalf of the family. It's only a poltergeist. Quite harmless.'

It occurred to me then that he was serious, and I didn't know quite what to say. You know how embarrassed you feel when you meet somebody who quite sincerely holds opinions that you've personally always regarded as rather a joke.

So I pretended to be impressed, though quite casual, and I said: 'Of course I've heard of them. Don't they throw things about and make noises?'

He looked uncomfortable, and I wished we hadn't opened the subject.

'The poltergeist,' he said, 'is just a mischievous spirit that makes its home in some chosen place. They had the idea in the Middle Ages with their Lob and their Puck. We can understand such things better now. This spirit has belonged to the district for years; some time ago it came into the house. I don't know when; but it was here when I arrived. It isn't any trouble to anybody, and it has only misbehaved twice. Once it did a silly trick with some break-fast dishes, and another time it took a hat from the hall and hid it in a kitchen saucepan. I wouldn't have mentioned it if you hadn't, because some people would be fools enough to regard the whole thing as a joke. Well, psychic matters aren't a joke, but they needn't be a trouble either. The best thing is to take no notice.' He completed his sentence with a sudden upward look and his attractive smile, and I made a murmur of agreement.

Then all of a sudden Miss Goff came in and we both stood up.

She looked at me, and said with a sort of demure firmness: 'Mr. Mertoun, I have a message for you from Colonel Barr.'

'Yes?' I asked.

'I told him what you had been doing,' she said, 'and what you told me this morning about the books not being valuable, and in such a state of confusion too. And he says that they're very valuable to him for sentimental reasons; that it has taken him a lifetime to collect them; and that he has been meaning to arrange and catalogue them for years. He wants it doing, very badly, and he wants to know if you can catalogue books.'

'Of course,' I murmured, 'I have done private libraries before——'

'In that case,' she said, 'will you undertake to arrange and catalogue these books for Colonel Barr? He hopes you will accept the commission. I'm to tell you that he will make it very well worth your while.'

Of course I was taken completely by surprise. I looked at Charlie Barr, and he seemed to be struggling between surprise and amusement.

'Queer idea!' he said.

The nurse took no notice of him, but kept on looking at me.

'Of course, if the Colonel really wants the work undertaken——' I temporized.

'He seems to have set his heart on it,' she said. 'I hope you'll do it, now that you're here, Mr. Mertoun.'

I still hesitated. 'There are catalogues and catalogues,' I said. 'You can have anything from a foolscap list to a proper card index with cross-references.'

'If you do this,' she said quickly, 'Colonel Barr will desire the best method.'

I was still turning the thing over in my mind, but I had already practically decided to accept, on the principle that only a fool refuses any job in these days. It only meant postponing my holiday.

'I should have to send to London for the cards, files, and so on,' I said. 'That would take a few days, but I could be arranging the books. I shall also have to send for some clothes. You see, the job will take me at least a fortnight.'

'That's quite all right,' she said. 'The Colonel said you were to charge the full fee for your time. May I tell him then that you'll take it on?'

I glanced at Charlie Barr, and I could quite understand what he was thinking. He smiled. 'From a practical point of view,' he said, 'it's a frightful waste of your time.' He turned to the nurse: 'My uncle gets some queer whims, Miss Goff. Do you think it's always wise——'

She didn't smile, but answered rather stiffly: 'In his state of health you have to give way to him. It might be fatal not to; the excitement of being denied.'

'I'm sorry,' said Charlie; 'I didn't understand. Of course he must have his own way.' He turned to me: 'I'm afraid you're in for a deadly and unprofitable fortnight.'

'I don't mind,' I said. 'I shan't have time to regret while clearing this litter.'

'Thank you,' said the nurse, and went out, quietly closing the door. So that was how I came to stay on at The Broch.

I've tried to give you the conversation in detail, for a reason that I'll explain later, at the end of my story. You see, the conversation must have a certain significance, though I can't for the life of me see it—yet.

Well, there I was, settled for another fortnight, and there wasn't any hurry to finish what I was doing. I was heavy and tired too that night, so I sat over the library fire with a book for the rest of the evening. I fished down an old history of Northumberland and quite interesting I found it. It had maps, and I was able to trace my locality. Charlie was also deep in a book. I read a good deal of history and local legend, though nothing I particularly noted beyond the fact that the original tribes were called the Ottadeni, and had fair hair, large limbs, and tattooed bodies. They were terrific fight ers, and were never actually conquered by the Roman invaders. The Romans kept their camps well in the south of the county and left the Ottadeni alone. I suppose these were the tribes who built the broch and other similar fortresses. It was all mildly interesting. Charlie asked me what I was reading and I showed him. He rather ragged me about it, and said that historians were pretty safe in speculating about those days. So I pushed the book back to continue it later, and we smoked a pipe and went to bed.

Like a fool I stood staring at the broch, because the sky behind it was livid with a kind of glassy moonlight and I never saw such masses of coal-black cloud. As a consequence I had a beastly dream. I was struggling with a thing that was half an animal and half a man, and suddenly I threw it off and saw that it had a tattooed body and long, fair, tangled hair. And the hair was dripping with blood. It wasn't my blood. There was something on the ground a little way away, something that still writhed faintly, horrible to look at. And then this savage came at me again, smelling abominably, and I saw a heap of dead men with red swords, and I was back in a shell-hole with the bombardment roaring like mad, and somebody shouting out, 'Mithras! Mithras!' So when I woke up in the dark I was shouting Mithras too, and I felt a frightful fool, and got up and got a drink of water. After that I went to sleep and it didn't come back. But in the morning I remembered it quite clearly, and I wondered about that 'Mithras' business; until it suddenly came back to me. Aren't dreams queer? There was a fellow in our battalion, Captain Curvey, who had a very fine baritone voice and he used to be in great demand at our concerts. He used to sing a rousing song that began, 'Mithras, god of the morning, our trumpets waken the Wall.' So that was the explanation, and yet Curvey hadn't been in my mind for over ten years. I say, that was the explanation—the simple one that I accepted after two days at The Broch.

The next day I was just a navvy, carting about masses of books. Masses and masses of books."

IV

"Nothing at all happened during the next two or three days. I'm not perfectly certain of the sequence of events because I didn't use my diary, but I seem to remember at least two very dreary days. I planned out the library shelves according to classified subject, and began to see the dawning of order. Once a day I went out for a lonely tramp, and then the man M'Coul offered to lend me his bicycle so that I could go farther afield. At least, I forget exactly when it was that he loaned me the bicycle, because the first time it really comes into the story was several days later when I fell off it. But I'll leave that for the present.

I saw hardly anything of Charlie Barr or Miss Goff. I suppose Charlie was working hard, and Miss Goff certainly was. She seemed to me to have an unconscionably hard time, and very rarely seemed to leave her patient's room. Of course I didn't know anything about the Colonel. He may have been exacting, but I remember hoping that she was well paid for her slavery.

I met her one afternoon on the stairs. She smiled at me rather warmly and I put my hand on her arm. She was twiddling the key of her patient's room in her fingers; she always kept his door locked against intruders.

'Come out for a walk!' I said. 'Just half an hour.'

She shook her head, but I thought she looked longing.

'Can't,' she said tersely.

'Oh, come along!' I said. 'Aren't you ever off duty?'

'It's a special case,' she pleaded.

'Is he so ill as that?' I said. 'Doesn't he ever take an hour's sleep? Do come with me. I'm bored.'

'Then . . . perhaps in a day or two,' she temporized.

'Wouldn't Mr. Barr sit with him?' I suggested.

She became frightfully professional, and I felt it was rather impudent of me to make these arrangements, as I supposed it appeared to her.

'You don't understand,' she said; 'the sight of any other person than myself would have the effect of a severe shock. It might be fatal.'

Of course I'd wondered what was the matter with the old man, and what disease necessitated all this seclusion, so at once I guessed that the trouble was mental, persecution mania, or something of the kind. Therefore I didn't pester the girl again. All my apparatus arrived from London; I think it was the next day, but I'm vague about that part of the chronology.

As I think I said, the nights came in dark and rainy, with gales of wind. The sea too was always noisy; in fact, there was a violent elemental symphony every night. I wasn't used to it, and I never slept deeply. I suppose those who were used to it would sleep like infants, just as when I'm at home all the bus gears and klaxons in London can't rouse me.

Well, I didn't sleep soundly and every unusual noise disturbed me; so one night I heard something and I woke. That's the baldest possible way I can express it, but that's the nearest I can come to it. This wasn't an elemental noise; it was a movement in the house. I couldn't place it, because the house was rambling and our bedrooms were far apart. I looked at my luminous watch, and it was 1.45 a.m. I suppose you'll say that there's nothing unusual in hearing someone moving in a house during the night, especially when there's an invalid and a nurse; but somehow this was—well, different. Sounds do convey a subconscious message, and this sound was heavy . . . furtive. It wasn't the *right* sound. I only heard it once, but it conveyed all that.

I didn't get up; I don't think I moved. In a few minutes I fell asleep, but I woke for good before dawn and the impression was perfectly distinct in my mind. And then I thought, 'I wonder if that was the poltergeist? Would it make a sound?' I hardly thought so, but I admitted I was a novice where mischievous spirits were concerned. You'll see that I had already accepted the poltergeist; or rather my attitude was that half my mind said, no, and the other half said, perhaps. Barr had unconsciously influenced me. After all, he was five-feet-ten and twelve stone, straight from materialistic New York, and he talked in a matter-of-fact way of spirits. I didn't really mind this poltergeist, one way or the other.

At breakfast I said: 'I believe I've heard your house-spirit.'

He looked quite interested. 'Honestly, do you mean that?'

'I heard the queerest sound in the night,' I said.

He nodded. 'That would be Gracchus. I didn't hear anything.'

'Gracchus?' I inquired.

His lips gave a humorous twist. He leaned over the breakfast table with planted elbows and fingers clasped. 'We have to call him something,' he said; 'Bingo or Rover would be too silly.'

The conversation might have become interesting, but at this

point a telegram arrived for Barr. I ought to have said that there was a village about a mile away, complete with post office and general shop.

He read his telegram and immediately said: 'Good. Splendid.' He turned to me. 'I've booked a room at the hotel at Keswick for the motor-cycle trials. I'm going to-morrow for a couple of days.'

'Good fun,' I said.

'Come with me,' he suggested.

'No,' I said; 'I never leave a job in the middle, and it would only postpone my getting back to town.'

'That's true,' he agreed.

It was a bright morning, and I saw the sun shining for the first time. The sky was particularly luminous and there was a faint sparkle on the wet hills and a dazzling shimmer on the sea. The lighthouse looked like a silver pillar against the blue-grey billows of the horizon.

In the middle of the morning I went up to my room for something or other, and ahead of me on the corridor I saw Miss Goff.

'Hullo!' I called.

She turned round reluctantly. I thought—or rather it was evident—that she looked pale and tired. There was a kind of anxious look in her eyes which I didn't approve of. Now—I beg you—don't think I was taking any particular interest in Miss Goff. She wasn't occupying my mind in the least, and this isn't one of those stories with a delicate thread of romance running through, as they say in the publisher's announcements. I suppose it was that I couldn't help being struck by the difference in her looks. In any case, I didn't comment, because women hate to be told they're not looking well. It means they're looking plain.

But as I passed her I caught sight of the back of her hand, and I deliberately took hold of it and turned up the sleeve. There was an ugly bruise running almost to the elbow.

'You must have pricked your finger!' I said meaningly.

She snatched her hand away. 'I have had a fall,' she said, very coldly; and went into the bathroom, bolting the door behind her. I heard the taps running loudly.

So I went along to my own room, and all of a sudden I felt

horribly ill. Giddy and faint. It was like being up for the first time after a sharp bout of malaria; in fact, malaria was my first thought, though I hadn't had a touch of it for ten years and it had never begun so suddenly as this.

I sat down on my bed and held my head. It was the vilest sensation I ever remember, and it brought with it a kind of ghastly depression. I seemed to be giving up the struggle and surrendering my mind to thoughts of hatred and horror.

Presently it passed away, and having nothing better I drank some brackish water out of my water-jug. But I still felt depressed. I was more than ever conscious that I detested that house. There was something wrong with it. That was as far as I went in my impressions. And yet I liked Charlie Barr and Miss Goff; there was nothing forbidding or repellent about them. Were they conscious of this 'wrongness' too? I came to the conclusion that Miss Goff was and Charlie wasn't. In spite of his poltergeist, which he certainly didn't regard as in any way sinister. Charlie evidently wasn't conscious of any such evil influence as I was suggesting to myself existed. But was Miss Goff, and could I get into touch with her ideas on the subject?

Then I pulled myself together and asked myself what real evidence I had for these suppositions. And in the end I decided that all the apparent evidence could be explained away quite simply. It was washed out by plain reason.

My first dislike of the house. Explanation: wet night, gloomy countryside, long cold journey.

The curious brain-shock I had experienced on my first evening. Explanation: heavy supper on a chilled, empty stomach.

Impression of 'haunting.' Explanation: superstitious servant-girl.

Curious behaviour of Miss Goff. Explanation: exacting patient.

Bad dream. Explanation: reading ancient history and looking at the moonlight on the ruined broch.

Mithras. Explanation: Curvey's concerts.

Noise in the night. Explanation: Miss Goff getting her patient a hot drink.

Bruise on Miss Goff's arm. Explanation: as she said, a fall.

My sudden illness. Explanation: touch of malaria.

The rest of that day was in every way normal. I didn't see Miss Goff again, nor Charlie until supper-time when we talked about motor-bikes. Afterwards he showed me some good card tricks in the library; I practised diligently, but I hadn't his knack. Then we talked about America and the American people. He agreed with me that they were charming individually, and more than dreadful *en masse*. We both deplored their sensationalism and lack of restraint. 'They're just adolescent,' he said; 'gauche.' He told me he had had people come by the hundred to his rooms in New York to be advised on the cure of their complexes and neuroses. All their nerves, he said, were in an appalling condition; the women because they had nothing to do but get involved in unfortunate love affairs, and the men because they couldn't make money as quickly as the other fellow. He used to send them away thinking beautiful, constructive thoughts, and his fee for a private consultation was twenty dollars.

His slightly cynical humour amused me immensely. I told you he was good-looking, and he said his age was thirty-seven.

'How did you drift into that profession?' I asked him.

He laughed. 'I don't know. I've always been interested in the impulses that govern action. Mind-control, and so on.'

'Hypnotism?' I suggested.

He swept up the cards. 'Heavens, no! That's getting too near necromancy.'

'Oh, come!' I said. 'Don't tell me those women weren't hypnotized?'

He gave a ringing laugh. 'In that perfectly harmless sense, yes. But as for the other—well, I once let myself be put in a trance by way of an experiment, but I wouldn't do it again. It was only for fun—or rather, to oblige a friend. . . . Will you excuse me if I go and pack a bag?'

The next morning he was gone quite early, and I missed what little of his company I had had. All the morning I worked on my indexing, and in the afternoon I slipped a poetry anthology in my overcoat pocket and went out for a tramp. It rained and I turned back, and then suddenly as I came within sight of the sea the sun blazed out of the clouds with a brilliance which seemed to fire the sad earth. A lustrous blue spread over the sky, and a bird began to cheep in the wet heather. The grey waves were rimmed with silver, and the sea-wind was fragrant. I never remember a more spring-like and beautiful moment. I found a sheltered hollow in the moor, and spreading a mackintosh I sat down. It was not in the least cold. I sat hugging my knees and looking out to that sparkling sea with its suggestion of cruelty and power. Then I opened my book at some favourite lines and read them with a thrill.

> 'The mountains look on Marathon
> And Marathon looks on the sea;
> And musing there an hour alone,
> I dreamed that Greece might yet be free;
> For standing on the Persians' grave
> I could not deem myself a slave.'

I was reading the line, 'A king sat on a rocky brow that looks o'er sea-born Salamis,' when I heard a footfall and Miss Goff appeared on the hillside just below me. I waved to her and she came up slowly.

'Hurrah!' I said. 'So you've really been persuaded to make a bid for freedom?'

She smiled. She was bareheaded and wrapped in a large tweed ulster. 'Isn't the sun glorious?' she said; 'it brought me out—only for a few minutes.'

'Share my mackintosh,' I suggested, and she sat down and gazed as I had been doing, out to sea.

'How the lighthouse glitters!' I said. 'The moving lamp shines into my room at night. It's a desolate life for the men. Are they local men?'

She shook her head. 'No. They haven't anything to do with this part. They come from Thorlwick, every three months, by boat.'

'By Jove!' I said suddenly. 'Look how the sun brings out colour on that cold, brown hillside! I thought of this place as hideous, but I'm inclined to think it could be fascinating in a subtle way.'

She followed my pointing finger with a rather weary look.

'Yes, it can be quite beautiful,' she said; 'but the sun doesn't often shine. The rain is terribly depressing, especially in summer.'

'Have you been here in summer?' I asked.

She nodded without speaking.

'But how long have you been at The Broch?' I persisted.

'Since about the middle of December.' She added: 'Of course, only since Colonel Barr became ill. But I lived only a few miles from here when I was a child.'

'Where is your home now?' I asked.

'My home?' She hesitated. 'I suppose I have one—but I don't see it often. There's only my father and my younger brother left. They live . . . some distance from here. I'm always in Edinburgh when I'm not out at a case.'

From where we sat we could just see the chimneys of the house.

'I wonder why they built in such a desolate spot?' I said. 'Somebody must have cultivated a taste for this particular part of England.'

'There have always been Barrs about here,' she answered. 'Their original house was on the other side of the hill. That was burnt down more than a hundred years ago, and they built again where the house now stands, facing the sea.'

'They must have been fond of that ugly Celtic tower,' I said idly. 'It certainly spoils the view.'

'The broch?' she said, rather sharply. 'Why, what's the matter with it? It's old enough to have a right to be there.'

'I suppose there are owls in it,' I said. 'Owls and moonlight always constitute a "haunt" in the country.'

She gave a strained laugh. 'Isn't it absurd? You couldn't get any of the local people to go within a hundred yards of it. Of course, that's only the most arrant superstition.'

'Said she, in a superior manner!' I laughed. 'How is the Colonel to-day?'

She pressed her lips together. 'He's asleep, or I couldn't have come out. I think I ought to go back now.'

'Please!' I protested. 'Do stay. He's a pretty frightful tyrant, isn't he?'

Her eyes flashed blue fire, and she said: 'Colonel Barr is one of the best and kindest men who ever lived. I've known him all my life. He was always good to my family; helped one of my brothers into a position; made it possible for me to be trained at Edinburgh. My father was poor and there were too many of us children. But for Colonel Barr I should have been a farm-girl, and my brothers swallowed up by the Tyneside pits. I owe him everything. None of my family can ever do enough to repay him. What's a little lack of my personal liberty when he needs me so badly?'

'I can imagine how you feel about it, if that is the case,' I said. 'I hope he isn't likely to die?'

She set her lips more firmly. 'He won't die,' she said. Her tone was curious; it silenced me for a time. We both sat quietly, watching the high waves crash into the unseen shore below the cliffs. Out on the horizon a black ship went by with its trail of smoke; dipped, and vanished. Behind us I felt rather than saw a growing darkness as rain-clouds rolled out of the west to smother the sun. And the coming of the clouds had the effect on me that I dreaded, the return of that chilling dislike to my surroundings which I've described before.

'Miss Goff,' I said suddenly, 'were you moving about in the house the night before last?'

She sat perfectly motionless, as though she were waiting for a blow to fall. There was something frightful in her very immobility. Her face was set; I couldn't read anything from it, but in a minute I saw her throat give a gulping tremor as though she were recovering her breath. Then she said in a flat voice: 'Possibly. Why do you ask?'

But she had told me what I wanted to know. I said: 'It wasn't you, Miss Goff. I know it wasn't you.'

She dug her fingers into the heather stalks. 'Who—who was it?'

I said dryly: 'I know, and you know. But I thought it was harmless?'

'Who told you?'

'Mr. Barr.'

'Oh.'

Suddenly I couldn't stand it any longer. 'For heaven's sake, tell me!' I said. 'Let's thrash it out. You're frightened—you're hiding it awfully well, but you are. I felt it too, almost from the minute I entered that house. It's a hateful house. Something seemed to get me by the neck . . . a creeping horror. I haven't even admitted it to myself until this moment. I've explained my sensations away, but now that you feel it too——! What is it? What is the beastly thing? Barr takes it lightly; a sort of jolly little house-spirit that plays tricks with the marmalade. That isn't the impression I've had. Is it malevolent, this poltergeist, as they call it? It must be. It brought that look to your face——'

She suddenly turned on me and the colour rushed to her angry cheeks. 'Mr. Mertoun! Have you gone *mad*?' she said. 'How can you believe in such rubbish? A spirit! The most utter nonsense. No intelligent person——'

I froze up instantly. 'Very well, dear lady,' I thought; 'but I call it rottenly unsporting of you.' It was her fault that I had given myself away; and then to draw back . . . Well, she wouldn't catch me twice.

I got up, and of course she had to, because I wanted my mackintosh; so I slung it across my shoulder and we went down to the house without saying anything, the heather stalks snapping under our feet. I held open the gate for her. 'Will you please forgive me?' she said unexpectedly. 'I don't know how——'

'Certainly,' I interrupted, pretty stiffly.

We both went in, and separated. I didn't see her again that day or the whole of the next; and in the evening to my relief Charlie Barr came back."

v

"Now this was the night of my first unquestionable experience. I haven't tried until now to put it into words. I suppose it is impossible to make you feel it as I felt it, but even now—hundreds of miles away—the chill of it is taking hold of me again. Don't think me more of a fool than you can help. I'm struggling with a string of memories that only free speech can relieve.

Very well, then. As I said, Charlie came back in the evening and he came back unlike himself, gloomy and almost morose. He nodded to me and went straight to his study, where he had his supper sent to him, but later he came to the library and made an attempt at conversation. Probably this attitude of his affected my own feelings. It was a horrible night too, gusty and raw, and the wind down the chimney filled the room with billows of smoke. We both coughed and bore it for a time, and then Charlie admitted to being desperately tired and we both went to bed.

Once in my room I discovered that I still had the poetry anthology of the previous day in my pocket, so I read myself to sleep with Cavalier lyrics and fantastic love lays. I slept soundly, and woke at the sound of a light tap on the door. It was pitch dark, and my luminous watch said it was a little before three. The wind was raging outside, and there was a dreary sluicing of rain on the window. A sickly beam from the lighthouse stole in for a second and was gone; the crashing of the breakers on the shore was very distinct.

Someone tapped again, very lightly. I got out of bed, put on a dressing-gown and opened the door. It was Miss Goff. She was wearing her uniform with apron and coif.

'Will you dress quickly, please,' she said quietly; 'I want to show you something.'

Of course I dressed and went out and joined her. There wasn't a light anywhere; I could see her white apron gleaming in the blackness of the corridor. I couldn't imagine where she was taking me, and to tell you the truth I wasn't thinking of anything sinister. You know how silent it is in a house in the middle of the night; instinctively you walk as softly as a cat. Neither she nor I made much sound. We came to the stairs and began to descend towards the half-landing on the way to the hall. There was a deep window on the half-landing and it made the stairs faintly light, light enough to see what we had come to see. 'Look,' Miss Goff said to me.

There was a large picture hanging on the wall at the turn of the stairs, some sort of a portrait in oils. I had noticed it several times. Now I saw that it was slashed almost to ribbons, as though it had been attacked with fiendish ferocity. There was something repulsive in those dark cuts, like wounds in human flesh.

Miss Goff stood quietly beside me. 'Was it like that when you went to bed?' she whispered.

'No,' I said, and I hardly recognized my voice.

'You see!' she said.

And then everything went black and I should have fallen if I hadn't clutched the banister-rail. 'It's here!' I heard myself say, and both her hands went into mine. They were as cold as ice. I felt myself fighting with a thick and hideous darkness that I could smell and taste. It was very old, slow-creeping, and evil. I couldn't move; I was waiting, waiting, for something to come and then I was going to give one mighty heave with my fists and end it, somehow. But it didn't come; there wasn't anything, any more than there is in a nightmare. That made it just ten times more horrible. How long it went on I don't know; probably several minutes. I know that suddenly I gave a choke that wrenched my throat most painfully, and opened my eyes, and discovered myself sane but feeling iller than I've felt for many a year. Miss Goff was drawing her hands out of mine. Her face was queerly contorted. I put my hand up to my brow and brought it away wet. And of course the first thing I said was something utterly absurd and inadequate. I said, 'So that's that,' and she gave a sort of a sob. Then we both stiffened up. Whatever the thing was, it had gone.

'Look here,' I said, 'how did you find out about—this?' And I pointed to the slashed picture.

'I thought I heard something,' she said quietly; 'so I came down to see.'

I admired her fearfully for making so little fuss.

'This is worse,' I said, 'than playing with marmalade and hiding hats.' She covered her face with her hand.

'Why did you come to me?' I asked her.

'Because I thought you'd understand,' she said.

'Thank you,' I said; 'I think I do. But I wish Barr needn't know, though of course he'll have to. Still, I don't think he'll realize the full significance of the thing, do you?'

She said slowly: 'I think he will.'

'You mean,' I said, 'he knows there's danger, but he's braving it out?' I could understand Barr's attitude completely now; deliberately making light of what he knew might prove to be frightful danger. 'I'm glad you didn't wake him,' I said, 'but I don't think he ought to come on this suddenly to-morrow morning.'

'You might go to his room and tell him,' she suggested.

I nodded. 'I suppose this is a portrait of a Barr?' I said.

'Yes. Some generations back. I think it was the one who built this house.'

'So it is malevolence,' I said. 'I wonder what the Barrs can have done?' She didn't speak, but her fingers were nervously turning the key of her patient's room. Suddenly I saw light. 'You're afraid for him?' I whispered.

Her face hardened. 'Please, Mr. Mertoun!' she said. I could see that there was a reserve which I should find it very difficult to penetrate.

All this time we were standing on the stairs in the cold, grey light before the slashed picture.

'Shall I take it down and put it away?' I suggested suddenly. 'The servants——'

'Leave it,' she said.

We went upstairs again, along the ghostly darkness of the corridor. I was thankful that Charlie Barr had heard nothing; it would have been so much worse for him, when even I still felt cold and shaken. Miss Goff unlocked the door of the Colonel's room and went in, and I heard the grate of the bolt inside. I had a faint feeling of resentment, as though she suspected me of a desire to intrude.

I got back to my room—I wonder what you're thinking!—with the appalling feeling, which properly belongs to nursery days, that something was at my heels. I remember turning the key in the lock—much good could that do me—and groping in the dark for cigarettes and matches. I couldn't go to bed. I threw up the window and let the wet, gusty air rush in; wild and salt from the sea, fresh and clean on my face. The night shadows were deep over the tangled garden and the crouching hill; above was a tattered sky, like a grey pool into which inky poison had been dropped. The cold revived me; I began to face up to things. I faced the fact that I had been afraid, with a fear which the guns of Loos and the gas-clouds of the Marne had never wrung from me. What was there that had power to make me afraid, afraid of—nothingness?

Hours went by, and then the dawn struggled over the hill and the stones of the old tower glimmered faintly on the mist of early morning. I heard the housemaid rattling at my locked door, but I found it too difficult to walk over and turn the key, so presently I heard her put down the can and go away.

Half an hour later I went to Charlie's room, but he was already gone. The bed was stripped and the window thrown up; the long curtains were flapping madly in the wind.

When I arrived at the head of the stairs I saw I was much too late. He was standing before the slashed portrait of his ancestor. He didn't hear me coming, even when I stood close to him. His face was quite calm, hardly curious, quietly considering. He stood like that for another moment, and then turning saw me.

'Breakfast is in,' he said. 'Come on down.'

'He's brave,' I thought; 'it's the northern blood.'

We ate breakfast rather quietly and read the papers. I got absorbed in the notice of a forthcoming sale at the Park Lane home of a ducal family, and I booked the date for future use. Charlie yawned, throwing down the *Daily Mail*.

'Do you ever begin the day,' he said, 'with an utter distaste for work? I suppose you'll say, Physician, heal thyself; but frankly I've never discovered the therapeutic procedure. Of course two days' holiday make a fatal break. How are you getting along? Have you nearly finished?'

'Far from it,' I said. 'I've only just received the files and cards from London.'

He shrugged his shoulders. 'Sorry you've got such a thankless job. You'll be glad to leave here.'

On that our eyes met, and I think he read something in mine which made him conscious that his final phrase might have an unfortunate significance. His hand flew up in a gesture I couldn't understand, and he left the room abruptly. I saw him no more that day, though I heard him making a savage protest in the evening; in fact, he was furious, and from what I gathered of the facts I didn't blame him. M'Coul had taken his sopping overcoat, slung it over an oven door to dry, and forgotten it. The house was full of the smell of charred wool and Charlie's coat was a back number. Not so easy to replace in those wilds, a good overcoat; besides, I had an impression—I don't know why—that money was tight in that house. And yet if so, why was the Colonel retaining me at my own figure? I couldn't explain it; perhaps it was only Charlie who was hard up.

That afternoon, feeling guilty of melodrama, I took an electric torch and searched the hidden corners of the house. I don't know what I expected to find. With my teeth set and a slightly choked sensation in my throat I dragged open cupboard doors in shuttered rooms, swept the torch's beam inside, and made myself look. But all that afternoon there was nothing; no horror but what existed in my own mind, and only the smell of dry rot which you couldn't call evil, though it is nasty.

From the front of the house I heard for the first time in my life the cry of the curlew, and saw the sad wheeling of that ancient bird prophet. That cry! What tragedy! It was like a lament for all the dead of the battle-scarred Border; the crying to Heaven of the blood-soaked heather of the North. I thought of the gallant swords that flashed for Hotspur and Stuart; and then of older and fiercer days when men of Naples and Rome had sobbed out their last breath under these sullen, foreign skies, and the ancient curlew on her nest had added their agony to her note. Poor bird, what tortured ancestral memories gave you that song? . . .

So after all my trouble I found nothing but empty and musty rooms, and I went back to my indexing; but on the half-landing I stopped before a square of deeper colouring in the faded red wallpaper. The slashed picture had been taken away, and I never saw it again. I now began to ask myself whether I seriously believed that there was some grim fate in store for the members of the Barr family. I only had my own psychic impressions and that slashed portrait to go on. Perhaps it was just chance that it was the portrait of a Barr, and yet those gashes had breathed malevolence. I could see again the pallor of the pictured face and hands, sliced to shreds. And then I immediately thought of Uncle Ian. Charlie had said that first his Uncle Bourdon died and then his Uncle Ian, and he had stopped short on the last name. Someone else too had broken off abruptly on that name—was it the chatty maid, or was it Miss Goff? There was certainly something unmentionable about Uncle Ian, though that didn't say it had any connection . . . however, you

can imagine how I reasoned. Futile! And at last I remembered how
the porter from Glasgow had told me that Uncle Ian fell over the
cliffs; and though that seemed to me an unpleasant end I didn't see
how, except by a stretch of imagination, I could connect it with a
malicious influence in the house. Accident put Uncle Ian out of
the running.

That night I had an absurd experience, and the fright of my
life. It was too ridiculous, and only my mental state accounted
for it; in fact, I was so enraged with myself the next morning
that I nearly threw everything up and came back to London. It
proves how when verging upon psychic matters, especially upon
debatable phenomena, the mind ought to be kept particularly bal-
anced and reasonable, clear-cut and logical. I nearly made a fool
of myself. The fact is, when I went to my room at night I saw
something moving at the foot of the Celtic tower, the broch, and
my spine shivered. Just a dark, low form, moving. I indulged in a
lot of mental madness. In the morning when I got up the sun was
shining and a mild wind blew. I dragged up the blind. On the slope
below the broch two ewes were feeding, each with a weak-legged,
new-born lamb at her side. Against the jagged, stained stones of
the tower a young man was leaning. He wore sacking across his
shoulders and held in his arms another lamb. Soon he stretched
out a hand to the sunlight, unflexed cramped fingers, lit a pipe, and
went swinging down the hillside. This young shepherd had made
a shelter for his early-lambing ewes within the thick walls of the
ruin. Simple, wasn't it?

I told Charlie at breakfast. 'One of your superstitious villagers
isn't so simple,' I said. 'A shepherd took possession of the ruined
tower last night for his lambing, and I saw him come out safe this
morning.'

He was amazed. 'It's almost incredible!' he said. 'There isn't a
man, woman, or child within miles will go near the broch. They
predict the most horrid fate for those who do—you know the kind
of thing; your cows will dry up, your crops rot in the ground, and
your wife present you with coal-black twins. And worse! I can't
believe it.'

'I'll tell you if he does it again,' I said. 'I'll fetch you to see.'

The very next morning I fetched him to see, but he seemed to have lost interest by then. 'Oh yes,' he said, evidently recognizing the man; 'an independent sort of fellow.'

Within a day or two the independence of this young man—Blaik was his name—was the topic of the village and countryside. I forget who gave me the gossip—oh yes, it was the girl, Gwennie, who said that whatever happened to that shepherd in the near future he would only have himself to blame. Blaik was a sturdy, shrewd type; read Tolstoy and Marx; had no imagination, and declared with the dogmatic assurance of his type of mind that he didn't believe in spirits. Personally, I rather applauded Blaik. I mean, to me that broch superstition was sheer village fable, and I concluded that once Blaik had had the temerity to quash the ghost story the rest of the local shepherds would be fighting for the use of such a convenient shelter.

However, the village community went on prophesying disaster for Blaik, and I seem to have gone two or three days out of my reckoning; so let's get back to where we were and I'll tell you how I came across Ingram, the doctor."

VI

"On the afternoon of the day I'm talking about—do you follow me? I mean the day after I saw the shepherd Blaik at the broch—I hunched myself on M'Coul's cycle and went for a spin across the moor. It was rather good fun. The roads were switchback, and though you might have to toil up a stiff rise there was a long, downward sweep on the other side where you could put up your feet and let her fly. The scenery was gloomy and unattractive, for the sun had forgotten to shine and the hills were correspondingly sullen, and the road owed little to anyone save the Romans who first made it; but I hadn't been on a bike since I was a kid, and it was glorious. Then a storm came on, and I had to climb down and wait, crouching in the lee of a boulder. I didn't get very wet, but unfortunately the clouds had swallowed up the daylight, and though it was only a little after three o'clock it never came light again. I mounted and began to grope my way back, but soon I hit a stone in the dark and did a rather good cartwheel over my handle-bars. The bike wasn't hurt, but those flint roads are the very dickens on the human frame. Like razors. I felt blood running, and found my left sleeve ripped and a three-inch gash in my upper arm.

However, on I pedalled, making a rather gory progress, with the one idea of getting back to the Barr residence, but when I arrived within about a mile of the village I decided it was hardly fair to hurl myself upon Miss Goff's tender mercies in this nasty state, so I stopped a rustic with a cart and asked him to direct me to the doctor.

'T'owld docthor's bad,' he told me. 'Bin bad for months. T'young felly's up to Crouchbothom while t'neight.'

It didn't look hopeful; however, I was turning away when he suggested that if my trouble was urgent I might go to the mad doctor. Village folks had been known to do so in an emergency. I thought he meant a kind of local wizard with a matted beard and a bunch of nasty-smelling herbs, but he assured me that this was a real doctor, though touched. Daft, he called it. He pointed out a small house shrouded in bushes, so I thought I'd take my chance.

I know these country doctors. They always wear farm corduroys and smell of whisky, and you don't have to look at the state of their hands; they've got the kindest hearts in the world, will regale you for hours with ghoulish stories of local cancers, and keep their instruments loose in the tool-drawer with the dog's collar and the harness-oil.

So Ingram came as a shock when I was expecting something quite different. He opened the door himself, heard what I had to explain, took me in—all without a word—and pushed a fan-backed chair in front of the log fire for me while he went to fetch his tool-bag. All this time he hadn't spoken, but he was as lean and clean as a greyhound and there was nothing rough or rustic in his movements. When he came back he looked at me and his eyes were dog-sad but quite sane.

'What made you come to me?' he said. A cultured voice. A north-country voice musically modulated.

'I understand the village doctor is ill,' I said, 'and the locum has gone to some distant case. They told me that you sometimes——'

'Yes. Of course, I don't practise. They pay—well, a friendly visit, you might say. Can't you get that coat off? Wait . . .'

He took his hammer and chisel, as you might say, and began. Efficiency. Marvellous hands. I didn't feel any pain in the absorbing interest of seeing an expert at work. An artist or an artisan, it thrills me if it's skilled labour. This man was an artist.

When he had finished I said: 'Please. What do I owe you?'

He looked slightly shocked. 'Of course—nothing! I thought I'd made that clear. You had better look in again to-morrow.'

I murmured something, rather confused, and he misunderstood me.

'Do you mean you're only passing through?' he asked.

'Oh no,' I said. 'I'm here for a short time. I'm staying at Colonel Barr's house—The Broch.'

Then his eyes went mad, and I knew what the village gossip meant. He stood quite still, his hands hanging, and those smouldering brown eyes searching me—red-brown, flickering, narrowing, crazy.

'Sit down,' he said.

I sat down. I was interested in the man.

'What are you doing there?' he asked abruptly.

'Cataloguing the Colonel's library,' I replied, with perfect and full truth.

'He's still alive?'

'Oh yes,' I said. 'Ill—but he has a good nurse.'

'Ah.' He seated himself opposite me. 'We'll have some tea. You'd like tea.' He rang a brass hand-bell, and putting it down hurled at me the amazing question: 'Has Vitellius Gracchus come back?'

'Yes,' I replied calmly; 'he came back the night before last and slashed a picture to ribbons. It was an old Barr portrait.'

Ingram fidgeted with his long, fine hands.

'Have they got into touch? So easy! What fortune!'

I didn't know what he meant, so I was quiet. The tea came, in the hands of a dour-faced native woman of middle age. China tea. The doctor poured. Only his eyes were mad, I assure you. Suddenly he poured out a torrent of words, the gist of which was to this effect: why didn't the Barrs have the case investigated? The creature, whatever it was, was so near; it did tangible and visible deeds. It would be so easy to get into touch with it, by means of a séance, a medium. Couldn't I induce Charlie Barr to have a séance and arrange for Ingram to be present?

What I couldn't understand was why all this was so vital to poor Ingram with his mad eyes. As I told you, while he was working on my arm he was as sane as you are. The explanation I'll tell you briefly now, though I didn't know it myself until later. He was constantly striving, without results, to get into communication with his dead wife and children; he thought that if his neighbour could arrange an effective séance with such promising material as 'Gracchus' to start off with, his own pathetic desire might be realized.

So after he'd pleaded for a while, and I'd promised to carry a message to Charlie, he got me to tell him again all about the slashing of the portrait.

'That's bad,' he said; 'that's bad. They'd better watch the Colonel carefully.'

'Miss Goff is most watchful,' I said. 'Nobody is allowed to see Colonel Barr. She keeps his door locked and hardly ever leaves him.'

'Good,' he said. 'Quite necessary. But what does young Barr think about it?'

'He has very little to say about it,' I said. 'When he does speak he makes nothing of it, but I think that's a gesture. I suppose he's rather brave?' Sheer fishing for information on my part.

He took no notice, leaning forward and stretching his hands to the fire. The cottage room was plainly furnished; a round table in the centre with a red cloth, and on it an old-fashioned paraffin lamp burning like a little moon and throwing a circle of light which barely reached us as we sat by the log fire. The curtains were not drawn, and outside the night looked dark and wild. But silent. I remember noticing how silent it was that night, because for the first time since I came to the moor I was undisturbed by elemental noises, particularly the drone of the eerie wind. Something moved in the shadows of the room and came pattering unsteadily to the fireside. It was an old, blind dog, grey-faced and toothless and with long claws that clicked on the flagged floor. I touched its ear and it bared its jaws at me.

Ingram sat back suddenly. 'It's a long time since I was in that house,' he said.

'At The Broch?'

'Yes. How did it strike you?'

'Gloomy,' I said, 'and cold. Perhaps—haunted. I don't know. I've tried to analyse my impressions without great success. I've never been in such a situation before.'

'In such a situation?' he repeated; 'Oh, you mean V. G.! There isn't anyone quite like him, is there? Did you feel when you first went into the house . . . but there, you wouldn't understand. I knew what to expect, so the last time I was in the house, which was on the occasion of Ian's funeral—not so very long ago, after all—I prepared myself for the chill, and it came. A slight brain-shock.' He put his hand to his head with a puzzled gesture. 'Or it may have been physical. I get so confused. You see, it's doubtful whether V. G. would have been present on that occasion. . . .'

He became silent again, while I listened to the heavy, monotonous tick-tock of a grandfather clock, the sound above all others that speaks to you of country peace and nodding sleep in an old arm-chair.

Ingram said suddenly: 'I've got some good books. I can lend you books if you've nothing to do in your spare time. That mixed collection of Barr's—terrible.'

'I know,' I said, 'but I'm hoping not to stay long enough to need your kind help in that direction. At present when I sit down to read I take up a *History of Northumberland*, which runs to about three hundred thousand words. It's Victorian, but quite interesting.'

'I could write a better,' he said. 'I wonder . . . perhaps some day. But it wouldn't be official, you understand. The unofficial history of Northumberland. An ill-fated county. Do you remember how Mary landed—poor soul—from Scotland, only a few miles from here? As soon as her foot touched the shore she was doomed. There were ghosts in the heather watching that boat; the Border dead and the Roman dead who cursed the soil in their dying and made it barren and cruel for all time. In Yorkshire now, in jolly Yorkshire, she might have been safe. Who knows? And you remember Flodden? Only a few miles from here. If they had fought on Scottish soil the flower of Scotland would never have been trampled into a bloodstained moor. The ghosts of Northumberland paralysed their sword-arms! An ill-fated county. And yet when I was a young rascal at Holney I never used to think about these things. Loneliness means too much thinking. . . . But go on telling me about The Broch.'

I laughed uncomfortably and said in a matter-of-fact voice: 'The broch? The latest news is that the spirits have departed from that unlucky watch-tower. A young shepherd—Blaik, they call him—is using it as a sheep-fold. He reads Karl Marx, hates the *bourgeoisie*, and doesn't believe in ghosts. So he's justified of his convictions and his ewes survive the cold nights.'

'I heard about him,' said Ingram; 'my housekeeper was interested.'

'At his temerity?' I said. 'So, I gather, is the whole village.'

Ingram replaced the tea-things on the table with scrupulous care. It was a joy to watch him handle anything, so deft and noise-less. He took up the hand-bell to ring for the dour woman, but thought better of it and put it down again.

'What were you saying about young Barr?' he asked, with one of his quick transitions of subject. 'Something about his being . . . brave, was it? I forget the context.'

'His careful carelessness,' I said, 'gave me that impression.'

Ingram repeated, 'Brave. Yes. He's the last of them, and if V. G. gets him before the Colonel the fortune will go into Chancery.'

'The Colonel is rich?' I said, ignoring the horrid suggestion underlying the sentence.

'Over a million,' he said. 'The Colonel's not a miser, but what they call in these parts canny. The fortune came out of the coal-pits. I lived in the county when I was a boy.' He stared into the fire as he was speaking, and the mad look faded out of his eyes to be replaced with something wistfully reminiscent, likeable. 'My father,' he said, 'was Rector of Holney-on-the-Wall.'

' "Mithras, god of the morning, our trumpets waken the Wall," ' I quoted, drowsy with heat and China tea.

'That's it!' he almost shouted. 'How did you know? The Wall,

and the chariots, and the sandalled soldier in his embrasure! The
nearest analogy in present-day warfare is a desert fort of the French
Foreign Legion—sentries on the watch for a savage horde closing
in across the wilderness of sand . . . I mean . . . the frozen moor.'
His eyes darted again, crazy, into mine. 'You must make young
Barr agree to—you know; what I said! It's to his advantage. He can
be too high-handed.'

'He's rather American,' I said; 'new to this old country.'

'Old country,' he repeated, brooding. Then he suddenly shot at
me, 'Tell me, is it true that Mackie saw V. G.?'

'Mackie?' I repeated stupidly.

'The doctor,' he said. 'The night that Ian Barr died.'

I felt I was on the verge of something. I tried to light a cigarette
with a glowing fragment from the log, but my fingers shook and I
dropped it.

'Have you been to see Mackie?' Ingram went on.

'No,' I said, puzzled. His vague and eccentric mind travelled too
quickly for me and left his meaning always just ungrasped.

'It cost him a dead mare, a fractured thigh, and a cerebral
hæmorrhage,' Ingram went on. 'If it wasn't V. G., then tell me
what made the mare shy? She was skittish, I'll admit, but she'd
been that road often before. Right up into the air she leapt, and
came down with the shaft in her breast. Alec Shawn shot her
when he came on the scene, and there was poor Mackie like a
pulp in the roadway. I went to see him when he came back from
the hospital. 'Ingram,' he said, 'the mare saw him, that deevil of a
Roman soldier.' You'll understand that Mackie's a bit broad in his
speech. Then he told me how he'd seen something flash, and he
got an impression of a man by the moorside—not a man in the
normal sense, you'll understand—and he wasn't even thinking of
V. G., but of a pneumonia case he'd lost. And then the mare gave a
squeal and shot up into the air, and it was all over. . . .'

He was silent for such a long time that I guessed the weird story
was done.

'And was it V. G.?' I said.

He gave me his queer glance. 'It was the night,' he said, 'when
Ian Barr—— But you'll have heard all about that.'

'No,' I protested; but either he didn't or wouldn't hear me. He roughened his grey hair with his hand, uneasily, as though his temples ached.

'I ought to go——' I began. Instantly he stopped me. His face became normal, friendly, quizzical.

'Oh, please!' he said. 'Need you? Mackie used to come and talk to me for hours. I've been lonely, since. Do stop. Where do you come from? What's your business in life?'

'I come from London,' I said. 'I'm a sort of glorified auctioneer.'

'London!' He laughed with a note of eager excitement. He didn't look mad then, only interested. 'Tell me!' he demanded; 'everything you can think of.'

I told him all about post-War London, the struggle for existence, good fellows—brave officers of the War—down on their uppers and selling lavender in Bond Street, the new rich without breeding or education lording it in Society, all the political clap-trap and the talk of the town.

'I shall never go back,' he said; and then the light of reason flickered out of his eyes, and I looked away because I had taken to the fellow, and it was painful to see him like that. He touched my shoulder gravely. 'Somebody I know is here!' he said. I nodded, just to please him. He couldn't have been more than fifty, a little past my own generation.

'Were you in the War?' I asked suddenly.

'I don't know,' he said, quite unmoved; 'I don't remember.'

Of course, Charlie told me why, afterwards.

He suddenly went back to the old subject. 'You'll help me?' he said, with the utmost seriousness. 'You'll try and arrange that séance? I'm almost certain that young Barr could get into touch with V. G.'

I took a new line. 'But what about Charlie Barr?' I said. 'Isn't it just hurling him into danger? I believe myself that V. G., as you call him, is a thoroughly bad character.'

'We should all be there,' said Ingram.

'Look here,' I went on, 'what have the Barrs done to annoy V. G.? He seems positively spiteful. Can you tell me why?'

'I suppose it's something to do with the house,' he said. 'V. G.

considers himself entitled to that piece of land. At least that's what I've always supposed. Of course, they've talked about V. G. in this district for a century, but we never thought he'd do any damage . . . until he seemed to concentrate on the Barrs. Even so, Bourdon's death was undoubtedly due to pneumonia. And he had a valvular lesion for years. . . ."

I got a cigarette lit at last.

'I know very little about these things,' I said; 'so tell me this. I always understood that a poltergeist was harmless. Just mischievous; not malevolent. How did I get that wrong idea?'

'Wrong idea?' he said. 'You're right. But why a poltergeist?'

'Well!' I exclaimed. 'What about the one you call V. G.?'

'A poltergeist!' he repeated. 'Of course they're queer little things. Thinkers have been studying them for centuries. In England, too. They rap, and throw things about, and play silly jokes; the irresponsible children of the spirit world. There was the Tedworth Drummer in the seventeenth century, a famous little fellow; and of course the well-known poltergeist of Epworth Rectory— you've heard of him? The Wesleys were intelligent and responsible people, but unfortunately they didn't know how to investigate, or what were the significant points to which to direct their attention. And nowadays the responsible investigator is never able to arrive on the scene until a crowd of enterprising journalists and sensation-hunters have queered the pitch. But why are we talking about poltergeists? Was it you who began it?'

'V. G.,' I said; 'Barr told me he was a poltergeist. He played tricks with hats and breakfast dishes.'

'Possibly,' said Ingram grimly; 'but if young Barr thinks he's a harmless poltergeist . . . but of course he doesn't! He knows all there is to know about V. G. I suppose he had to tell you the simplest story for your own sake. He wouldn't want to scare you off, or to give himself away.'

'Why do you call him V. G.?' I asked.

For the first time a faint smile twisted his well-cut lips.

'Vitellius Gracchus, if you prefer it,' he said; 'but it's a slipshod age. You had better ask young Barr. Ask him to show you the stone. And I'm relying on you to arrange that séance.'

This made me uncomfortable, and soon after I left, promising to call again next day to show my arm. In the last two minutes I spent with him he was completely sane and rather admirable."

VII

"Now that was a queer conversation, you'll agree, and a queer character to find in the middle of a moor. It all added to my sense of unreality. Unreality. I was by then living in another world, and by and by all other worlds faded. When I came back to London two days ago I had the most curious feeling that I was still there, in the North. It won't leave me; I feel now as though I'd been forcibly disembodied. I'm not myself, so you'll have to be indulgent.

Well, I came out into a hard night. The rain-pools were freezing. As I rode along, the black lake of the sky was shot with curious lights, like lurid flashes from the crackling stars, beaten out by the hammers of the frost. Twice I thought that I saw fires starting on the moor's horizon, but it was only some weird effect of cloud and moonshine. When I came in sight of the sea it was as bright as steel and strangely still, except where a wave seemed to leap under the wandering beam of the lighthouse, sweeping along its circuit. It was becoming very cold, and my breath rose in sad little wraithlike shapes. A strange sensation to watch them flickering away from the handle-bars. When I came to the house there was a terrific altercation in progress between Charlie Barr and Miss Goff. They were carrying on this 'argy-bargying' in the hall for anybody to hear, and at the time I arrived they had both completely lost their tempers. Nerves, you see. They were both strung up. As usual in a domestic riot there was something to be said for both sides, though in this case I was privately rather inclined to sympathize with Charlie.

'Go on,' I said, as I slung my coat over a stag's convenient antlers; 'don't mind me.' So they went on.

'It isn't any use, Mr. Barr,' the nurse was saying, 'so you can argue till doomsday. I've made my rule, and I shall stick to it.'

'And you call yourself an intelligent woman?' Charlie blazed.

'But, of course, that's just like a woman—to put the letter of the law first. A fetish——'

'If the papers are as important as you say they are,' she said icily, 'I'll take them up now to the Colonel, and if he's well enough he shall read them over. But see him you shall not, nor anybody else in this house or this village, but me.'

'But I tell you, the papers need an explanation——'

'Then you can write it and give it to me——'

'Look here, Nurse, once and for all I won't have tyranny from anyone employed in this house. Come with me at once to my uncle's room, or give me the key and let me——'

'I shall not!'

'Then consider yourself dismissed, and leave the house to-morrow!'

'I shall not do that either,' she said coolly. 'Colonel Barr employs me, and no one else has the right to dismiss me.'

There was deadlock for a moment, and then Charlie said, quite reasonably, I thought: 'Will you please to tell me what harm it could possibly do my uncle if you were to prepare him to see me, and I were to go in and talk to him quietly for five minutes? Or three would be sufficient. Just tell me that.'

'No one!' was all she said, and her blue eyes were hot under the starched coif across her forehead.

'But me! Me! Will you tell me why I——'

'Who knows,' she said deliberately, 'from whose hand it will come?'

Their eyes locked for a moment, and then with a stifled exclamation he wheeled into the dining-room, to return in a moment with a slim sheaf of papers. He thrust them into the nurse's hand. 'Here they are. Tell him to make what he can of them, and that I should have *liked*—remember this part—should have liked to have discussed them. They deal with transference of investments, quite a simple matter. If he approves, a mere yes is sufficient. Thank you, Miss Goff.' He made her a stiff bow, but his lips were unsteady, and I was secretly sorry for him. She went upstairs with her usual unhurried step.

'What do you think of that, Mertoun?' said Charlie.

'High-handed,' I said. 'They all are.'

'Yes, but this is carrying things to excess . . . beyond all reason,' he said, with a worried frown. 'I suppose you gathered from what you heard of the edifying conversation that it was the old topic of my uncle's complete seclusion. I was really angry this time, Mertoun. Do you think I'm justified?'

'I quite see your point of view,' I said, 'and I admit I think Miss Goff is unreasonable. But she regards it as her duty——'

He gave me a swift, burning look. 'Mertoun,' he said, 'I'm worried. I don't trust that woman.'

I said in amazement: 'Why, she's got a face as frank as a summer sky!'

'Yes,' he answered curtly. And that was all.

After supper we sat by the library fire, and I said: 'Barr, when are you going to tell me who V. G. is?'

'V. G.?' he said. 'Who's been talking about V. G.? There's only one person calls him that, and it's Ingram, the good old madman. You've been calling on Ingram. No one knows what *he's* going to say next. How did this happen?'

'I fell off M'Coul's bike,' I said, 'and split my arm. This muscular protuberance is a dressing—in fact, Ingram's dressing. He was the only doctor available. What an amazing man!'

'Yes,' said Charlie. 'He once had his plate in Harley Street, London. I don't know it myself, but I guess it's the goods in his profession, isn't it? Lost his wife and family in a motor accident during the War, came up here, buried himself, and quietly went mad.'

'That,' said the voice of Miss Goff from the doorway, 'is hardly fair to Doctor Ingram.'

Charlie flushed, and said quietly: 'I was summarizing the situation, Miss Goff. Is it necessary for you always to misjudge me?'

I was completely in sympathy with Charlie.

She turned to me. 'Perhaps you will let me tell you a little about Doctor Ingram. Strangers can so easily misunderstand.'

'Of course,' I said awkwardly. What else could I say?—though Charlie was looking thoroughly uncomfortable, through no fault of his own.

'Thirteen years ago,' said Miss Goff, 'Doctor Ingram's beautiful wife and three children were burnt to death in a blazing car while he was serving at a Base Hospital in France. Against the advice of his friends he came here . . . he had been a boy in this county . . . and buried himself in the cottage where he still lives. He was alone and companionless. If he had stayed in London with his friends he would have recovered. Instead of that, solitude and one other thing led on to slight derangement. Hereabouts they have no half-shades. They call him mad. The mad doctor. Two years after that tragedy he became a victim of the mania known as spiritualism; that was directly responsible for his lapse from sanity—the mad, unreasonable craving to get into touch with those poor departed spirits which he had adored and lost. Charlatans encouraged him; it was wicked. Of course, he never got any satisfaction; he's still searching, pathetically hoping for the impossible. Two years ago some friends of his from London came and tried to get him away. He became violent. They had to leave him. You see, it's tragic. He was a genius, and such a very lovable man. There must be people who remember him at his best and care for him still, but he shuts his doors against them now. He thinks they're his enemies and want to take him away. And he talks pathetic nonsense about the moors around here being peopled by the ghosts of the dead who died in the battles of the old, savage times. When he's working he's sane, but talk of spirits. . . . They've filled his poor, bewildered brain——'

Charlie made a gesture of distaste to silence her. 'Please, Miss Goff! I think that's enough——'

She hesitated, and said in a different tone: 'Here are your papers. The Colonel has studied them, and he says that he approves.'

'Thank you,' said Charlie curtly. She went out, with a flick of the heavy door-curtain. Charlie pushed the papers into a drawer. 'I'm angry,' he said. 'I'm being treated like a bad child.'

'Forget it,' I said, 'and come here, push your feet to the logs, and tell me about V. G.'

'What do you want to know?' he asked thoughtfully.

'Everything,' I said.

He shuddered slightly, and looked towards the window. 'I'll say it's cold!'

'Freezing,' I said.

'Snow!' he grumbled. 'You should see this place when it's cut off by drifts three feet high. Like a circle of hell. No wonder the folks grow morbid. But you want to hear about Gracchus?'

I suddenly remembered. 'The stone,' I said. 'He said you were to show me the stone.'

'The stone!' he repeated. 'Well, you see, it's covered, and I haven't been near it myself for months. I've been kind of hoping . . . that it would disappear. It may have disappeared; we'll go and look to-morrow morning. Can't go to-night in the dark. But Gracchus, he's a different matter.'

'He's no poltergeist,' I said.

He smiled. 'Of course I deceived you,' he said, 'Naturally. You don't tell such things to strangers.'

'You don't look upon me as a stranger now?'

'Somehow—not,' he said. 'Besides, I might have guessed that you couldn't come to this cursed place without getting an inkling. . . . You'll have to know. Lucky for you, it won't affect you. You'll be gone in a week or two, and it'll be forgotten. It's half legend; half truth.'

I kicked at a log which fell in a little inferno of blue flame and glittering sparks.

'Come!' I said. 'For a beginning, who *is* Vitellius Gracchus?'

'The powerful spirit,' he said, 'of a mighty man; a centurion of the third legion, the Augustine, stationed at Corstopitum in the south of the county some sixteen hundred years ago. . . .' He paused for a minute. 'That's all,' he said abruptly, as though—how shall I explain it?—as though he were addressing himself, a cowering, beseeching Charlie Barr, shrinking in the shadows of the room.

'Oh no!' I said; 'oh no. That isn't all.'

With an outflung hand he snatched back the scarlet silk shade of the electric standard, so that the clear white light broke into the room with its crude glare.

'There!' said Charlie. 'That's better.' He thrust his hands deep down into his pockets. 'I don't know why you stop in a place like this, Mertoun. Other men would have thrown up the job long ago and got out—while the going was good. Other men would look upon us here as a lot of half-crazy devils. So we are. But even we didn't believe that such things could be . . . until they came to be. You go, Mertoun; go to-morrow. We shan't blame you. I speak for my uncle, whom I'm not allowed to see!' The last phrase held a note of bitterness.

'I'm not going,' I said; 'I want to meet this Gracchus.'

His dark eyes withdrew under frowning brows. 'Meet Gracchus and die—as they say in these parts.'

'Very well,' I said; 'I'll abide by the local rules.'

He gave a short, unmirthful laugh. 'I wish I were back in New York. The American part of me pulls that way, but the English roots are as deep as the English rocks. I honestly don't want to tell you any more. You'd much better go away.'

But by then I knew that curiosity alone would hold me there to the bitter end, though I was far from foreseeing what that end would be. So by and by he told me the historical story of Vitellius Gracchus, which half legend, half fact, was harmless enough so far as it went; just a battle story that might belong to any century and any land.

This Roman officer, a man of outstanding personality and military ability, was stationed at the great camp in the south of the county, the headquarters of his legion. To the north was a fearsome desert of moorland, populated by fighting tribesmen. The order was for penetration and conquest, and the establishing of Roman outposts. Gracchus, with a column of a hundred and twenty men—his own company—and half a dozen sub-officers, was sent out to discover and relieve a force which had disappeared in this unknown and perilous region. In those fog-bound, wintry hills this little company was ambushed, miles from the friendly Wall, miles from aid, within sound of the moaning North Sea and the screeching, hostile wind that haunts those waves. They threw up an earthwork and defended themselves; and so they waited and the tribesmen waited. No help came. Some died of starvation, and others of heart-break for these cold northern skies and the memories of golden Rome which they would never see again.

After a week Gracchus led out his men to die in battle. They

marched out in their tattered glory, and once on the open moor
they formed their square, some sixty of them, drew their swords
and waited for the onrush. Hordes of howling tribesmen with tattooed bodies and streaming yellow hair swept down from the hill
crests. The square was never broken, but in a few minutes it was
a square of the Roman dead. Last of all to die, though none had
been more cruelly wounded, was that mighty man the centurion,
Vitellius Gracchus. He lay gasping on the broad surface of an English rock, and with the point of his short sword he carved the one
word ROMA!—and beneath, his name.

'And perhaps it's only a legend,' said Charlie Barr, 'but some
few years ago the Society of Antiquaries, excavating for Roman
remains, laid bare that rock a few feet below the surface. And
where do you suppose they were excavating?'

'I don't know,' I told him.

'In the cellars of this house.'

I started. 'Oh. Then this house . . . ?'

'—Is pitched on the site of Gracchus's last battle—the piece of
earth which he won for Rome. Well, it belonged to Rome for all
anyone cared but the curlews, until the old house on the other
side of the hill was burnt down some hundred years ago, and
my ancestor built again, and chose this place. It was an unlucky
choice. The Gracchus legend had been active in this neighbourhood before then, and suddenly it broke out like a prairie fire. We
can't tell why—which is disappointing—because it was all so long
ago, and nobody kept a record. I sometimes wonder if there was
some sort of manifestation. . . . Anyhow, the new house got an ill
name before the plaster was dry.'

Barr got up suddenly and began to poke the fire with unnecessary violence. 'They say,' he said, 'that a spirit by patient waiting,
even for centuries, can draw to itself more power. Gracchus is
waiting—for his hour. I can't tell you any more until you've seen
the stone.'

'What can there be in the stone——?' I began.

'I'll show you to-morrow,' he said, and his voice had become
strained. 'I told you, I haven't seen it for months. . . . I've been
hoping . . .'

So we both sat over the fire, smoking, in that unpleasant house, and for the life of me I couldn't keep my mind away from the nasty story Ingram had told me about the doctor's mare, and what she saw—or didn't see—on the road.

I said suddenly: 'What do you think, Barr? Ingram told me about the doctor's accident from which he hasn't recovered yet. Did the mare see something? What's behind it all?'

He paled suddenly and his dark eyes gave me a horrified glance.

'Don't ever speak to me about that night!' he said, and he stretched out his foot and clattered the fire-irons into the hearth as though he couldn't endure the silence. So then I knew there was more in it than the doctor's accident. Because previously I had rather suspected Mackie of having come straight from the village pub.

'Look here!' I said. 'You won't be offended, Barr, but I promised poor Ingram I'd mention a matter to you. He has it on his mind, and wouldn't let me go until I promised. I don't know how you'll take it, but don't be hard on the poor fellow. He wants you to have a séance.'

'A séance!' he repeated, half incredulously, half cynically.

'Yes. He thinks it would be easy to get into touch with Gracchus and find out what he wants.'

Charlie took the suggestion lightly, to my relief. 'Tell him,' he said, 'that my Latin isn't equal to it. Classical education isn't a strong point in the States.'

'Surely,' I said, equally lightly, 'after sixteen hundred years in this country our friend ought to be able to oblige us with some proficiency in the vernacular.'

'Pooh!' said Charlie, twisting a spill and plunging it into the reddest furnace of the flames.

'He was very much in earnest about it,' I said.

Charlie suddenly flared. 'I know! He wants to get in touch with his wife. He thinks he'll do it through me and my private ghost. What about me? He doesn't think of what Gracchus might do if we gave him that much liberty! I won't be caught. There'll be no séance.'

The spill which he had forgotten burned down and caught his

fingers, and he used some fine Yankee oaths, until I had to laugh.

'Do you believe that it would be a real danger?' I found myself asking, almost as if I were pleading Ingram's cause. I don't know what had brought me round to that attitude; perhaps my natural obstinacy had been piqued by Charlie's opposition, though it was reasonable that he should oppose the scheme. I granted him that.

'I won't have it, Mertoun,' he said firmly; 'I won't have anything to do with mediums, trances, telekinesis, or controls. So take the whole conjuring outfit away, and tell Ingram to go drown himself at Salt Lake City. And I don't mean maybe.'

So that was final enough, and we parted and went to our rooms. The whole moor was freezing then and the sky looked high and bitter. During the night snow began to fall, coming thicker and faster while we were asleep, and when I looked out in the morning there were great billows of snow rolling away into the hungry mist of the wild moor, and the deadly frost-wind was tearing at the bowed laurels in the garden. A cruel morning. I went down to the dining-room and found Charlie Barr sitting with his head in his hands. He lifted it as I entered. His eyes looked as though he hadn't slept, and there was something wrung about his mouth.

'Mertoun,' he said, 'something's happened. I got thinking about that séance last night, and in the dark I heard someone laugh. I hope I'll never hear that laughter again. He was glad . . . that I wasn't going to track him down.'

M'Coul's footsteps were heard coming along the hall. Charlie snatched up *The Times* and hid his face. Just before the servant entered he said: 'Go and see Ingram to-day, and tell him that we'll have a séance.'"

VIII

"'I want to see the stone,' I reminded Charlie.

So we went down to the cellars, which would have housed an army, provided the army was not particular about darkness and damp. All those old houses are built on a huge foundation of cellarage. These flagged chambers opened one from another, and very dirty they were as well as miserably dank and cold. Char-lie carried an electric torch, for though it was the middle of the morning there wasn't a gleam of daylight in those horrible vaults. I commented on this, and he showed me the reason. The barred windows were buried deep under a dead weight of snow, and as Charlie flashed the torch I could see the greyish mass behind each frozen pane.

There was a wooden trap-door about a yard square let into the flags and this Charlie raised easily with the aid of a ring, and flashed down the light of the torch. I noticed that he himself didn't look down. He rather withdrew.

'You look,' he said. 'Tell me just what you see.'

So I looked, and a couple of feet down I saw the grey surface of a flat rock, bright under the glare of the torch.

'It's there!' I said. 'And I can read the words quite plainly . . . ROMA . . . and VITELLIUS GRACCHUS. . . . Barr! It's amazing . . . almost incredible.'

'What is?' he said in a curious flat voice.

'Why, of course, that those words carved sixteen hundred years ago by a dying man should be not only legible to-day, but clear. May I look more closely?'

'Certainly,' he said, in the same queer, lifeless way. 'Take the torch.'

I went down on my knees and flashed the torch into the cavity. The words were deep and clear, though dark with earth and moss.

I suddenly knelt back. 'What did you expect to find, Charlie?'

'I was hoping that it would have disappeared,' he said, 'as suddenly as it came.'

'As suddenly as it came?'

'When the stone was first uncovered,' he said, 'the traces of an inscription were found. They were quite illegible. Gradually, over a period of years, the words formed. Early last December they were found to have become clear, as you see them to-day. As you see them to-day, Mertoun.'

I gave him back his torch, he closed the trap, and we left the cellar. I didn't ask him anything more. I felt chilled and wretched, not for my own sake, but for his.

In the afternoon I set out to keep my appointment with Ingram. You never saw such a landscape! A rolling plain of grey, windswept snow, and a rolling grey sky over all. I kept to the road by following the tracks of a cart that had brought milk from the village, but the drifts dragged at my feet and nearly brought me to my knees. I thought of London with its swept streets, and it seemed like a place I had seen in a dream years ago. I plodded on, hunched like an old shepherd.

At the junction where the main road branched off to cross the moor I saw a Ford car buried to its axles. The driver was my friend the Glasgow out-porter, who acknowledged me with a surly nod. In the front of the stranded car, huddled into a coat of curly grey fur, was a fair-haired girl, the loveliest girl I think—no, I know!— that I ever saw in my life.

'Hullo!' she said, staring straight at me.

I grabbed at my hat, but honestly my fingers were so frozen that in pulling it off I dropped it in the churned-up snow where the car had made wild plunges in its efforts to escape.

'How do you do?' I said. 'May I help?'

'You jolly well can!' she answered promptly, with an exquisite smile. Her eyes were grey, with long curling lashes, and one blonde tress had escaped from her scarlet béret. 'Can you get me out of this catastrophe and up to Doctor Ingram's house? If you'll be good King Wenceslas I'll be the world's model page. I can leave my luggage.'

'I'm going to Doctor Ingram's,' I said. 'It's a mile from here, and under present conditions we'll do it easily in two hours.'

She laughed eagerly. 'Angel!' she said. 'I'm adoring this adventure.'

So we set out to walk. She was the gayest, prettiest thing you ever dreamed about. Her name was Joan Hope, she was nineteen, and had had one 'perfectly gorgeous' season. Her father was President of the First National Experimental Hospital in Boston, U.S.A., but she herself lived in London with her aunt, Mrs. Thelma Marchant, the popular Member of Parliament. She also explained to me what had brought her to this God-forsaken region. Ingram and her father had been great friends; in fact, it was Joan's father

who had come, as Miss Goff had told me, to try and persuade
Ingram to go back to the healthier influences of his old life and
friends. Joan's father had been badly received, but where he had
failed Joan, with the superb confidence and optimism of modern
youth, hoped to succeed. She had been devoted to Ingram as a
child, a little companion of his own children, and he had made
a fuss of her. So she had packed her things, taken French leave
of her aunt's house while the worthy lady was away touring her
constituency; and here she was in the wilds of Northumberland,
ploughing through the snow-drifts as happy as a lark in summer,
giving all her confidences quite frankly to the first stranger she
met—who, thanks be to Allah, happened to be me!

'He'll be glad to see me,' she kept on saying. 'He'll simply adore
seeing me. I'm glad I'm easy to look at.'

She certainly was that. I was half in love with her myself in
the first ten minutes—I, of the cynical, war-weary, post-war-weary
generation; and afterwards . . . well, I loved her to distraction, and
though I'll never tell her so, for she's meant for some young, happy
boy of her own age, and though I may never see her again, I'll
carry the little snapshot she gave me as long as I live. Sentimental?
Thank God, yes.

Well, we arrived at Ingram's cottage; and while I was discreetly
knocking she, with the divine impatience of youth, rattled the
latch, found it open, burst in, and with a cry of 'Cheer-oh, Uncle
Peter!' threw her arms round the mad doctor's neck and kissed
him heartily.

'It's me!' she said. 'It's Joan. I've come to stop with you a bit.
What a heavenly cottage!'

He grew pale and stood as though he had been turned to stone.
Then he caught sight of me. 'Oh, your arm, Mr.—er——' he said.
'If you'll come this way I'll fix you up with another dressing. No
discomfort, I hope?'

'That's the spirit!' said Joan gaily. 'I'll breeze off and unpack.
And I'd adore some tea; the restaurant car was a swindle.'

He looked at her with a marvellously softened look. 'I don't
quite realize,' he said slowly, 'who you are.'

'Oh, my *angel!*' She clasped her hands to her scarlet béret. 'Did you think I was a potty patient? You must have done. I'm Joan Hope, of course; old Philip Hope's little bit of trouble. Don't you remember playing with me at Forest End?'

'Forest End?' he said. 'Oh, God!'

'Darling,' she inquired, 'where do I strew my suitings? And may I have tea? I'd offer to make it myself, but I can't boil water without burning it.'

'I'll ring for Mrs. Corlett,' he said, as though in a dream. 'There's a nice little spare bedroom.'

She squeezed his arm. 'Splendid. Now you give the kind gentleman his cough mixture, and I'll be back in half an hour. You haven't said you're glad to see me yet, but I've heard of people being stunned with joy. Cheer up. Your lucky number's in the home.'

His eyes, I noticed, followed her to the door. She pulled off her béret with a gay whisk, and her blonde hair caught up all the light in the room. He stood silently for quite a minute, and there was a new look in his eyes now; not madness, nor heavy sadness, but a kind of sweet recollection struggling with the darker memories.

Then he dressed my arm with the swift, pleasurable efficiency of the previous day.

'Thanks most awfully!' I said. 'Will you let me send you something, a small memento, when I get back to London? A charming miniature of Marie Antoinette. It isn't valuable, but you'll love to look at the face.'

He nodded. 'I'll accept that, with pleasure. And you'll have forgotten there was anything wrong with that arm in a week, unless you're idiot enough to shovel snow with it. I've been shovelling snow all the morning. How are you for drifts at The Broch?'

'I understand the outer doors wouldn't open,' I said, 'until M'Coul climbed out of the scullery window with a shovel and got to work. Charlie Barr's working in his study. I don't think it would worry him if the drifts cut us off. He certainly wouldn't shovel snow; he says white is the most depressing hue on earth.'

The mention of Charlie Barr was enough.

'Did you ask him?' Ingram flashed at me, and his face grew avid with unhappy eagerness.

I felt suddenly sick of the whole subject; as though I didn't want to discuss it or ever hear it discussed again. I didn't ask myself why, or whether the coming of Joan Hope had been like a ray of clear, rainbow light penetrating our darkness; but because of what had happened yesterday I had to say: 'Yes. He'll have a séance.'

'When?' he asked eagerly.

'He didn't say.'

He began calculating. 'To-morrow . . . Thursday . . . not enough time. I know of an excellent medium. Hunter of Holney would bring him. They could be here by Friday. Will you ask Barr if Friday night would do? You'll press it, won't you?'

I said that I'd pass the suggestion on to Charlie. You'll notice that I hadn't gone into any details of my conversation with Charlie, or mentioned how at first he'd absolutely vetoed the séance, only to change his mind this morning after some rather disquieting experience or impression during the night. I thought it was enough for Ingram to know that Barr agreed.

But I wasn't going to get away from the subject easily. Ingram made me sit down in one of those comfortable old high-backed chairs before the log fire, and light a pipe; and, truth to tell, I wasn't anxious to hurry away, for I rather hoped to be present when a refreshed and settled Joan Hope made her reappearance.

'That's a charming girl,' I said. 'She told me she was the daughter of an old friend of yours, and had suddenly taken it into her head to dart up north and pay you a visit. I found her in the station car, stuck in a snow-drift, so I helped her out and that was how we happened to walk in on you together. Modern young girls are rather sudden.'

He shook his head. 'I ought to know her,' he said; 'but that all belongs to something I've forgotten.'

'You won't be dull with her in the house,' I said; 'I wish she'd descended on The Broch.'

'The Broch?' He caught me up at once. 'Did he show you the stone?'

'Um,' I said.

'And is it——'

'The inscription,' I said, 'is quite deep and legible. When did you see it?'

'For the first time,' he said, 'when the Antiquaries uncovered the rock. I remember how we pored over those queer marks, too broken to be recognizable as letters, except for the R and the V, which certainly looked like Roman capitals. The second time was about ten months ago when Colonel Barr sent for me to see a curious sight; it was that faint inscription, now easily discernible and legible under a magnifying-glass. I remember how we all stared at each other, wondering what it meant, that gradual appearing of the words after long centuries. Mackie was there as well as myself and the Colonel, Mr. Ian Barr, and young Charlie Barr. Mackie crossed himself hastily—he's a devout Catholic—and said, "Merciful saints! That Roman devil's loose among us, and here's his hand to it!" And the third time I saw the inscription—well, it was on the day of Ian Barr's funeral, and the stone letters were as you saw them this morning, deep and clear, though dark with earth and moss. Mackie was groaning in the hospital by then, and the Colonel, Charlie and I stood by the rock. "Cover it up!" said Charlie; "cover it quick. It may fade, here in the dark." But I think he hadn't much hope of it fading. It must have been a shock to him when he saw it this morning, and the Colonel so ill. He's living, I suppose?'

'Oh yes,' I assured him. 'The nurse says he's certain to recover so long as he has absolute quiet. I should have thought Charlie himself was in the worse position.'

'Ah yes.'

Ingram snapped his fingers to the blind dog, who came lurching across the floor, his claws clicking on the flags, and flopped down with a grunt on his master's feet.

'There's only one story I want to hear,' I said boldly, 'and that's what happened the night Ian Barr died—fell over the cliffs. The station porter told me that much. But there's more behind it, isn't there?'

'Of course,' he said promptly. 'There was Mackie's accident.'

'Oh!' I said. 'Then there *was* a connection.'

'I shan't forget that night,' he said, staring at the logs; 'the twelfth of December last. Things had been very quiet in the countryside; we hadn't had anything to talk about for weeks. I'd had a particularly desolate and disquieting time myself, because someone I knew had been trying to come to see me and they wouldn't let her through. I think that was on account of the moors being so dark on winter nights. . . .'

This made me uncomfortable; I had to head him off from this subject, so I said quickly, 'Yes. The village. On the twelfth of December, wasn't it?'

He looked up, almost gratefully. 'Yes, the twelfth of December. The winter nights closed in very early, round about four o'clock. It was fine, cold weather with just a slight winter mist, not enough to prevent one seeing, say, twenty or thirty yards ahead. That's important when you think of Ian Barr. . . . However, just before eight I put old Sturdy, here, on the lead and set off down to the village for some tobacco. You get it at the smith's, you know, where they also sell kettles and candles, which always seems a queer thing to me. So while the smith was serving me he said, with all the importance of a village news-bearer, "Have you heard the tale?" "What's that?" I said. "Why, they're saying," he said, "that Doctor Mackie's smashed himself up coming over from Tibby's farm in the dark. Alec Shawn came in a while ago and fetched some of the lads. Alec says the mare's dead and the doctor as near to it as doesn't matter. Mrs. Mackie's rung up the cottage hospital to send an ambulance, so young Mona at the post office is telling me. Bad job, isn't it?" "Very bad," I said, "what can have happened?" He shook his head. "Deil knows," he said. "It's a clear road and the doctor's been over it more times than I've got whiskers." When I got out into the village they were all in little knots, waiting for the ambulance and talking as fast as they knew how. Then Alec Shawn came along and told how he'd found the mare on the road bleeding with the shaft in her breast, and the trap overturned, and the doctor underneath it. "The mare," he said, "she must have jumped clear up into the air. But why? There hasn't been so much as a motor-cycle that way this night." After they'd taken Mackie away I went along to the Fox and Hounds and sat there. Somehow I seemed to want company that night. The men were talking, and I sat quietly in my corner. "Believe me," one of them said, "it was no human thing that frighted the doctor's mare. There's things on that moor 'ud drive a man's wits into his gullet and choke him." They all seemed to agree. "What about that Roman felly," another said, "that put a curse on old Geordie's mare so that all her foals were born with five legs?" They considered that idea with approval; and remember it wasn't until weeks later when Mackie came back from the hospital that he told us what had really frightened the mare. It was undoubtedly the Roman ghost, and you must mark the fact that this was his first recorded manifestation. . . .

But to go back to the night of the accident; you'd think enough had happened to give one village a topic for conversation; however, as we were sitting at the inn the door opened and Colonel Barr looked in. He didn't see me at first. "Hullo, fellows," he said, "have any of you seen my brother?" No one as it happened had seen Ian Barr that evening. Barr told us that his brother had left The Broch at four o'clock to walk over to a farm to see some spaniel puppies. He was fond of walking, was Ian, even in the dark of winter evenings. He had promised to be back by nine, which was the supper hour. It was now almost eleven and he had not arrived. What was more surprising, the Colonel while walking down to the village had met a labourer from the farm in question who said that he had seen Mr. Ian Barr leave the farm at eight o'clock. The homeward walk shouldn't have taken more than an hour. "I made sure he'd dropped in here for a crack," the Colonel said, looking in a disappointed way about the inn parlour which was veiled in tobacco smoke. Then he noticed me, called me out, and offered to walk home with me. So he brought me to this gate and we parted there. His last words to me were, "He's sure to be at home when I get back." He wasn't in the least apprehensive.

The body of Ian Barr was discovered at five o'clock next morning by two lads hunting on the shore—poaching, I should say—for lobster-pots. He had obviously fallen over the cliff, for there were the scuffled marks on the brink above. The place where he had fallen was at least a dozen yards from the path he must have been taking on his homeward way; he knew every step of the path; and it was a mystery how and why he should have come so near the edge of the cliff as to fall over. The mist was so slight, one couldn't blame that. Ugly rumours began to float round. Suicide. But it was absurd on the face of it. Ian Barr was a contented man, fond of his hobbies and of country life; a healthy man, if not over-strong not subject to any disease. However, when it was broad daylight, they found in a patch of loose earth at the head of the cliff footmarks; those of Ian Barr, who had fallen, and of another man, and at that the whole countryside became like a boiling pot. It was murder. The men with their guns scoured the moorland for miles around. Women locked themselves into their houses, afraid of some desperate villain at large. But when we came to look closely at those mysterious footmarks it was easy to see they were made by a shoe the like of which was never worn by modern man. Though a Roman sandal could have made such prints. . . . Then a panic broke out, and somebody asked again what it might have been that the doctor's mare saw, coming over the moor road. The terror was loose among us; a fierce, earth-bound spirit, struggling through the centuries to take shape. So that was the end of Ian Barr, and what his last moments were, no one will ever know . . . unless another Barr meets the same fate. One knows of no precautions. . . .'

'I should be interested,' I said, 'to hear the verdict of the coroner's jury. I suppose there was an inquest?'

'It was adjourned twice,' he said, 'and then in the end they brought in death by misadventure. An extraordinary verdict, but it was all so confusing. Some of them even tried to make it out an Act of God.'

'I suppose it didn't occur to anyone,' I said, 'that Ian Barr might have been dazzled by a sudden light. Supposing the beam of the lighthouse had flashed full in his eyes, it might have bewildered him sufficiently to account for a twelve-yards divergence from the path to the cliff-edge.'

'It might,' said Ingram; 'but you didn't see the footmarks!'

Now that was more or less the end of that conversation, and I suppose I'd found out by this time all I wanted to know; my imagination could fill in the blanks.

As I left the cottage I was hailed from above. Joan Hope was leaning out of an upper window, her pretty head framed by the sere ivy.

'What's your name?' she called. 'Where do you live?'

So I told her, and also that I was stopping not far away.

'Shall I be seeing you again soon?' she asked.

'I hope so,' I said.

'Will you come for a walk to-morrow morning?'

'No,' I said; 'I shall be working.'

'To-morrow afternoon, then?'

'Rather!' said I. 'But what about all this?' And I waved my hand towards the ocean of snow, obliterating the paths.

'Oh, that makes it more fun,' she said promptly. 'I'll meet you in that comic village we came through, at two o'clock. Bung-ho!'

'Bung-ho!' said I.

So on the whole I went back to The Broch with my mind, as they say in the best novels, in 'a whirl of conflicting emotions.'"

IX

"You were asking me, what had happened to Miss Goff all this time. As a matter of fact, I'd seen very little of her. She seemed more attentive than ever to her patient. I'm bound to admit that there was something else too; whereas at the beginning she and I had seemed rather drawn together—you'll remember the occasions from what I've told you—now there was a definite reserve in her manner when she happened upon me in the house. I'm sure it wasn't my fault; it must have been hers, and I wasn't in the least able to account for it. In fact, I didn't try to account for it, because if I was conscious of it I wasn't troubled by it. I do remember wondering once if she had taken offence—heavens, how women do take offence!—at my having rather allied myself with Charlie in criticizing her rigid ruling in the case of the Colonel's seclusion. Certainly, I did think she was overdoing it, and I'd have told her so if we'd been on anything like familiar terms; but I gave her the credit for her devotion to what she thought was her duty, and for her anxiety on the Colonel's behalf. She evidently had a great personal regard for him, and was eaten up with a superstitious fear which her profession wouldn't allow her to admit. Poor Miss Goff. Deep down, I had a sincere liking for her. When I get to the end of my story, and you read for yourself the letter I had from her this morning, you'll realize what a difficult job I'm having now in making an impartial estimate of her motives at this stage of the affair.

But I must tell you about my walk with Joan. When I got to the village to keep the appointment, I found her already there, leaning against the palings of the Institute and biting the corners off one of those big blocks of Cadbury's milk chocolate.

'Here!' she said, in the last stages of impatience; 'chop this thing up. Thanks frightfully, but bigger lumps, please. I've been out here half an hour and every man, woman, child, and cow in the village has been along to inspect the exhibit.' She was worth inspection too, in nice little Harris tweeds with a yellow scarf and golden hair in smooth, gleaming waves. No hat. I told her she'd get a mastoid, or something, in that east wind, and she laughed with pure delight and said, 'Darling, don't be too utterly antediluvian!' So that was that.

'I'm having a heavenly time at the cottage,' she said, as we set off briskly. 'I thought poor Uncle Peter wasn't quite so blue at breakfast this morning. I haven't made him laugh yet; but if he doesn't like me, at least he doesn't mind me. Oh, and I must remember, that means something quite different here. It's the biggest jape in the world. What would you say, Billy, if I asked you, "Do you mind my face?"'

'I should reply,' I said, '"My dear Joan, for the sake of your feelings I shall try to endure what is your misfortune rather than your responsibility."'

She shouted, 'Isn't it gorgeous! And it only means, "Do you remember me?" I'm going to try it on everybody in London.'

She began kicking up the loose snow with her shoes and getting herself very wet, which she seemed to enjoy; and suddenly she waved her hand to the whole of that vast, desolate, bristling, snow-smothered moorland, with the cruel grey sky above, and cried: 'Isn't this the jolliest place you ever saw?'

'If I'd just escaped from Devil's Island,' I said, 'I might say yes.'

'Don't you like it?' she said, very astonished.

'I rather hate it,' I told her.

'Oh, but it's so big. I never felt so free in my life. Look here! Can I smell the sea, or am I under chloroform?'

'Probably you can,' I said; 'we're not a mile from it.'

'Oh, please let's go where we can see it!' She grabbed my hand. '"All the king's horses, all the king's men!"' she sang, and laughed in my face when I told her she was quite mad.

'Where's the house where you're staying?' she asked.

'Not far from here.'

'House-party? Is it jolly?'

'Heavens, no,' I said; 'I'm cataloguing a library for an old man who's ill in bed.'

'How divine!' was her inappropriate comment. 'What's the house like? I like houses.'

'Just gloomy and old,' I said.

'It sounds ripping,' she said. 'Is there a ghost?'

'No.'

'Oh, how deadly uninteresting for you!' she said. 'I was stopping at a house in the country last summer where they had a perfectly marvellous ghost. Lady Robinetta. Isn't it a wonderful name? She used to walk about the garden at night, wringing her hands, with pond-weed in her hair. Of course, nobody had ever actually seen her, but it was fun to pretend you were fearfully scared when you went out in the garden alone after dark.'

'That wouldn't happen to you very often,' I said.

She widened her eyes, clasped her brow, and pretended to be enduring torments of concentrated thought. 'Oh, I get you. Heavy Victorian compliment intended. Well, don't be afraid of me. I think those old customs are rather sweet. And no, as it happens, I wasn't particularly lonely that time. . . . My dear!'

'What is it now?'

She pointed. 'Thalassa! Thalassa!'

'How terribly classical of you,' I said.

'Young brother,' she said curtly; 'Harrow. Bit of an ass.' She pirouetted in the snow. 'Look, aren't the waves savage this morning? If it were summer I could stay up here for hours, watching the sea. In one of my lives I was a conger-eel.'

'No,' I said; 'one of those charming rainbow fish that flick their little tails in the sunny southern seas.'

She liked that. Her lovely eyes sparkled. 'Oh!' she cried, 'a lighthouse. Wouldn't I like to go! Billy . . . Billy, get a boat and take me out.'

'Alas,' I said, 'it cannot be. No visitors allowed on his Majesty's lighthouses.'

'Why?' she demanded.

'For the same reason,' I told her, 'that most of the things in life that you most want to do are forbidden.'

'That wouldn't prevent me,' she said, 'if I really wanted. But things are very well as they are. I'm frightfully happy—always.'

'Probably,' I said, 'you have everything in the world to make you happy.'

'It isn't that,' she replied quickly. 'Of course I like fun, and clothes, and the cream-bunny side of life—but I think it's chiefly places.'

'Places?'

'Well, yes. You don't have to pay to look at sky and water. Isn't it jolly to think of all the different places there are left for me to see, and every one a different thrill? This, for instance. And two days ago I didn't know it existed. I think it's glorious. Miles of lovely snow, and leagues of lovely sea. Oh, I'm so happy I could shout! Shout, Billy! Whoop—like wild Indians!' And she actually shouted for joy, until those grim old hills seemed to shudder at the unexpected sound.

She slipped her arm into mine in her sudden way.

'Miserable, Billy? What have I said?'

'Only old age,' I said, 'and not being able to see things through your eyes, Joan.'

'Why don't you like this place?' she asked.

'Because it's cruel,' I said; 'cruel to people I rather care about.'

'Oh, you mean Uncle Peter!' she cried. 'But I'm going to alter all that. It's because of his wife, you know, and the two little boys and the baby. He thinks they're here and he has to stay with them, and he talks to them in the dark. I heard him last night. She was called Cynthia and I just remember her; she was perfectly lovely. To-night I'll make him talk to me about her, and then I guess he'll feel better. You needn't worry about Uncle Peter; he'll be all right. Buck up, Billy.'

You can guess how I 'bucked up.' We tramped on across that snowy moor without noticing how far we were going until we came to a small hamlet which must have been forgotten from the beginning of time. There was a tiny pub, and she dragged me in and demanded ham and eggs. The squarest woman I ever saw— she was about a quarter of an acre—brought us a huge rasher and *eight* eggs. Joan and I consumed this meal—honestly we did—at four o'clock of a winter's afternoon, in a little parlour the walls of which were stiff with yellowed funeral cards. Joan ate three eggs and I ate five, and then arm in arm we read all those funereal inscriptions, the annals of a forgotten village. Then we sat by the fire and she told me ridiculous stories about the school she had been to at Lausanne and the tricks those terrible girls used to play on the German governess.

'Come on,' she said at last, quite suddenly. 'Let's go home.'

It was dark now, and misty. I took her to Ingram's door and waited until I saw her safely into the house. Rather a marvellous afternoon. It's difficult to explain the effect it had on me. It was as though Joan's presence was a talisman against all evil; against darkness, fear, cruelty and death. You couldn't think of these things in connection with her. As I turned away from Ingram's gate the picture that was clear in my mind was Joan, standing on a rock and radiant as a beam of light, and beyond her all the tossing, greedy billows of the grey North Sea. I could hear her pretty ringing voice for hours after, just like a strain of music, adorably ridiculous . . . 'and there was old Fräulein, Billy, looking exactly like an ossified beetroot . . . a pound and a half of *petits fours* in her shoe locker, the *pig* . . . and Madame was such a mixture of heavenly piety and earthly fascination, my dear, like Saint Teresa and Mistinguett in one. . . .' Ridiculous. Divine. Joan—just nineteen.

Another of those terrible winter nights was closing in as I tramped back through the treacherous snow. The thaw was beginning already, and there was a noise of hidden streams. The village lights waned behind me through an encrimsoned fog. I felt like an explorer in a nightmare country, striding into the unknown. Before I was back at The Broch the old horror was on me, and I was thinking of nothing but the vivid story of Ian Barr's death and the prints of the Roman sandal. I don't know how it struck you, but to me all the terror of the narrative seemed to cling round that ominous print. That sandal-print seemed to give the whole story a cold veracity, whereas the tale of a sheeted figure seen slipping away from the scene of the crime would merely have made me laugh. A sandal-print, cold under the moon, and a wilderness of empty heather! Do you remember how in the old story Crusoe saw the footprint in the sand? Just a thrill of horror, and then— nothing. An empty horizon. That was how I felt about the Roman ghost. And I couldn't forget that down in the cellar below me was the living stone. I wondered why Charlie didn't take a load of earth and tip it into the cavity; perhaps he had more control, was less headlong, than I.

The library was in darkness as I looked in on my way upstairs. Just as I was going on I saw someone sitting by the fire, bent, with his head buried in his hands. It was poor Charlie. He must have heard me, for he suddenly jerked up, and said savagely: 'Don't stand there, M'Coul, curse you! Switch the lights on!'

I switched them on, and when Charlie saw it was me, he averted his head quickly and pretended to be examining a book. I went away. Poor old Charlie. I don't know to this day what had happened, or whether I had just surprised him with his brave mask off.

That night I slept well. I was tired from my tramp in the keen moorland air, and emotionally excited. When I woke next morning, believe me, I wasn't thinking of ghosts or of death, nor even of poor Charlie—heartless of me, that—but of Joan. Youth is exhilarating . . . young companionship.

I worked all the morning with one idea in my mind, to see her again. I wanted to forget horror, and laugh at things as we'd laughed together in that stuffy little moorland inn.

Charlie came in to lunch with me, and after we'd discussed the China question, and the Irish question, and the Labour Party, and the Soviet, and all the other newspaper ramps, he began to tell me about a ruined abbey five miles away to the west, and so well worth a visit that I ought to inspect it without delay. It makes me smile now to remember my state of apprehension while he went on to describe the peculiarities of the cloister and to tell monkish legends, sinister and merely rapscallion. I thought he was going to offer to take me over that afternoon; and I was making wild plans to include Ingram and Joan in the expedition—and to lose Ingram and Charlie.

However, I soon realized that Barr hadn't any intention of scouring the country with me. It was just a gallant effort on his part to make conversation, and when I realized what he was doing I admired him for it. I couldn't get out of my mind the picture of him sitting there in the dark of the previous night, head in hands, and the ashes of the forgotten fire paling at his feet. So I talked easily and lightly for his sake, and summoned a laugh, and felt a hypocrite and rather hated myself that I could cheerfully leave him and his tragic house to go in search of adventure with a gay young girl.

I said: 'I've completed a large section this morning. I suppose you won't mind if I take a breather this afternoon. I can go on with my index for two or three hours after supper.'

'You're going walking?'

'Probably.'

He smiled wearily. 'You must be fond of walking! But do beware of the moors . . . they're treacherous.' He caught my eye and added, 'I don't mean anything sinister. But men have disappeared and from absolutely natural causes. The heath is full of pits, and the pits are full of stones, and I can't imagine a nastier death than starvation with a broken leg in a twelve-foot hole. It has happened.'

'I'll be careful,' I said. 'Then I have your permission to be away?'

'But of course. This house is gloomy enough without your being a prisoner in it. You must think longingly of your Whitehall Club!'

He smiled stiffly and left the room. In ten minutes I had seized cap, stick, and overcoat, and was swinging out of the drive gates on the road that led to the village.

Joan knew no conventional reticences, and I wasn't going to be bound by any. If I couldn't find her in the village I should go boldly to Ingram's house and tell her I wanted her.

But I found her, quite easily, in the village. Nobody in that village could have missed her. She was the centre of a skipping-match on the green. Two great hulking youths—pop-eyed from their unusual exertions—each held an end, and a mass of mixed juvenility between the ages of five and fifteen leapt and shrieked with delight above the whiz of a flying rope. Above those black and brown Northumbrian heads rose the blonde shingle of my girl. She was shouting louder than the loudest; she yelled as her little brown brogues cleared the rope, and her excited laughter was so full of mirth that it would have made a stone gargoyle split his sides.

I stood laughing myself for a full minute. Suddenly she saw me. With a ringing halloo she flung off all her motley young playmates and came twirling and skipping to my side.

'Hullo, Billy,' she said, not even breathless; 'I'm a hoyden.'

'I see you are,' I said.

'Please, where are you going?'

'I'm going to see a ruined abbey.'

'Oh, how divine. Are we going to have tea there?'

I burst out laughing, and promptly she slipped her arm into mine and marched beside me, with a gay shout that you couldn't call singing . . . 'Some *talk* of Alexander, and *some* of Hercules! . . .'

We left the village behind us. She said: "Billy, I can think of some ghastly spectacles, but I honestly can't think of anything worse than a ruined abbey. Is that really your idea of a jolly afternoon?'

'It's historical,' I said. 'The monks——'

'I know,' she said, long-faced; 'their lives became drearier and drearier, until with a yell they leapt from their cell and eloped with the Mother Supe——'

'Stop it!' I snapped. 'I'm disgusted with you. You've no sense of tradition.'

'Billy——' she said, thinking deeply.

'Yes?'

'I could have had a sense of tradition, but I never had a chance. I've always longed to belong to one of those hoary families with limpets on the keel, that came over with William the Conqueror, so that I could go to the Three Arts Ball as my ancestress, the Lady Guinevere, who was shot for treason in 1066. She sent a cable to King Harold—her old love, you know—that William was approaching Eastbourne. As dawn's rosy fingers stole into the eastern sky she faced the Norman arrows. Her last words were . . . oh, Billy, it's too sad. I can't go on. I only made her up a minute ago, and she's so beautiful I can't believe she never lived. Oh dear! What a divine ancestress!'

'Her last words,' I said, 'were, "A woman, by the mercifulness of Allah, is not responsible for her descendants."'

'No, Billy,' said Joan in a subdued voice. 'She only spoke French, poor darling. She may have been ambidextrous, but I'm quite sure she wasn't polyglottous.'

Perhaps it all sounds ridiculous as I tell it now. Remember that I was in a wrought-up, imaginative state, and that Joan was just an excited child full of the heady wine of freedom.

I said: 'You've spoiled my afternoon, and now it's up to you to suggest something better. I haven't any ideas.'

'Then let's go and examine the local haunt.'

'The—what?'

'That weird tower thing near where you're staying. The boy who brings our milk told me it was full of ghosts.'

'I wouldn't take you near that place for a thousand pounds,' I said.

She opened her eyes. 'Billy! Why? . . . I say, you *don't* believe our milk-boy? What a joke.'

'It's a particularly unsafe place for you to go,' I said.

She jerked her arm out of mine. 'Please don't be chivalrous to me. It gives me a pain in the neck.'

'Now, Joan——'

'I know. When men don't want to do something to please you they always pretend they're being chivalrous, and it makes me so mad I could chew a tea-cup.'

I told her she was behaving like a spoilt child, and that sobered her considerably. She said: 'I don't want to be flippant. I want to have a really serious afternoon, and walk along the moor road to the cliffs and think about the ghosts of the Roman dead, and the Border dead. . . .'

I broke in: 'You got that from Ingram?'

'Yes, he was telling me last night. It's rather terrible, isn't it? This
is a haunted place, Billy—in spite of my laughing at the milk-boy. I
can almost feel it—quite a different feeling from the time when we
used to laugh about Lady Robinetta in the garden at Chesley Park.
She was just a joke; this isn't. Honestly I'm serious, Billy. There's a
great giant of a Roman soldier stalks these moors at night . . . has
done for hundreds of years. It's true. Did you know?'

'I've heard,' I said; 'I wish you hadn't.'

'Why not? It thrills me. I wouldn't mind seeing him . . . if I had
hold of your hand. Though nobody has actually seen him, have
they?'

I thought of Doctor Mackie . . . and of Ian Barr.

'I don't suppose anybody ever will,' I said.

'And he lives in the tower on the hill,' she said.

'I never heard that story!' I exclaimed.

She swung half-round. 'Look! Can't you believe it?'

The unwalled road on which we were walking ran clear across
the moor, and the air had that lurid clarity which comes before a
storm. The blackened heather was exactly like an angry sea, waves
of it, rolling under the wind with its sighing, crackling sound. To
the east, perhaps a mile away, rose the mound, and on the mound
the broch, a blot with jagged edges. The sky behind it was livid; it
looked alive.

'Not canny,' I said. 'Yes . . . I'll give it credit for being the home
of your monster.'

'Let's go and see.'

'Not on your life, girl!'

She dug her hands in her pockets. 'Funk!' she said clearly; and
leaving me she plunged into that swelling tide of heather. For a
few yards she made rapid progress; but then the stalks and the
hidden stones caught her feet, and she suddenly fell to her knees
with a cry of impatience.

'I could have told you so,' I said calmly. 'You'd much better
come round with me by the road.'

Her eyes sparkled. 'We're going then?'

'We're going to explore every stone of that ugly place,' I said.

This was nothing but a mean deception on my part and I'm

almost ashamed to tell it. I knew that a heavy storm was coming and would be on us long before we got to the broch. I wasn't going to take that reckless girl into any doubtful adventures.

'Good,' she said. 'Come on, stout Cortez.'

We swung along at a good four miles an hour . . . and the storm delayed. I reckoned that it would take us about forty minutes to walk round by the road to the broch, and I hoped that the storm would be on us in ten. It didn't come. I set my teeth. Soon the stones of the ruin were clearly visible, and the tangled, stripped hazel-bushes at its base.

'Do we storm it?' said Joan fiercely. 'Or do we ambush it on hands and knees?'

'It's a sharp climb,' I said. 'You'll tear your shoes to pieces.'

'What,' she said, 'are shoes for?'

'I hope you like it better,' I said, 'on closer acquaintance.'

She stood still. 'There's something horrible about it, Billy. Honestly there is. I'm not in a funk . . . but we ought to have a torch. It's pitch-black in there.'

'It's pitch-black everywhere,' I said; and at that moment the storm broke. Such a storm as I never remember in my life before and hope I shall never face again. We simply dropped where we were and crouched like wild rabbits, and around us all the storms of the world congregated together and went mad. Joan shrieked something at me, and I couldn't hear a word. It was no use trying to talk; the yelling of the wind and the crashing of the thunder, and in a few moments the booming of great seas on the rocks, drowned and deafened us. We both pressed our hands to our ears and crushed ourselves against the ground to keep from being blown away like bits of paper. The sky was jet black until the lightning ripped it open, and then it blazed with blue and white electric flashes. I thought, 'Wait till the rain comes!' The rain came. It was as though the sea had leapt over the cliffs and descended upon us. Wall after wall of water until the heather-tops rose and writhed above a yellow torrent. It swirled round our waists as we crouched. And this wasn't a momentary experience. The deluge, lightning, thunder, and tempest continued for nearly three-quarters of an hour. Then gradually, gradually it faded; a little light, grey and wraithlike, crept out of the ravaged sky; and in a plaintive, falling rain, mild and infantile, Joan and I rose up and faced one another. She looked as though she had been taken out of the Thames. So, I suppose, did I.

I said: 'Are you wet?'

'No thank you, dear,' she said sweetly. 'Where did you put the lobster mayonnaise? Underneath the ice-cream freezer?'

She shook herself and shrugged her dripping shoulders. Then she gave a distinct shudder.

'You'll get your death,' I said. 'Let's go, and quickly.'

'I'm not cold,' she said; 'but I've learned a lesson.'

'What do you mean?'

'Not to interfere. That awful place . . . it showed us clearly it didn't want us.'

'You think it was the broch——'

She shivered. 'Don't ever talk to me again about Roman ghosts. I'll never forget this. Look at that horrible tower.'

It loomed, as black as a carrion crow, on the mound above us, and the sky behind it was a violent purple slashed with the colours of storm. Many of the hazel-bushes were stricken and looked more tangled than ever. From the ground there rose to the jagged crown a frosty mist, hanging on the lips of those ill-fated stones. I thought of the temerity of the shepherd, Blaik, and I believe if I had been alone I should have charged the tower at that moment and satisfied my curiosity.

I had to confess. 'I never intended to take you, Joan,' I said; 'I knew the storm would be on us before we arrived. It's too horrible a place for a picnic. The Roman ghost is a tragic fact to the family where I'm staying, and one member of it has already met his death . . . nobody knows how . . . except that he was quite alone in the black desolation of this moor and within sight of the North Sea. Some people say he saw what nobody has yet seen. We'll never know. But I don't feel inclined to make a jolly spook-hunting party out of an affair like that.'

'I'll forgive you,' she said with a curt nod, still staring at the broch. 'What about this man who uses it for a sheep-fold?'

'I suppose you heard about that in the village?'

'Yes. I thought where he could go, I could go. They say he's either in league with the Thing, or daring it. Is that nonsense?'

'Probably,' I said.

She tried to dry her face on a sodden pocket-handkerchief.

'I hope nothing will happen to him while I'm here. They were prophesying awful calamities in the village, and I laughed. I think perhaps there are some things in the world not meant to laugh at. This has gloomed me, Billy.'

'Let's go home,' I said. 'A bright fire will make things look different.'

She said: 'Are they jolly people where you're staying?'

'Rather sad people,' I said; 'a sick old man, and a very brave young one who's putting up a fight for his house and his tradition. I hardly know them. I'm a stranger.'

'Are they afraid of the ghost?'

'Not afraid. They're defying it. It's a long strain . . . a waiting game.'

'I think you're plucky to stay there.'

'It's my job,' I said, 'and I rather admire the Barrs, especially the young one.'

'Should I like him?'

'You'd probably find him good company. He's a charming man. He comes from New York.'

'New York!' She opened her eyes. 'Say, I could shoot him the glad mitt, couldn't I? Why did he come to England?'

'Because this house . . . ghost and all . . . tragedy included . . . is his family inheritance, and he'll hold it till he drops.'

She nodded approval and said no more, so we tramped on in silence; but Joan could never be downcast long and almost as soon as we were out of sight of the broch she was making jokes about my draggled appearance and quite forgetting her own.

'We look like Lord and Lady Mud going to Court!' she cried; 'I ought to have a bouquet. Why isn't there anything to pick?' She caught sight of some cabbage-like weeds sprouting at the moor's edge and snatched a handful. 'Look, Billy!' She struck an attitude . . . 'Lines from Dante Gabriel Rossetti. She had three lilies in her hand, and the teeth in her head were seven.'

'I've no use for you,' I said. 'You can't respect English poetry.'

She tossed the weeds away and turned on me with flashing eyes.

'I do. I can. Beast, to say that! Cadski!'

So we reached the village exchanging happy abuse; and after tea and toast at Ingram's and a chat about everything on earth but Roman ghosts, I went back, wet clothes and all, to Charlie's unhappy house."

X

"Now I'll come straight to the séance on the Friday evening. It will take a lot of explaining, that mixture of charlatanism and dread reality. I don't want you to read into what I'm going to tell you any of my supposed views on the reliability of mediums; that is a matter entirely beside the point. The medium who came was a decent, highly strung fellow, an artist to his finger-tips. I was sorry for him. He was paid to get results and he had to work to order. An artist, to work to order! I believe he was sincere, and if under the circumstances he supplemented his psychic powers with a little intelligent conjuring—well, I don't know that I blame him. In the end, poor fellow, he got more than he bargained for. The only part I hated was the Cynthia part, which grated on every bit of good taste I've got, but you can judge for yourself. . . .

Well, there were Charlie and I on the Friday evening, waiting for the car that was bringing these people from the station. Dinner was to be at eight. At half-past seven Ingram arrived, looking very pale. He hadn't a word to say to either of us, and when he found himself in the library, took down a book at random from the shelves—which by now I had resolved into fairly decent order—and buried himself in its pages.

It was a dismal night, following a dark, raw day. The thaw was well under way, and ugly, sombre patches showed all over the hills where the livid snow had melted. I was tired of the seeping, gurgling sound of running snow-water and of looking out over that untempting landscape, and I was glad when the curtains were drawn and the library fire made up for the night. Soon we heard the grating brakes of the car on the gravel sweep and Charlie went out. When he came back to the library he brought three men with him and introduced them. Mr. Wedgwood. Mr. Hunter. Mr. Harkness.

Wedgwood was a retired schoolmaster; stout, with a moon-shaped, hairless face and prominent, inquiring eyes. His fat hands were restless, and his two thumbs worked incessantly on their respective sets of fingers as though he were rolling cigarette papers. He had the retired pedagogue's habit of addressing the company as though it were a class of adolescents.

Hunter was one of those queer, wizened, wiry little fellows who take a bird-like interest in everything that is out of the ordinary. He told me that fortunately he had never had to adopt a trade or profession, his private income being sufficient for his needs and his hobbies, which had ranged from brass-rubbing to moth-collecting. He had written a book on English grasses before he took to psychical research. He was apt to twitter and had no sense of humour.

Harkness, the medium, I more or less described before. He looked not too strong, was immaculately dressed, and had little to say.

While they were all warming themselves at the fire and there was still five minutes to go to the gong, Charlie came over to me.

'Mertoun,' he said, 'will you go and ask Miss Goff if she'd care to come down to dinner? I don't want her to think I'm shutting her out. I ought to have thought of it before.'

'Of course,' I said, 'but after——'

He read my meaning. 'The séance? Well, of course I should like her to stay to that too. In fact, I hope she will; she has a right to first-hand knowledge of anything . . . if anything . . .'

I went upstairs. All was silent. I knocked very lightly at the door of Colonel Barr's room. Instantly her voice answered sharply: 'Who's there?'

'Mertoun,' I said. 'May I speak to you for a minute?'

She hesitated, and then said: 'Go into the big window embrasure. I'll join you in a moment.'

She meant the big window which overlooked the front of the

house, so I went there and sat down on the wooden window-ledge. It was dark there and draughty, and looking out I couldn't see anything but the bushes of the garden beaten down by the snow, and the dark, patchy-looking hillside beyond, with its rivers of melted snow. She came along in her uniform.

'We're going to have dinner at eight,' I said. 'Mr. Barr will be pleased if you'll come down.'

'No, thank you,' she said, with that air of hers of aloofness, demureness, coldness . . . oh, I don't know what it was! Rather maddening, anyway.

'Oh, come along,' I said; 'we've lots of company to-night. Sit by me. You may be amused.'

'I'd rather not come down,' she insisted.

'Then the séance——' I began.

'I'm certainly not coming to that!' She sounded quite determined on that point.

I shrugged my shoulders. 'Not even any natural curiosity, Nurse?'

'I suppose I can do as I please?'

'I think that your presence would please Barr,' I said.

Her face hardened. 'I couldn't possibly leave my patient for so long.'

'The old excuse!' I bantered her.

'If you like,' she said coolly.

I held my ground, and said: 'Well, I think you might come, if only to support me. After all, you led me into something the other night——'

She turned white and bit her upper lip. 'I wish I hadn't,' she said.

'But you did. You weren't afraid then; and I don't believe you're afraid now. You're a brave woman. Be a sport too. Come down.'

'No,' she said.

'Please, Miss Goff!'

She shook her head. 'Holding hands round a table . . . it's too absurd.'

'Then treat it as a game, and come.'

'No.'

'But what shall I tell Mr. Barr?'

'Tell him that Nurse Goff presents her compliments and is on duty this evening——'

I interrupted her. 'When did you first come here, Nurse? Was it after Mr. Ian Barr died?'

'Yes. I came on the fourteenth of December, the day after the Colonel had his stroke. But I had been staying in the neighbourhood for several weeks, looking after my aunt, Mrs. Clytie at Adam's Cranny. Why?'

'Nothing,' I said; 'only I know now how Ian Barr died.'

'Then you know more than most people,' she said dryly. 'I suppose even you will admit the circumstances were unusual!'

'We shall get to the bottom of it,' I said. 'Something is going to happen.'

'To-night?' she asked cynically.

'Who knows?' I said.

Her blue eyes flickered scornfully. 'There's the gong. Don't miss your soup.'

'Please come down!' I begged.

'I wouldn't think of it.'

'I'm sorry,' I said; 'I thought we were rather friends.'

'We might have been,' she said.

'What exactly do you mean by that?' I demanded.

'Nothing. You'd better go down. I'm very busy.'

Queer woman. I went down, and said to Charlie briefly: 'She won't come.' He shrugged his shoulders.

Harkness, the medium, wouldn't take dinner, but asked if he might have a little fruit juice. This led to a momentary domestic crisis, until the worthy Mrs. M'Coul had the presence of mind to open a tin of Californian peaches. Harkness took this nourishment in silence and the rest of us dined, with the usual sort of desultory conversation—weather, trade, politics, and the various subjects that comprised Hunter's hobbies.

After dinner we went into the library. The fire had died down to a scarlet glow, and Wedgwood screened it off effectively. When the lights were switched off the room was totally dark except for a faint luminosity on the ceiling above the hearth.

We took our places in a circle.

'Sitting by me?' Charlie whispered.

'Shall I?'

'Or shall we divide ourselves among these fellows to see that there's no flummery?' he asked.

I agreed that that would be better; so when we sat down I was between Ingram and Wedgwood, and Charlie between Hunter and Harkness. That put Wedgwood next to the medium and Hunter next to Ingram. Ingram's lean, clever hand was in my left, and in my right was Wedgwood's pudding, vainly trying to work its thumb and finger movements. We sat in that darkness for what seemed about seven minutes, but was probably only two or three, and then I heard the medium make a sound between a cough and a cry, and a perfectly new and rather high-pitched voice began to talk.

'Good evening, gentlemen. I hope you are all well, working hard, and thinking brave thoughts.'

This, I must explain, was Harkness's control; a French poet called Gaston who had starved to death in a Paris garret about a hundred years ago.

'Is that you, Gaston?' said Wedgwood.

'Yes, yes, yes, yes.' (I'm not reproducing the extraordinary accent.)

'Have you a message for us to-night?'

'Yes. Work hard. Very tired. Very happy.'

'Is there anyone else on that side who would like to give us a message?'

'Yes. Bippy.'

'What do you mean by Bippy?'

'Bippy. Very jolly. Ha-ha-ha.'

'Bad spirit,' Hunter broke in. 'Are you still there, Gaston?'

'Yes. Bad spirit. Very tired.'

'Can you bring us to the spirit we are seeking?'

'Yes. Charles.'

'Here I am,' said Charlie's level voice. 'Who's trying to speak to me?'

'Margaret.'

'I don't know any Margaret.'

'Oh, yes you do. Hudson River. Blue eyes.'

'What does Margaret want to say to me?'

'Margaret says very happy. Doing beautiful, useful work getting ready for those that follow. Flowers.'

'What about flowers?'

'Blue flowers.'

'Is that all Margaret has to say to me? Isn't there anyone else?'

Gaston's voice was suddenly replaced by a woman's, an uneducated voice too. However, this wasn't Margaret. This was Grace.

'Grace wants to tell George. Grace wants to tell George.'

'What?' said Hunter suddenly.

'To-morrow.'

'What about to-morrow?'

'To-morrow.'

'Is it something I'm to do?'

'In the G.'

'In the garden?'

'No. Go away.'

Gaston came back, this time gabbling French, quite unintelligible. Honestly, by this time I don't know whether I was most amused or disgusted. It was so childish, so farcical.

'Bourdon is here,' said the high-pitched voice.

'That's my uncle,' said Charlie. 'What does he want?'

'Wants to warn Charles. The stone. Very careful.'

'But my Uncle Bourdon doesn't know anything about the stone!'

'Yes. Knows. Watching.'

'Ask him,' I found myself saying suddenly, 'if we shall fill the cavity with earth.'

'Yes, yes,' came the answer. 'Fill with earth. Lock.'

'Lock what?' said Charlie.

'The door. All the doors.'

'Thanks very much!' said Charlie dryly. 'Very useful, I'm sure.'

'Bad spirit near,' said Gaston abruptly, and treated us to more crazy French. Then came the bit I didn't like.

'Cynthia is here,' said Gaston suddenly; and I felt Ingram's hand in mine grow icy.

'Tell her to speak!' said Ingram's voice hoarsely.

'Can't speak. On higher plane, this spirit.'

The man's hand shook in mine. 'Tell her to speak!' he implored. 'Just one word in her own voice.'

'Cynthia says, go back to London.'

'But I can't. I can't leave her here.'

'Cynthia in lovely garden. Very bright. Says she meet you in London. Go to London. Go to London. Go to London.'

Ingram's hand slid out of mine and he collapsed in his chair.

'Put the lights up!' I said angrily. 'This is going too far.'

'Nonsense!' said Wedgwood; 'he's all right. He wanted results, didn't he? You can't interrupt the trance.'

'I'm all right,' said Ingram; 'tell them to go on.'

But there was dead silence now, and all we could hear was the medium's painful breathing and the howling of the wind outside the curtained windows. The night was becoming wild. Crash! Wedgwood's fat hand quivered in mine. A brick had fallen down the chimney.

The medium gave a sharp cry.

'He's coming round,' said Hunter.

'No,' said Charlie; 'he's going to speak.'

Harkness, deep in trance, twisted in his chair. 'They won't find you,' he said; 'I shall watch you up the moor, and then I shall fire my pistol in the air, three times, and I shall open all the doors and run out towards the cliff, and they'll all come streaming after. At the crossroads you'll find a mare. Nelly. Call her Nelly and she'll come to you. Good-bye. The pistol. No, no, no! No! Aaaaaah!' It ended in a long scream. Harkness writhed in his chair, wringing his hands as though in bodily torment.

'Wake him up,' I said; 'it's beastly.'

'No,' said Charlie; 'just some undiscovered piece of family history. It's getting interesting. The walls speak.'

And the next moment the walls spoke with a vengeance! Above the howling of the wind and the creaking of the windows and the soughing of the streams, a voice like a warrior's shout positively rocked the room. The screen fell forward across the fireplace, and I felt the ground shake under my feet.

'I, Vitellius Gracchus, am here!'

It was huge, triumphant, terrible. Suddenly I couldn't bear the feel of Wedgwood's hand in mine any longer, so I snatched mine away and gripped the arm of my chair. The darkness was shot with blinding sparks and everything was reeling round me.

'I, Vitellius Gracchus, am here!'

And then I heard Charlie's voice, brave and faint and far away: 'What do you want, you fiend? Deal with me! I'm your man!'

The arms of the chair seemed to slip away from me. I was choking. Peal after peal of insensate laughter was tearing through the room, and then I seemed to hear the clash of battle and shouting voices, and finally a terrible, deafening crash. And everything went black.

The flashing on of the lights brought me to my senses. I was sitting on my chair, with clammy hands pressed to my cheeks. Wedgwood, in a paralysis of fright, was standing petrified beside me. Hunter was crouching in the window embrasure, with tears running down his cheeks, jabbering to himself. Ingram, pale as death, leant against the mantelpiece, his face hidden in his hands. Charlie, very white and with blazing eyes, stood with one hand on the electric switch; and stretched across the floor lay the twisted body of Harkness, the medium, with ashen face and all the appearance of death.

'Get that man up!' said Charlie sharply. 'Come on, Mertoun; give a hand into the dining-room with him. Ingram, we shall want you.'

Ingram lifted his face slowly. 'Me? You want me?'

'Yes. This man's ill. Pull yourself together. Now, Mertoun!'

Charlie's authoritative voice did as much as anything to restore us to our normal selves. Between us, he and I picked up poor Harkness, and as we opened the library door we came face to face with Miss Goff, standing as white as a ghost, a yard away from the threshold. How long had she been there? And what was she doing there? I was furious with her.

'Get some brandy,' said Charlie curtly.

She nodded and fled. When she came back we began to drop brandy between the poor fellow's lips with a fountain-pen filler, but he was too far gone for immediate aid. It was two hours before he came round. He shuddered and tried to speak.

'Don't talk,' said Ingram, calm by now; 'just lie down and rest.'

'Too strong for me!' the poor fellow gasped. 'Too strong!'

'The brandy?' I asked; 'I'll get some water.'

'The spirit! The spirit!'

We got him to bed, and Wedgwood and Hunter, who flatly refused to go to bed, offered to sit with him during the night.

When I came downstairs again Ingram was gone.

Charlie, his eyes still hot in his white face, turned to Miss Goff.

'And now,' he said, 'I should like to know what you were doing outside that door?'

'If I told you,' she said, 'that I had been there for exactly sixty seconds, I suppose you wouldn't believe me?'

'What brought you down at all?' he demanded. 'You couldn't come down when you were properly asked.'

'I came when I heard the noises,' she said.

'What noises?'

'The noises of hell let loose in this house,' she said.

'Nurse,' I said, 'Vitellius Gracchus has been here.'

Her blue eyes were like needle-points. 'Has he?' she said stonily. 'I thought somehow he would be.'

'So that was why you wouldn't come down!' I said.

'Under such circumstances,' she said, 'I thought my place was with the Colonel.'

Charlie started. 'Oh. My uncle. Is he all right, Nurse? Did the noise disturb him?'

'He didn't hear anything,' she said calmly.

'He didn't hear anything? Are you sure?'

'Quite sure,' she said; 'quite certain.'

Charlie hesitated. There was always something rather maddening about this woman's replies, as though she were purposely enigmatic. I think myself it was just her manner, but it had an irritating effect on me, so what it must have had on Charlie. . . .

However, it was midnight by now, and Charlie said: 'The lights are still on in the library. We'd better straighten that furniture before we go to bed.'

So we all three went into the library, where the chairs were lying overturned and the fire had long ago burned itself out. The minute I entered the room I felt queer; then in the glare of the electric light I saw something on the wall high above the mantel-piece, a dark, projecting thing.

I said: 'What's that?' But I knew it was something horrid and unnatural. Charlie's shoulder brushed mine, and I felt a kind of galvanic shudder run through his muscles.

He said: 'It's . . . the hilt . . . of a knife. In the wall.'

We all three stood staring up at the thing.

'Pull it down!' said Charlie. I think he was speaking as much to himself as to me, but I took the suggestion literally, and climbed on a chair.

'It is a hilt,' I said; 'it looks like brass, but it's green and encrusted with age.'

The thing, however, was hard and firm in my grasp, though I instinctively shrank away as I touched it. I pulled, but I couldn't move it. Couldn't move that thing, driven into the plaster of the wall! You won't believe it. I heard my voice saying queerly, 'I can't move it!'

'Pull!' said Charlie hoarsely. 'Pull, man, can't you!'

'I'm pulling . . .' I protested.

I got down off the chair and the sweat was running down my temples. Charlie took one glance at me and climbed up in my place. At his first touch the thing came away and he stood there grasping it in his two hands, his eyes downcast and his face inscrutable. It was a short, broad-bladed sword, dark and corroded with age—with centuries of age.

'It was driven so deep,' I heard myself saying, 'that I couldn't move it. You got it easily, Charlie.'

'Yes,' he said in a strange voice; 'I got it easily.'

Miss Goff was standing motionless, her lips a thin line, her hands clasped before her on her white apron.

Charlie pulled open a desk drawer with a clatter and flung the sword in. 'There! Let it stop there!' He rammed the drawer in with his knee.

I picked up a fallen chair and set it in its place against the wall; the nurse took another; Charlie a third. Soon the room was perfectly orderly. Then we looked at each other—three swift, unreadable glances—and moved towards the door. Charlie switched off the lights and we went upstairs."

IX

"You can guess how much sleep I had that night, though for warmth's sake I tumbled into bed. I was down by seven next morning, but Charlie was before me; in fact, now when I remember his appearance, haggard, chilled, tight-lipped, all his assurance of the previous night gone, I am pretty certain that he had not been to bed at all.

He was 'warming' himself at the pale flames of a newly lighted fire, and when I entered the room he didn't even look up. I could understand his feelings.

'Charlie,' I said, 'you know it was never my intention to intrude upon your private affairs.'

'I know,' he said; 'you couldn't help it. You've been thrust into this. I ought to apologize. I don't know how to.' These staccato sentences came jerkily with awkward pauses between.

'So long as you understand,' I said, 'that I haven't been deliberately inquisitive.'

He made a gesture for me to stop. 'I quite understand. In the first place, you ought never to have been brought here—to a place like this . . . a perfect stranger. It was my uncle's whim. I was dumbfounded when I heard you were expected; I hoped you'd only stay for a day or two . . . and then this ridiculous cataloguing business turned up! It isn't decent to bring strangers into a family like ours—a house like this! Well, Mertoun, I tell you frankly, I hope you'll soon take yourself away. Brutally speaking, I want you gone. You only embarrass me while you're here, and when you're gone I hope you'll make it your business to forget anything you may have seen or heard in this wretched place. I don't doubt that you will. How much longer are you going to be in that library?'

'A few days should see me through,' I said; 'three or four.'

He looked relieved. 'Three or four? Good. I hope we'll keep the peace undisturbed for that short period.'

At that point M'Coul walked in with the coffee. I felt flat and disappointed, as though I were being dragged out of the theatre during the second interval of a thrilling play; and yet I couldn't help admitting Charlie Barr's point of view. After all, I was a stranger and had no real right to be there; and the affair wasn't a play, it was a matter of life and death to Charlie. No wonder he wanted to be rid of spectators.

He said suddenly, as though to himself: 'There's one thing to be said for it; once back in London, this place and its associations will seem like a dream. In a week you'll have persuaded yourself either that you dreamed it, or accidentally got yourself involved with some mad people of whom the less said the better. I know what city clubs are—that is, New York ones, which probably don't differ very much from London ones. I needn't tell you that a man who talks in his club about having heard and seen the evidences of spirit presences is gently carried home and talked about in hushed whispers. So forget it, Mertoun; and good luck to you. You've behaved very well under the circumstances. When I think of the blundering sort of fellow you might have been, it makes me shudder.'

'I ought to tell you,' I said, 'that I have heard about your uncle—Mr. Ian Barr's death.'

'From whom?' he asked.

'From Ingram.'

Charlie nodded. 'That's all right. Ingram would give you an unbiased story. What did you make of it?'

'The sandal-print!' I said. 'That seemed to me both terrible and conclusive.'

'So it did to everyone else—with imagination,' said Charlie. 'My uncle the Colonel—upstairs—came home and had a seizure. I shan't easily forget the days that followed.'

'It's horrible!' I said hotly. 'A man like Mr. Ian Barr, whom I gather was a kindly fellow and liked by everybody. I suppose he left the farm in the dark, to walk home along the path he knew well——'

'Knew well!' Charlie echoed. 'He'd been walking that path all his life.'

I admit that I was so interested by now in my theory that I forgot myself. I said: 'But what actually happened? Was there a struggle on the cliff-edge? It looks like it; but don't you see, Barr, that presupposes the—the attacker in a material form! Can you conceive of such a thing?'

Charlie turned away his ashen face. 'Conceive of it! Hasn't it haunted me? The spirit of Gracchus attaining, after centuries of struggle, the power of materialization. Just once, so far as we know. Just once. But if once . . . oh, stop it, can't you? Stop it!'

'I'm sorry,' I muttered.

'No, you're not!' he almost shouted; 'you're wondering at this minute whether Gracchus still walks the moors at night, and whether he'll get me in the end! . . . Whether . . . he'll get . . .' He choked, and in his turn said: 'I'm sorry, Mertoun. You can see now, it's high time you went back to London.'

I wondered what had happened to make him lose his composure like this; I mean, ever since I had appeared in the dining-room he had been unlike himself, first morose and then violent. It came out a few minutes later in the course of conversation. I believe he was wanting to tell me all the time, and yet hating to. But he told me in the end. The sword of Gracchus which he had shut up in the library drawer had disappeared during the night. He had gone there first thing, while it was still dark and there was no one about; and the drawer was empty. And though he was shocked with a kind of dull horror, somehow he wasn't surprised. What did I think? I said that I wasn't surprised either; one just had to accept the fact. But if either of us could have foreseen where in less than two days that sword would be found . . .

'I should be obliged,' said Charlie, 'if you'd give me your word not to mention this sword business to anyone.'

'Of course,' I assured him. 'But Miss Goff——'

'Least of all to Miss Goff,' he said; 'I don't think that she'll speak of it of her own accord.'

I noticed that he was eating nothing, and was now pouring out his third cup of black coffee.

'I hope Ingram got home safely,' I said casually; 'I wondered afterwards whether we ought to have let him go alone. But we were so occupied at the time, or I could easily have walked with him.'

'Oh, Ingram would be all right!' said Charlie. 'He's used to roaming about at all hours.'

'I was thinking of his state of mind,' I explained; 'I rather hated that allusion to his wife. I can't help wondering what effect it would have on him.'

Charlie shrugged his shoulders. 'I agree with you that it was a particularly nasty bit of hocus-pocus. But it can only have one of two effects. Either Ingram didn't believe in it, in which case he won't regard it as of any consequence; or he did believe in it, following which he'll probably feel compelled to go back to London, which is what his friends have wanted all along, isn't it? But if you're anxious about him you can walk over there this afternoon. As for me, I feel rotten, and I'm going to spend the day in the study. I don't want to see or hear anybody. Miss Goff can give any necessary orders. Will you do something for me, Mertoun?'

'Willingly,' I said.

'Then just see those fellows upstairs off the premises. I've told M'Coul to serve their breakfast at nine, and there's a car coming for them at nine-forty-five. There's nothing to do except see them off. Ingram is going to pay the medium himself. I didn't want him to, but he insisted. Just a whim, but he's a man you have to humour. You don't mind?'

Well, Charlie went off to his study, and at nine the three visitors came down. I gave them the morning papers to read, and we didn't discuss the previous night at all! Harkness, the medium, looked very ill, with purple stains round his eyes. He ate nothing, but like Charlie drank black coffee. The other two made quite a hearty meal. The car came round to take them to the station, and off they went into a raw and misty morning. And that was that.

I went into the library and worked. Good atmosphere for work, as you can imagine, after the doings of the night before. But strangely enough, I wasn't so disturbed as you'd think. The room was light and orderly, and there was a good fire in the grate. I took out my card index and got to work on the letter T. Thiers, Marcel. Some Contemporary French Essayists. By the time I'd written that, I was feeling level-headed. I don't think I had any thought beyond my work during the rest of that morning.

When I went upstairs after lunch I saw Miss Goff sitting in the window embrasure on the first floor. She was looking out over the dismal garden and the wintry hillside, and didn't see me pass. There she was, all the time within easy reach of her patient's door, keeping her faithful and pathetic watch. Queer creature. Had she such faith in herself? What did she suppose she could do if that terrible hand chose to strike? But still she went on watching, guarding the helpless man for whom she had such deep regard and affection. I couldn't fathom her; I haven't fathomed her yet, and the letter I had from her this morning adds to her mystery.

Very well then. I walked as far as Ingram's place, through a nasty creeping fog that swirled and writhed over the hollows of the moor, and I was relieved in my mind when Ingram himself opened the door.

'Come in,' he said; so I went in and sat down by the fire as before.

'How's Barr?' he asked.

'Knocked up,' I said.

'I'm sorry,' he said. 'It was my fault. And all for nothing, I'm afraid.'

'For nothing?' I echoed.

'Yes. I don't believe the medium was genuine.'

With that he relapsed into silence. I had better say here and now that I received the definite impression—which I'm sure was the truth—that Ingram had no recollection of the Gracchus episode of the night before. It simply had passed him by, with all its noise and significance. He had gone to the séance with one object only, to get into touch with his dead Cynthia, and everything beyond the mention of her name had found his mind closed and unresponsive.

I tested him. I said: 'Poor Harkness, the medium, was very exhausted. Weren't you alarmed when it took you so long to get him out of his trance? Unusual, isn't it?'

'Was it long?' he said. 'He hadn't much constitution; that probably accounts for it. Tell Barr I'm sorry if I've put him to a great deal of trouble.' He hesitated, and then said abruptly: 'You know . . . I may go back to London, after all.'

'Because of . . . the message?' I stammered.

'No, not that. I couldn't accept that, because it wasn't Cynthia's own voice. It's since Joan came. She keeps telling me that Cynthia isn't here. I'm almost beginning to believe it.'

'I hope you will believe it,' I said, trying to say the right thing. 'I feel sure that your place is among your old friends, and hers.' I nearly said Cynthia's.

'But I've been here ten . . . twelve years——' he began; and then Joan flew in with a gay shout: 'Hallo, Billy! Where have you been all these years? And what do you mean by keeping Uncle Peter out till midnight at your smoking-party?'

'I hope you didn't sit up,' I said.

'Of course I sat up!' she flashed; 'and I hadn't anything to do except the crossword puzzle in the *Daily Mail*. Invite me next time, please.'

'There won't be any next time,' I said, glad that Ingram had misled her as to his real purpose at The Broch; 'I'm going back to London in two or three days.'

'Good!' said Joan; 'so are we. We must meet in town, Billy. My aunt is rather desiccated and doesn't give parties, but we could make up a four and go to Monseigneur or the Kit-Cat——'

'My child,' I said, 'I don't dance.'

She put her head on one side, looked me over intensely, and an expression of painful horror widened her eyes.

'My poor darling,' she said, 'have you seen a specialist? Well, never mind. We'll do something quite elderly, if you prefer it. Dinner and a show. But meanwhile, what do you think? I've telephoned a cable message to my Papa in "Bawston" to come over and meet us—me and Uncle Peter—in London. He'll be over in a week——'

Ingram interrupted. 'No, Joan. Not so soon. I couldn't go so soon. You don't understand. Suppose *she* spoke to me, and told me to stay?'

'She won't tell you to stay,' said Joan gently; 'because she isn't here. I keep on telling you she isn't here.'

'How can you know that?' he said impatiently.

'Because I knew Cynthia,' said Joan; 'I was only a little girl, but I remember her quite well. And where did she like to be? In the middle of a moor in the snow? Not likely! It was on top of a bus riding round Piccadilly Circus, with the flower-baskets, pink and red and yellow, down below; or else in Kensington Gardens showing us the rabbits that dance round Peter Pan. That's where I'd look for Cynthia.' She bent down to get a fresh log for the fire, and muttered to me: 'My old man says that he'll cure him in twelve months if I can only get him to London. So back me up, ducky.'

I said to Ingram: 'I think this girl is your good fairy.'

'Joan?' he said wistfully. 'I hope she won't go away.'

'I hope she will go away,' I said, 'and you with her.'

His fine lips twisted into a half-smile. 'Perhaps!' he said; and we both watched that lovely child ruining her shoes by kicking the logs into place.

Then she turned to me. 'Billy,' she said, 'are you a magician?'

'Absolutely,' I said; 'try me.'

'I want to sew,' she said; 'to make a pink jumper with sleeves into a pink jumper without sleeves. And to do that I want a reel of pink silk. And this appalling little shop in the village only sells black and white cotton, and keeps that in the same box as the carbolic soap. What shall I do?'

'What do you want?' I demanded; 'I may be dense, but——'

She flung out a supplicating hand. 'A reel of pink silk, a loaf of bread, and thou.'

'If you can wait until to-morrow afternoon,' I said, 'I think I can promise you all three. Miss Goff, who is a sort of nurse-housekeeper-secretary person at the house where I'm staying is always doing sewing of some kind. I'll ask her if she has what you want. If so, I'll be round to-morrow about two o'clock; we'll go for a walk to another charming pub where the loaf of bread will be newly baked and accompanied by ham, eggs, and strawberry jam; and as for me, well, if you want me I'm always your humble and adoring servant, Joan.'

'That's the nicest speech I've heard for a long time,' she said; 'I do love the Victorians.'

As a matter of fact, I went away that afternoon hopelessly in love with her, and just twice her age. I even kept on asking myself, did that matter frightfully? I mean, people do it in these days. But I knew we hadn't a thing in common really; it was just madness. But I dreamt about her that night—this is mad too—dreamed that we were sitting on the moor above the sea; only it was summer and the heather buds were pink and humming with little shimmering flies; the sun was pouring down, the sky was golden with rosy clouds, and the sea was glittering like glass. She said, 'Billy, I love the sea.' And I sat there dumb. Then she said, 'Billy, I love you.' So I kissed her mouth and it tasted like flowers, and I remember wishing in the dream that the moment might go on and on for ever. Even in the dream it lasted a long, long time; so long that when I woke I couldn't forget it, it seemed so real. You see, if it could have happened it would have been just like that. And queerly enough, before that day was over I did kiss Joan and she kissed me, but it wasn't in the least like the dream. It was out in the mist and the melted snow, and all over before I had time to realize it, and to realize too that a girl of Joan's generation will give a kiss as lightly as a handshake to a man she likes. It doesn't mean a row of beans to her, but she shouldn't try it on defenceless Victorians. It might hurt.

However, when I got up that morning I knew that in the corner of my collar drawer there was tucked away a reel of pink silk, borrowed from Miss Goff the night before. I was ridiculously pleased that I'd been able to get Joan what she wanted. I got up early and did an hour's work before breakfast. As I intended to take Joan out to tea I felt that I owed it to Charlie Barr to make up the full amount of work for that day. So I forged ahead with the letters U, V, and W. Charlie sent down a message at lunch-time asking me to excuse him; he had a lot of writing to do and was staying in his study. I read between the lines and realized that he was suffering badly from reaction after that wretched séance, and wanted to be alone until he was himself again. I tried to put myself in his place and wondered what I should have done. Run, probably. Run away. It made me admire all the more that dogged bravery which kept Charlie at his post, defiant to the last. If there should be a last

. . . which was a thought that made me cold. But this was Charlie's home and Charlie's tradition, and I believe he had no other thought but to stick to it. Well, I made up my mind not to start out until I'd finished letter W, and it took me longer than I'd expected. I'd told Joan two o'clock, but it was nearly three when I reached Ingram's house and asked for her.

'Why, didn't you meet her?' Ingram said. 'She got tired of waiting and set out to meet you half an hour ago.'"

XII

"'I must have missed her in the village,' I said; 'I'll go back and find her.' So I turned back, but to all appearances the village was as deserted as when I had first passed through it; a raw, cloudy, misty afternoon, and every door closed. I went to the shop, but she hadn't been there, and I glanced into the Institute where two lads were happily punishing the billiard-table, only to learn that Joan had been seen going in the direction of the coast road some forty minutes ago. So I set out expecting to overtake her at every bend of the road; and in the end I got right back to the gates of The Broch and hadn't seen a sign of her, or in fact of any living creature. Surely, I thought, she hadn't gone to the house and asked for me? Well, of course, she hadn't; but as I was there I borrowed M'Coul's bike and pedalled back to the village, thinking that she would have returned to Ingram's place by now. It was well after four o'clock and the sky was darkening to the close of an overcast and wintry day.

I walked straight in. 'Has she come back?' I said; 'I haven't found her.'

Up to that minute, believe me, I hadn't had an anxious thought; but now it all seemed to break over me. Sheer panic. And Ingram too.

'Good God!' he said. 'Where is she? It's getting dark.'

'Look here!' I said; 'I'm going out to search for her.'

'So am I,' he said; 'I don't like this. You go east at the fork and I'll go west. Meet here again in an hour's time.'

In the village we couldn't find anyone who had seen her after she set out along the coast road to meet me. Soon I was out alone on the moorland road, calling her, going deeper and deeper into the wilderness and the night. My voice seemed to carry for miles in that desolation, and it gave me a certain amount of satisfaction, because I thought if she had stumbled into a ghyll and couldn't get out, she might at least hear me and reply. But there was utter silence. I scanned the road carefully in case there was a trace of her, a dropped handkerchief or a bit of coloured wool from her scarf. Soon it got too dark to see, and I grew rather frantic. I kept standing to face that ocean of rough moorland, and crying at the top of my voice, 'Joan! Joan! Are you there? Can you hear me?' Once or twice I left the road and struck out into the moor, but you know what that means. You top a ridge and see another before you, and beyond that another, and a few yards ahead you can lose yourself never to regain the road. If that was what Joan had done, I was terrified at the thought. Stumbling on over that treacherous heather in the dark, where the ghylls were veiled in misty shadow, she might easily have missed her footing and fallen unconscious into one of those rocky death-traps. I yelled myself hoarse, and all for nothing.

I don't remember when it was exactly that the deadlier fear grew on me. I think it was the sudden recollection of that awful sandal-print and Ian Barr's dead body at the foot of the cliffs in the darkness of just such a misty evening as this. Horror had me in its grip. I stood still, I remember, frozen at the thought of Joan . . . and that monster who had spoken to us, only two nights ago. It seemed to me then that from the first I'd been too unutterably light-hearted about the whole affair of the Barr tragedy, as though I'd been watching a rather thrilling play in a theatre. Now it was coming home to me, and believe me, from that night—those few frightful hours when I searched for Joan—I haven't been the same man. I got more than a few grey hairs that night.

I tried to be coldly reasonable, and asked myself why the Thing should attack Joan who after all had no connection with the Barr family; but you know yourself how useful it is trying to be reasonable when you're in a panic, particularly in the middle of a moor at night with all the powers of hell let loose. I think I went rather mad. I know I shouted to the Thing to come out and face me like a man so that I could stand up to it with my fists. And then I thought of the picture-slashing, and the knife in the wall of the library— the knife that had been *fetched* during the night—and I went crazier still, running and shouting and beating about among the heather.

I must have covered miles. I suddenly remembered that I had agreed to come back and meet Ingram within the hour, and consulting my luminous watch I saw that I had been out for three hours. It was nearly half-past seven. With my pocket compass and torch I found my way back to the village. Ingram was at his house; had been back two or three times expecting to find me. If there was anything good in that welter of anxiety, it was to notice how Ingram's mind had been taken completely off its own preoccupations. He said to me the sanest thing I had ever heard him say. 'When I find her,' he said, 'I'll have no more of this kind of thing; I'll take her straight back to London and hand her over to her father.'

'You know these moors,' I said, 'what—what harm could come to her?' I wanted desperately to be reassured, or else to have someone share my horrid fears.

'Anything!' said Ingram. 'Anything.' He paused, and added: 'Men have been lost on the moor and wandered till they died. Hardy, local men. And she's only a girl, a stranger, and unused to exposure. I shall have to call on the village for a search-party.'

We were both strung up to the highest pitch by then, and for my part I was ready to do battle with anybody or anything, and quite prepared for a night on the moor, with or without a village search-party. But, as you know, real life is simply a series of anticlimaxes; no artistry, no sense of drama. All that is left to fiction. So instead of some tremendous end to this adventure, all that happened was that a trap stopped outside the door and we heard Joan's voice and saw her climbing down.

'Hallo, Billy!' she said, catching sight of me; 'I've had an adventure.'

I was dumb. I think she must have read something in my face, for she stopped still before me, and put her hands on my wrists.

'Now what's the matter? You don't mean to say you thought I was dead? You dear old pre-War fusser, I believe you did!'

And then I lost my head completely, and did the most idiotic thing. I fumbled in my pocket and pulled out the pink silk reel. 'Look, Joan,' I said; 'I got you this.'

She gave a gay cry. 'Billy, you're a wow!' And she slipped her hands up to my shoulders and kissed me—lavishly. So I kissed her too, in a dazed sort of way, as though I were seeing the light after years in an underground dungeon. Presently she said: 'That'll do. Lay off it—as they say in "Bawston." There's Uncle Peter looking as if he'd been pole-axed.'

She ran into the house, pulling off her yellow scarf. 'I've had a ripping tea,' she cried, 'at a farm. Lucky, wasn't it? You see, Billy, I set out to meet you, but when I got to the fork I took the wrong road, and I didn't realize it until I'd gone about two miles. So I turned back, but I somehow got on to another road and this time I walked about seven leagues and it began to get dark. So I thought, "Well, here's little Maria all alone in the Sahara. Let's give a view halloo." So I hooted a bit, and then somebody hooted back, and it was a nice farm-boy called Harold, with a cart. So he took me to the farm and they were just going to have a scrummy sort of meal, jam and hot girdle-cakes, and did I say no? I'll say I didn't. And then the young man brought me back in the trap, and here I am, about four hours too late for our walk, Billy. Better luck next time.'

'There'll be no next time,' said Ingram sternly; 'I'm going to take you to London.'

'You might have been killed,' I said, rubbing it in. 'Your uncle and I have been scouring the moor for hours. We thought you were lost and wandering. Strong men have wandered there until they died of exposure. If you'd fallen into a ghyll with a broken leg you might have lain there for days. We've been horribly anxious.'

'Billy,' she said, 'don't do the heavy parent. It doesn't suit you. And now I'd better go and pack if we're starting for London to-morrow.'

'We can't go yet,' said Ingram; 'I have matters to arrange.'

'In that case,' said Joan calmly, 'we'll have some supper. You'll stay, Billy, won't you? Especially as I did you out of your tea. Sorrow!'

And at that, I realized that it was nine o'clock and I had been away from my duty at The Broch all those hours without giving it a thought. Barr would be justified in thinking it more than casual of me. So I excused myself to Ingram and Joan, and set off on M'Coul's bike at a terrific bat, which of course I couldn't keep up after I was through the village, owing to the darkness and the potholes of the road.

As for my state of mind, I felt cold and angry. Reaction after all my excitements and heroics. Just flat and cold and furious and unimaginative; remember that. It was a rotten night; raw and damp, with a wispy mist lying in patches on the moor. The sky was cloudy and wild, and on her back in the cloud-rack lay a weeping half-moon. It would rain before morning. I was thinking of nothing beyond what a vile day I'd had and how hungry I was, and how I ought to apologize at The Broch for having absented myself so long. As a matter of fact I needn't have worried, as it turned out. Nobody but M'Coul had missed me, as Charlie had spent the whole day busy in his study. But I didn't know that as I went pedalling over that moorland road, swerving round the potholes I could see and lurching across those that took me unawares. I met no living creature on that journey; few people are abroad in the country at nine o'clock—and later—of an evening.

But in that frame of mind, fearless, unimaginative, preoccupied, and in cold blood—in that frame of mind, pedalling a heavy iron bicycle across a wicked moorland road in the darkness of a raw night, I saw the Roman ghost."

XIII

"Think of it. And Joan, so gallant and gay, only just safe. It was when I was not more than half a mile from The Broch and the road ran perhaps fifty yards from the cliffs which overhung the sea. The tide was in, because I could hear the thundering of the waves on the rocky shore far below. As I rode I was suddenly dazzled by a strong light which flashed into my eyes for a second and passed on. I saw the long, white beam travelling away across the rough shoulder of the moor; it was the ray from the lighthouse. Sixty seconds it took to complete its revolution, and then it was back again from the sea and sweeping across my path. And this time as I followed the travelling beam of light, I saw where it caught the edge of the cliff, fifty yards away; and there, framed for a moment in the white radiance he stood, Vitellius Gracchus, brilliant against the dark night. He was still, but not with the stillness of a statue; the pose was tense, the powerful shoulders drawn back, the arms flexed. It was as though a single lime in a darkened theatre had picked out one poised and glittering figure on the tenebrous stage.

First I saw the glitter of his helmet with the sweeping neck-guard; and then the gleam of his cuirass with its falling thongs of leather and brass, and beneath the thongs the flutter of a scarlet tunic; and then the high, laced sandals. No face. Only a grey blur, like smoke, for I looked particularly. The whole effect was big, powerful, menacing. And yet he was unarmed. I looked in vain for the high shield with the letter of his legion and the painted eagle, for the spear which once must have lain across his shoulder, and the short sword at his side. Vitellius Gracchus was unarmed, and yet unspeakably terrible, standing there on the cliffs above the North Sea, haunting the blood-stained moor where he and his legionaries had died. Here in twentieth-century England for a moment the old, savage England raised its head. And the change-less wind blew across the moor. I was off the cycle now, staring at that brooding figure. And all this, which has taken me several minutes to describe, took place in about a second in the light of the travelling beam from the sea. The beam passed on. Darkness. I breathed as though I had been running; waiting, waiting for the return of the light. A long, long minute and again the white ray swept the cliffs. He was gone, and the tangled heather lay empty and bare. The bicycle clattered down in the road and I began to run across the moor to where he had stood. I stumbled and fell. The heather lashed and entrapped my feet. But I found the place— I think it was the very place—and there was nothing. Not even the print of his sandal. I listened, but I could only hear the creep-ing of that eerie wind. Then there came a wild gust, and the rain fell.

At that, terror seized hold of me and I couldn't move a limb. I thought I should suddenly see him rising out of the mist within a yard of me . . . and hear his voice of thunder again . . . and this time see his awful face. I knew that he wasn't far away. How I blessed that lighthouse lamp! While it swept the sea I waited, with the sweat pouring off me; when it returned to land I made a leap and ran for the road as though hell were at my heels. Do you think me an unspeakable coward? I'm telling you it exactly as it happened. You don't see a sight like that and feel the same afterwards. I've seen, and I know. I've twice faced a line of charging bayonets; then my blood boiled, now it froze. Coward if you like. Coward a thousand times. I don't care.

I don't know whether I rode the cycle or whether I dragged it after me. I got to the house somehow, and tore at the bell. M'Coul let me in, impassive as usual.

'Have you had supper, sir?' he asked.

I gasped a curt reply.

'Then if you would have it now, sir, I could clear away. It is waiting in the dining-room.'

Surprisingly, once in the house I felt serene, and pleasantly hungry. I had my supper, smoked a couple of cigarettes, and went into the library. 'I dreamed it,' I said to myself. 'No. I swear I didn't. It wasn't just *a* Roman soldier I saw; it was an individual. I could see the dints in his cuirass, and the neck-guard of his helmet was wrenched awry. I couldn't have dreamed that.' I looked at the clock; it was half-past ten. Presently I heard the slam of a door above and footsteps on the stairs. Charlie Barr was coming down. I was flipping over the cards of the index and for the life of me I couldn't say a word when he came in. He offered me his cigarette-case—he always smoked very good cigarettes, fat, brown Russians with gold tips—sounds rather precious, but he wasn't at all like that—and I took one and lit up. Then I said: 'Barr, I saw the ghost to-night. On the cliff. Gracchus.'

Too sudden. Down went the cigarette-case, clatter-clatter on the parquet.

'I don't believe it!' he rapped out.

'Oh, yes you do!' I said.

He went over to the fire, lit his cigarette, turned his face away, and said: 'Tell me.'

'I was coming back from Ingram's,' I said, 'a little after nine o'clock. As I came over the moor-road the lighthouse beam came sweeping round, and in the light of it I saw *him* standing on the cliff about fifty yards away. It wasn't an imaginative effort. My thoughts were far away from him at the time. He was there, quite, quite distinct. I could see the dints in his armour. Then the light passed on, and when it came again he was gone. I even went to the place where he'd been, but he'd vanished. I don't think he meant to show himself to me. I think that he is just . . . abroad.'

Charlie said nothing, but presently I saw his unsmoked cigarette drop into the fire, and without facing me he said sharply: 'Have you told anybody?'

'No,' I said; 'I've only seen M'Coul since I came in.'

'Then don't, please . . .' He added, half-hopefully. 'Perhaps you'll disbelieve it yourself to-morrow.'

'No,' I said firmly; 'I saw him. It's a sight I shan't forget.'

Charlie shivered, and then with a gesture of anger pulled himself together. 'Please tell me—I'm curious—what was he like? His face . . .'

'That's a curious thing,' I said; 'he had no face. Between his helmet and cuirass there was only a grey mistiness. It was a face of smoke. The armour and the tunic looked almost material; the man himself was a wraith.'

'Tall? Powerful?' he asked.

'The impression I got was of height and power,' I explained, 'but on second thoughts I believe that was the effect of the armour. He was about your own height or mine.'

'Supposing,' Charlie went on, 'that he'd been there on the cliff when you got to him, Mertoun! What would you have done?'

'Grappled with him,' I said.

Charlie laughed bitterly. 'I wonder whether a man could! I've half a mind to go out.'

'Don't,' I said tersely.

He laughed, more lightly. 'Then I'll stay. But he's getting nearer, Mertoun. I wonder if I'll be the next to see him?' He turned a few papers over restlessly, and said: 'How's your job? Made much progress?'

'I shall finish to-morrow,' I told him.

He nodded in a preoccupied manner, and left the room. A few minutes later Miss Goff came in and stood just inside the door, waiting with a kind of frigid nonchalance until I looked up from my writing.

I said: 'Do you want anything, Miss Goff?'

She said coldly: 'Mr. Barr tells me you are leaving the day after to-morrow. He said I was to tell the Colonel, with regard to your account. The Colonel wishes to know what he owes you.'

Well, of course, taken completely by surprise like that I was at a disadvantage; but I didn't see why I shouldn't be well paid for my work by a man who was perfectly able to afford it, and Ingram himself had told me that Colonel Barr was a millionaire, though close with his money.

So I said: 'I prefer to leave that to the Colonel, Miss Goff. I haven't had a commission quite like this one before, and I shall be satisfied if he pays me what he thinks my work is worth. Of course it would be more satisfactory if he could see it—and me—but under the circumstances perhaps you'll tell him that his books are now properly arranged and made up with a complete card index, in these boxes, with cross-references to author and subject. When he can see them for himself I think he'll be pleased. Kindly tell him that. Also that my charge for the original valuation which I came here to make is five guineas.'

'Very well,' said she, and marched out.

In about half an hour she came back, still more tight-lipped.

'The Colonel,' she said, as though carefully quoting her instructions, 'says that he prefers you to name your figure. He hopes you will do so now.'

My hopes of a lavish cheque disappeared, so I accepted the situation and said promptly: 'Then will you tell him, five guineas for the valuation, and fifteen for the catalogue, including the cost of the cards and boxes.'

'Twenty guineas in all,' she said; 'thank you.'

And then, to crown this engaging conversation, she came a

third time and said that the Colonel had my London address and would send me a cheque for twenty guineas, and that was that. The last phrase, of course, being mine. I thought the Colonel was rather a cool card, but I couldn't very well say that I would much, much rather carry that cheque away with me. I hoped for the best, and said, 'Thank you very much.' And I felt like adding, 'Tell him that Vitellius Gracchus is out on the moor!' Which would have been slightly Lower School of me, after all.

I sat up late, reading and smoking. And thinking, rather against my will. That last short interview with the nurse had given a hint of finality to my stay in that strange part of the world. To-morrow was to be my last day at The Broch, and then London, and the memory of a queer, unfinished adventure. Or should I one day wake up in St. John's Wood and realize that the whole affair had been a dream? No. The characters were too distinct to be dream-like. Charlie Barr, Winifred Goff, Ingram, Joan. People I should never forget. And the man I had seen to-night; the man from an age of savage strength, passion, brutality, vengefulness, with his dinted armour and swordless hands; the man whose name was carved in living letters on the rock hidden deep in the heart of the house; the man whose voice of thunder had flung us all to the ground like dead men; the man who had wrestled with poor Ian Barr on the cliffs above the dark North Sea. The insatiable, brooding, blood-lusting Gracchus.

And in strange contrast, I remember thinking how lovely a place this might have been with summer lingering on a purple moor, and shifting deeps of azure and sapphire in sky and sea; to wander and dream and hear Joan laughing from morning till night; to pull the gorse and read an old book. But now it was endless winter and the rain was falling coldly from the sad sky.

Early next morning I was wakened as usual by a tapping at my door, but this tapping went on insistently and obviously required an answer. I called, 'What is it?' and M'Coul put his head in. 'If you please, sir, will you come down? The policeman wants to speak to you.'

'The policeman!' I said. 'What's the time? Where's Mr. Barr?'

'I thought I'd better tell you before rousing Mr. Barr,' the man said; 'it's six o'clock only, sir. And they've found a dead man, sir, on the moor. It's young James Blaik.'"

XIV

"You remember who James Blaik was—the young shepherd who had defied what he considered superstition by sheltering his flock at night in the ruined tower on the hill. I threw on the minimum of clothing and bounded downstairs. It was still dark, of course, and very cold. In the hall a stout country policeman accosted me and asked whether he might make use of the 'phone to call up the Superintendent of Police at Heaviburgh and also a doctor—Mackie's locum, in fact. Of course, I told him to go ahead and quickly, so when he'd done that he began to explain to me what had happened. Two labourers on their way to a distant farm had come an hour ago upon the body of a man, sodden with rain, lying out on the moor. It was James Blaik, the shepherd. They had shown no more surprise then than did the officer of the law now in telling it to me.

'He's been asking for it; now it's come to him,' the policeman said. Gruesome fatalism! But I told you before how the country-side had prophesied some kind of disaster for Blaik ever since he ventured into the ruined broch with his ewes.

'Where is the place?' I asked.

'Not above half a mile from here,' I was told; 'just between the broch, there, and the cliff-edge.' I felt a kind of sinister shiver.

'Can I come back with you?' I asked.

'If you like, sir. Can't do with a crowd, of course.'

'Wait!' I said, 'I must tell Mr. Barr myself.'

I went up to Charlie's room and knocked. In rather a surprised voice he told me to enter, and I found him in bed, sticking a puzzled head above the sheets.

'Something's happened,' I said abruptly, and for the life of me I couldn't keep the ring of the unusual out of my voice. He lifted himself on his elbow and looked alert.

'Happened? What?'

'Young Blaik, the shepherd,' I said; 'he's been found dead on the moor. It's only just past six o'clock.'

'Dead? Do you mean they've brought him here?'

'No,' I said; 'two labourers found him and they're staying with the body. The constable came here to telephone. He's below now. I'm going up with him to see. I shouldn't come if I were you.'

'Why not?' he asked in a curious voice.

'Because I don't like the sound of it,' I said. 'You remember what the village has been saying about Blaik . . . and you know what I saw last night. I think it's about the same place.'

He swallowed convulsively and his eyes widened until I could see the white eyeballs above the dark pupils. He well understood what I meant.

'I'll come . . . later,' he said; 'you go, Mertoun. And find out. . . .'

I nodded and left him. I took my torch and the constable had a swinging lantern. By the light of these we tramped through the rain up the slippery moorland road. Across the heather we could see the dark forms of two men against the greyish, livid sky. The place, as the policeman had said, was between the ruined broch and the cliffs. One of the men came to meet us, a rough labourer with sacking round his shoulders and corduroys tied at the knees with string.

'How did you find him?' I asked.

'Me and Dordy was gangin' ower the moor to Hurstin's,' he said, 'when Dordy sees summat dark juist awa' theer from sheep-path. So we comes up and we sees 'tis Jamie Blaik, on his back and deead. Starin' up. Wet and clarty, like he'd been theer all neet. So he munna, for sheep havena been folded; broch or no broch. So Ah bides, and Dordy gangs to fetch pollis. And when Dordy's awa, I sees as Jamie's a-liggin' in a puddle o' his own bluid.'

'That'll do. That'll do,' said the constable. 'None of that till the Superintendent comes.'

So a few yards farther on I saw James Blaik face to face for the first time, the man who'd given me such a jerk when I caught sight of him prowling round his sinister sheep-fold. He was lying flat on his back with his arms outflung, and his peaked face tipped up to the sky; a young, ashen, jutting kind of face; rigid, and glistening with rain. His poor clothes were sodden; he must have lain for hours. It was a starkly hideous thing to see. And behind his shoulders, in the strong light of my torch, the heather was darker still and gave a crimson gleam. I whipped the light away.

'No touching him till the doctor comes,' said the constable.

Then out of the grey stillness of that grisly morning came the rattle of wheels—the doctor's trap. It was the young locum, a bumptious lad in his late twenties, with an exaggerated manner. He looked distastefully at the sopping ground, and went down on his knees with an exclamation of disgust as the icy moisture struck through his trouser-legs. His brief examination was soon over, and with a kind of lofty indifference he heaved the body over and said, just as though he were reprimanding the rest of us for a breach of etiquette, 'This man has been stabbed in the back.'

Of course, that was obvious at once to what is generally described as the meanest intelligence. I mean, when you see a pair of hunched and sodden shoulder-blades with the hilt of a knife sprouting out between like some monstrous growth. . . .

I didn't look for long, because I saw at the first glance that it was the same hilt. In the library that night . . . I'd tugged and tugged at it . . . and Charlie had finally wrested it out of the wall and tossed it into a drawer. . . .

About then the dawn began to creep, very yellowish and smoky, over the beaky brow of the moor; and a thunderstorm broke—as it often does at dawn in the hills—with violent slashes of lightning and ceaseless growlings of thunder. There were five of us now, standing as mutely miserable as wet cab-horses, round the dead man; and with the growing light and the electric flashes, faces came where before there had only been pale, blank ovals, and I remember noticing that one of the labourers, the one they called Dordy, had jutting red eyebrows which reminded me, for some lunatic reason, of the cliffs of Devon. Those rusty red eye-brows, and the rusty red heather, and our grim half-circle with the little, uppish doctor adjusting his tortoise-shell goggles and telling us that the death had taken place between nine and eleven hours previously. I could have told him that . . . for when I saw the Roman at nine o'clock he was without his sword. And I must have passed within a few yards of this very spot when Blaik lay warm, and perhaps still breathing. But I didn't say anything. I was as dumb as a clod.

The Superintendent of Police came, and we had the whole story again; and then a curious, gaping straggle of ghouls from the village, and among them a draggled, loud-mouthed woman— Blaik's sister. She took one look at the corpse, and wiped her lips with a dingy cotton handkerchief. 'It's a judgment on him,' she said; 'allus knew better than his elders, he did. An' now it's got him.'

'What's got him?' somebody snarled.

'How should I know?' she snapped. 'Them 'at meddles with the powers of darkness'll come to a bad end any road. That's the devil's own knife in him, I'll be bound. Never seed one like it before, any of you! And who's to be telling his poor wife, I'd like to know, and her brought to bed with her fourth only this morning. Went out as jaunty as you please, he did at half-past seven. That's the last I or anybody seed of him.'

She was voicing the general opinion, that Blaik had met his death through his foolhardy disregard of the sinister legends which surrounded the ruined tower where he had persisted in sheltering his sheep. That leering audience on the moor wore I-told-you-so expressions. It was rather horrible; a sort of ghoulish satisfaction in the fulfilment of their nasty prophecies.

They were lifting the body into a flat cart when I saw Charlie coming up the road from the house, wearing an old ulster and a pulled-down hat. Only the lower part of his face was visible, and that was unshaven. He ignored me and spoke to the Superintendent.

'What's all this?' he said; and I suppose it was obvious as he half-turned his head to the backing cart. 'What happened?'

'Stabbed in the back.'

'How?'

'Dunno, sir. Queer sort of knife. Queer sort of felly he was.'

'A knife? How—queer?'

'See here, sir.'

'Thanks,' said Charlie grimly; 'I don't want to see it. Wasn't this the man who came every night to the broch?'

A sort of shudder ran through the crowd of village people; half of them answered him. 'Ay, sir. Ay, sir. This is him.'

'But you don't believe——'

'Ay, sir. We do.'

'You——' He turned to the two policemen.

'Well, sir, there's queer things happen hereabouts, there's no mistake.'

I said in a low tone: 'I ought to tell them.'

'If you think so,' he said.

'But don't you think so?'

'I hate it,' he said; 'but I suppose it's necessary.'

I said aloud: 'I saw the Roman soldier on the moor last night. It was about nine o'clock, as I was coming back from the village.'

Someone let his breath out in a sharp sigh.

I said: 'It wasn't a dozen yards from this place.'

The young locum was staring with his mouth wide open. The last flickers of lightning died out of the sky, and suddenly it was light and the rain was pelting down with renewed vigour.

Someone said: 'So he's back again! Well, we know now.'

The constable was suddenly at my side. 'What's your name, sir?' He began to write on a page streaked with rain, and I read over his shoulder. 'William Mertoun, 14, Richmond Mansions, London, N.W.8.'—I had to spell all that out for him—'He says he saw the Roman soldier on the 7th inst. at nine p.m. within doz. yards of scene of crime.'

Everybody began shouting and chattering at once; a hideous uproar, like a fair-ground.

I said to Charlie: 'It's the very place. I must have passed within a few yards of the body last night. If I'd known . . .'

His shoulders twitched with either dread or disgust. 'Did you see this knife?'

'Yes,' I said; 'the same . . . the library wall . . .'

'Let's go,' he said.

At that moment I saw Ingram and Joan come round the bend of the road. 'Oh, look!' I said; 'she mustn't come here. I must go and send her back.'

'Who is it?' Charlie asked irritably.

'It's Ingram, and a girl who's staying with him. Daughter of a friend.'

Unfortunately Joan had caught sight of me and came running up to us. I had to introduce her and Charlie, but he barely acknowledged the introduction. It was an awkward moment.

'Please go back,' I said; 'this isn't a place for you.'

'What's happened?' she asked in her gay young voice. 'We heard there'd been an accident and Uncle Peter thought he might be wanted. So I came along. Sheer curiosity.'

'I'm taking you back,' I said; 'there's a man—been killed. Come along, Joan!' That dreadful cart was creeping up behind us.

She looked rather shocked, but stood her ground, and the cart actually passed us. They hadn't even covered Blaik's face. I wouldn't have had it happen for a hundred pounds, but by the time Ingram joined us her curiosity was more than sated! Her knees had given way and she was clinging to my arm with her face hidden on my shoulder. 'I'm sorry!' she gasped; 'I . . . I'm a fool. Oh, I must sit down . . . please!' I could feel her slipping to the ground.

'She'd better come to the house,' I said to Charlie. It was less than half a mile away, you'll remember.

'I'm sorry,' came from the corner of Charlie's lips; 'we've no accommodation for a lady. She ought not to have come.' He swung round on his heel and took two paces; then turning said to me in a muffled voice, 'You see, I'm all in!' And went striding away towards his house.

However, that little incident revived Joan completely.

'What a hateful man!' she said, with the frankness of her age and generation.

'You don't understand,' I said. 'Mr. Barr is going through a very dreadful ordeal.'

Ingram suddenly supported me. 'Yes, indeed!' he said; and lowering his voice added: 'I heard something as I came along. Can it be true?'

I nodded.

'Then it was V. G.!'

I nodded again. Words failed me.

'We'll go back,' he said. 'Will you come?'

I suppose I nodded again, because we all walked along together, Joan rather pale and with bitten lips. I had never known her so silent before. Ingram, on the other hand, was fiercely interested, and would talk. He wanted to know everything that had happened to me since I left his house the night before; all about V. G.; where I'd seen him and when, and how, and what I did after that, and what I said to Charlie Barr and what he said to me, and what we both thought about it; and was Charlie taking any precautions such as not going out alone after dark, or was he just sitting down under it, waiting for what might come?

Ingram then advanced a wild scheme he had just thought of; getting together a party of sufficiently interested people and going out that night in search of V. G. I told him he could do what he liked about it, but he could count me out. I believe in the end he did try something of the kind, but had to give it up as nobody in the village was hardy enough to join his crusade; but he did tell me a day or two later something from which I should have done my best to dissuade him if I'd known of it in time, that he'd taken out his bicycle round about midnight and cycled slowly to and fro along the moor road where the lighthouse beam fell, in the hope of repeating my experience. But he hadn't seen anything.

We went as far as his house, and I went in and had some coffee which I was glad of, as I'd gone off without breakfast. Then I said meaningly to Joan: 'I hope I'll see you in town soon. This is my last day here. I'm going back to London to-morrow.'

'Good!' she said briefly; 'I'm rather sick of the place too.'

Ingram said: 'But they won't let you go until after the inquest.'

I looked blank, but he was quite right. The inquest was fixed for two days hence, at the pub where they had a big room, and I had to stay.

By now I was wondering about Charlie, and decided that I'd better get back to the house. Rain. Rain. Rain. And a road like a quagmire. Nobody much about by now; they were all discussing it indoors, and the house where the wretched wife was lying was probably packed with busybodies. I tramped back to The Broch, and when I walked into the flagged hall I heard a movement, a kind of rustling above, and got the impression that someone was looking down at me between the banisters. So I ran up, and at the top of the flight was Miss Goff with a face like death and both hands clutching the bodice of her uniform.

She gasped at me, 'Mr. Mertoun! Mr. Mertoun!'

'Good heavens!' I said; 'what is it now?'

She stared at me. 'This awful thing . . . it's true?'

'Yes, yes,' I said; 'I thought for the minute it was something worse.'

She shuddered. Heavens, how she shuddered; and gave a short moan.

'Miss Goff!' I said. 'Don't give way like that! Did you know this Blaik? He wasn't anything to you, was he?'

'No,' she said, with a sound like a gritting sob. 'No . . . no . . . no. It's too terrible. I'm crazy . . . crazy, Mr. Mertoun. I can't bear it. I must go. I'll have to go.'

So that was it. She was going to leave in a fit of hysterics.

'You won't go,' I said calmly; 'you'll stay here where your duty is. If you left you'd never forgive yourself.'

'You're going!' she muttered, her eyes brilliant with fear.

'It's a different case,' I said; '*you'll* stay right here.'

She put up her hands to steady the quivering of her ashen cheeks.

'Dead . . . stabbed . . . dead . . . oh, what shall I do? I don't know . . . I don't know. . . .'

'Have you had breakfast?' I asked.

'No!'

'Then have some strong tea,' I said; 'you'll be better.'

She shook her head. 'No. Never. It's coming nearer . . .'

'Where's Mr. Barr?' I asked sharply.

'Who?' Her teeth chattered.

'Mr. Barr. For heaven's sake, Miss Goff. . . . Didn't you see him come in?'

'He's in the study.'

I went along to Barr's study; it was the first time I'd disturbed him there, but I forgot everything except the occasion and he didn't resent my intrusion. He at least looked sane, and had had breakfast and a shave. His desk was a muddle of papers.

'Well?' he said. 'Have you heard anything more?'

'Only that the inquest is the day after to-morrow, and I'm expected to stay. Will you mind?'

'Not in the least,' he said; 'it's necessary, though it's a bore for you. What does Ingram think?'

'He's talking of getting a party together,' I said, 'to hunt for V. G. And he wonders if you are taking precautions.'

'I?' said Charlie. 'Precautions!' And he laughed; rather an ugly sound.

When I went to my room that night I looked out and saw moonlight, greenish and gleaming like ice, poured into the rugged crannies of the broch that crouched on the hill. It was lonely now, and lonely it would be. A generation or two would pass before another man became so venturesome; grass and nettles would grow high inside that haunted circle of stone, as untrodden as the peak of Everest."

xv

"The day of the inquest came, and the room at the back of the inn was packed an hour before the coroner arrived. And who do you suppose the coroner was? It was Mackie the doctor, whom the excitement of the moment had so electrified that he found himself sufficiently recovered from his accident to undertake his duties. In fact, he gave the impression that he would have died of chagrin at having missed this inquest. He was carried in an arm-chair by four men from his house to the inn; and when the jurors came forth rather shakily from their ordeal of viewing the body, Mackie set the tone of the whole proceedings by holding up that stained, brass weapon, the Roman sword, and saying impressively, '"Twas the glint of this in the hand of that deevil my poor mare saw the night Mr. Ian Barr was murdered.' A sigh of horror went round the room, and the coroner crossed himself. After that the atmosphere was seething with superstitious fear. The jurymen were so frightened over their duty that all they longed for was a quick verdict and a stiff brandy in the comfortable privacy of the bar-parlour.

Ingram was there, leaning forward, his chin propped on his fists and his eyes alight with scientific interest. I felt myself that if Gracchus had strode in at that moment with clatter of cuirass and swirl of giant limbs, Ingram would have registered nothing but delighted curiosity.

The formal witnesses came first; the labourers who had found the body, the constable, the young doctor in his horn-rims giving his first medical evidence with a good deal of unction and an Oxford accent. This part would have been funny if it hadn't been so tragic; I mean, hard-boiled old Mackie, Irish Catholic, and this young blood from Bloomsbury having a wordy sparring match in exaggerated dialects. It would have made a marvellous music-hall turn.

Then the woman came on, Blaik's sister, and told a long tale about the time her brother left his cottage and what sort of a fool she had long since considered him. You could feel the stagnant air of the room quivering, and I felt that if Mackie crossed himself again I should have to relieve myself by kicking Charlie Barr who sat beside me, his arms folded across his chest and his face stony. He kept his eyes down. I wondered if he were thinking of that other inquest on his uncle, not so long ago; it must have resembled this one too strikingly to be easily bearable. How many more? That thought struck me a blow . . . but I was going away and probably should never know.

Then I was called, and I told my story in a hush through which I, pausing, could hear the faint, faint noise of a winter-bound fly stirring on the dirty panes. I suppose I must have told it with conviction; I couldn't help it, a story like that, so vividly remembered. When I described how I groped to the spot where a minute before Gracchus had stood, and fell on my knees, frozen with something worse than fright, to wait desperately for the life-giving lighthouse beam, a woman screamed and a score of throats growled for silence.

The coroner held up the exhibit. Did I recognize this knife?

I said: 'When I saw the Roman his hands were empty. It impressed me forcibly that he was unarmed.'

Well, everybody knew what that meant; it set the time of the murder before nine o'clock.

I asked: 'Excuse me, sir, but as a matter of curiosity, are there any prints on that knife?'

There were not. Ghostly hands leave no prints.

Then the verdict. To you, the incredible verdict. Death by stabbing, with insufficient evidence to show whether or not self-inflicted.

As though they were afraid of offending the spirit and bringing down on themselves the wrath of the mighty Gracchus. And it was all over; Blaik in future would be nothing but the memory of a hushed whisper. Charlie Barr had not been called, for which I was thankful and I'm sure he was.

We walked home in silence, and I sensed no despondency but a kind of new sternness in his attitude. When we got within a few yards of the house this was explained. He said: 'Mertoun, I want you to come with me to see my uncle. I insist.'

I said: 'Of course that's your affair.'

'Yes,' he said, 'it is my affair. That nurse is insufferable. I shall send for her directly we get in and have the matter out. I'd like you to be present. I don't want to be alone with her—if there's a scene, you understand.'

'So long as you don't expect me to take any part,' I said.

'That's as you wish,' he said gravely. 'If you consider that I'm ill-treating her you'll probably fly at me, so I'm taking a great risk.'

I was prepared for a scene; remembering the other night on the stairs, quite a formidable scene.

Charlie rang from the library. Would M'Coul tell Miss Goff that Mr. Barr desired to see her? We waited. She came down, looking particularly frozen and unapproachable. Charlie didn't waste words. He said—as far as I remember, his exact words—'Miss Goff, Mr. Mertoun and I are going up now to see my uncle. You can prepare him, if you like.'

The battle that followed was an absolutely silent one, and lasted only a few seconds, but you could feel the tension. Terrific. Then she gave way. She said: 'Very well, Mr. Barr.' I dare say you've noticed how often that happens; when an interview you've dreaded and screwed yourself up to goes off like a song.

She stood on one side then and hung her head down.

'Aren't you going up?' Charlie said.

'Oh, certainly not, Mr. Barr!' said she, very low and mordant; 'I wouldn't think of it.'

I thought again what a strange woman she was, with her face as white as paper—with temper, I suppose—and her eyes blazing, what you could see of them under the lowered lids.

I stood back.

'Come,' said Charlie.

So I followed him up the stairs to that closed door of mystery. But the greatest mystery was still to break upon us. Mystery, I said. That was the least of it. The surmise was the worst. For when we opened that door we found an empty room. An empty bed. Empty and yet undisturbed, the sheets coldly spread. I heard Charlie say in an astonished, echoing voice, 'Uncle! Where are you?' As though the missing man had stepped playfully behind a window-curtain! And then the emptiness spoke to us both simultaneously, and we knew that the Colonel hadn't 'stepped' anywhere . . . except perhaps out of life. Charlie took a pace towards me and the blood rushed up into his paled cheeks. The words broke out, 'You . . . Mertoun . . . do you know anything about this?' I was dumb with surprise. Then of course he found himself again, and said, 'I'm sorry. A ridiculous question. It was only the shock . . .'

'Miss Goff . . .' I muttered, and with one accord we went charging down the stairs; that gaping door, so long closed, now wide behind us and the curtains whipping in the wet wind. The nurse was standing in the library doorway, with her hand on the portière. Charlie caught her by the shoulder and she shook off his hand. She always hated to be touched.

'He's gone!' said Charlie. 'By hell, where is he? I'm asking you!'

She stared and stared at him as though she didn't understand, her eyes like hard blue stones; but at last it got through, and she gave a queer mutter and fell back, clutching the portière. Which of course came away under her weight, and, falling, she saved herself and groped for a chair.

Charlie was almost raving at her. I pulled him by the arm.

'Don't you see?' I said. 'Her shock. She knows no more about it than you do!'

'What!' he shouted. 'You mean, my uncle was ta . . . disappeared just now, while she was down here with us?'

'Ask her,' I said, 'when she was last in his room.'

She heard what I said, and gasped, 'Perhaps . . . an hour ago.'

'An hour ago!'

The nurse hid her face in her hands then, and burst into tears.

Charlie pulled her hands down. 'Stop that! We've got to talk—do you hear? And we've got to find him. You can hunt as well as any other.'

I had never seen Charlie so—shall I say, beside himself? He seemed frantic, and his face was full of unrecognizable lines.

'It's no good, Mr. Barr,' said the nurse in a low, shaking voice; 'it's come. I knew it was coming.'

'What do you mean?'

'Ever since Mr. Ian . . . and then poor young Blaik . . . I knew. He was the next. He was doomed.'

'Don't talk in riddles,' demanded Charlie; 'say what's in your mind.'

She said: 'He's taken the Colonel. The Roman soldier.'

Charlie gave a sharp 'Aaah!' and his fist flew up and dug a pit between his eyebrows. His lower lip was gripped between his teeth. He looked as though lightning had struck him into that attitude; so did the nurse. It was left for me to speak. I said: 'I'll go out and scour the moor! I'll rouse the village!' I hardly knew what I was saying. I was talking for the sake of talking, to break the strain between those two. Neither of them answered me. I had the chilly experience of hearing my own words die slowly away in the trembling air of the darkening room.

After long minutes Charlie stammered, as though after ponderous attention to my burning remark, now ashes: 'We—we must do . . . something.'

The nurse turned her head slowly, with a kind of pantherish scorn. 'Yes . . . something!' she said. 'Against that Gracchus!'

Charlie plunged down upon her words. 'What do you mean—Gracchus? You and your Roman soldier! You glib, superstitious . . . Repeating village gossip. . . . My uncle . . . in broad daylight. . . . There's something at the bottom of this.'

She set back her shoulders with a small shiver. 'You should know best, Mr. Barr,' she said in that thin, cold voice of hers; 'and as for whether the Roman soldier is village gossip or not, and as to whether he has a grudge against this house, well, didn't he speak to you with his own voice just a week ago from this day, and didn't Mr. Mertoun see the living form of him stalking at large about the moors? And didn't you with your own hands, before my eyes, take the Roman sword from the moulding of this room? What became of it after I never did ask, but its owner must have come for it, or else I'm mistaken in guessing it was the very blade that stuck in the back of the shepherd. The night Mr. Ian died he was abroad, as you very well know and I don't ask you to discuss; and I may be just a village gossip and a superstitious girl, but I know and you know that you may go out now and search the moor as you like, but you'll not find either the Roman soldier or the Colonel's body. And after all that's happened, what can we do in this house but stand and wait? Wait for what's coming.'

'Are we all going mad!' said Charlie, clenching his hands. 'Mertoun, will you be so good as to go and ring up the police-station——'

'—and tell them,' said Miss Goff, massaging her cold fingers, 'that Mr. Barr is anxious to know how long they'll be before they catch the Roman ghost, for he's harrying this house like a dog in a sheep-fold.'

'Don't go!' said Charlie to me, abruptly. And then to the nurse: 'Your services aren't required any longer, Miss Goff. You can leave to-night. I don't need your kind direction and oversight when I go out to find my uncle, and the less interest you take in the outcome of this business the better it will be for all of us. And, Mertoun,'—he turned to me—'I hope you won't misunderstand or take any offence when I tell you that I want this house clear. If you can find it convenient to pack your things now and ring up the station at Heaviburgh, they'll send a car in the morning in time for you to catch the London train.'

I agreed. I knew then that this was the end; that I couldn't delay my going any longer. My part on this wintry, northern stage was played, and I would pass out, perhaps never to know the close of the drama. Such a departure of the actors! The nurse; myself; soon

Ingram and Joan. And I seemed to see, as though leaving it behind, a great, mist-encircled arena and two figures groping there . . . converging nearer and nearer . . . Charlie Barr and the Roman ghost. Already I was looking over my shoulder, reluctantly as I moved away. It was like—forgive the crudeness of the analogy—like leaving a theatre in the middle of the last act to catch a train. You've done that? You'll understand.

The nurse went ahead of me up the stairs. I knew that in a minute I should have to say a few appropriate words of farewell to her. It was difficult. I tried to plan it . . . 'Well, good-bye, Miss Goff, and good luck.' Then other sentences . . . 'I'm sure you've done your best . . . You've had an ordeal . . . You mustn't blame yourself . . . The circumstances have been exceptional . . .' It was all too terribly banal; I'm ashamed to recall it. However I saved myself in time, and when it came to the point I said nothing but, 'Well, good-bye, Miss Goff . . . and good luck.' Hollow and unconvincing it sounded. She hardly looked at me; put out an almost reluctant hand and said a swift good-bye.

I didn't see her again; she was gone within the hour in a farmer's trap.

I sat down in my room and wrote a few lines to Joan.

My dear Joan,—[I scrawled]

I'm off to London in the morning and haven't time to see you again before I go. My calamity! Try and get Ingram away as soon as you can, and write to me at the address I gave you. I shall be sitting on the mat, holding my hand under the letter-box, so be a little sport and save my life. To please me, don't go dashing about the countryside now I'm gone. Call it dog-in-the-manger if you like, though it isn't that. Put in the time making pink silk jumpers and red flannel hug-me-tights. I'll make it up to you when you get to town. Salaams to Ingram and undying devotion to yourself,

Ever yours,

Billy.

I went down to a lonely evening in the cold old house, an evening of which every minute dragged. At about eight o'clock the hall door clanged. I ran to the window, and saw Charlie's back disappearing into the gloom, muffled in an overcoat, hands thrust deep in pockets, a loose ash-stick slung on his wrist by the crook. Where he went I don't know; I never shall know, because I never saw him again. I don't mean that anything sinister happened to him, for he was in the house when I left next morning, though he didn't come down to speed my departure with the usual amiabilities. He let me go without a word, which I felt was understandable and a fitting close to an association which from beginning to end was beyond the ordinary range of conversational amenities.

I suppose you are thinking that this ending to my adventure is an intolerable anticlimax. I ought to have warned you that I wasn't giving you the plot of a novel with its neat parabola of sensation. Life suddenly dumped me at the doors of The Broch and as suddenly hurried me away. I carried off only what I've given you, a fragment of a history, an arc of the parabola. I never knew such patience as yours . . . the way you've listened. You see, ever since I got back to London I've been thinking; a wheel of thoughts going round and round without arriving anywhere, and sometimes the wheel gets red hot and I can't bear it another minute. Telling you has . . . well, slowed down the wheel. But one thing keeps me restless; I haven't heard from Joan. That needn't mean anything, yet.

Then this morning I had what I didn't expect; the strangest letter, from Miss Goff, written on a sheet of flimsy, cheap paper like you'd find in a cottage, with a corroded and scratchy pen. It reads so glibly, and yet so stiffly—if that isn't a contradiction in terms—that one suspects she made half a dozen rough attempts and laboriously copied out the final production. The heading is 'Adam's Cranny, Little Thruston, Bellock, Northumberland,' and I imagine that is the address of the relatives she told me she had in the neighbourhood. Without comment from me, this is what she says:

DEAR MR. MERTOUN,—

You will be surprised to get this from me because you will be expecting to get a cheque to pay you for the work you did at Colonel Barr's house. This is to tell you that there won't be any cheque. I expect you will think you have been defrauded, and so you have. If you go to the police about it you will be quite within your rights, but if you will be generous enough to wait I will pay you the twenty guineas a bit at a time. Because it was all my fault. Colonel Barr never sent for you to do any work at his house. It is true that you were recommended to him and he wrote that letter and left it in his library. It was just about the time before Mr. Ian was killed, so the letter was never sent and never would have been. Then I was frightened and desperate and wondered what I could do. So I found that letter one day a long time after and I knew who you were because my brother Douglas who was in your Company had always been talking about you all those years ago in the war-time. You were like a hero to him, and when I saw your name there on the letter I thought it was like an answer to all our difficulties, and I thought if you were in the house you would help me and there would be no more of this dreadful tragedy. So I addressed the letter to you, because Colonel Barr had written your address at the bottom, and I sent it and nobody knew it was done by me. The Colonel never knew you came. It was all a fraud by me because I was frightened. So when you came you were just like Douglas said, and we talked about Douglas, and I thought it was all going to be all right, and when you said you were only going to stop a day or two I didn't know what to do, so I went away and thought what I could do. So I invented about the library catalogue because I knew that would keep you in the house a long time. And then in a day or two I knew it was all no good and you were going to fail me. And you did fail me. I knew the night the picture was cut. So I hope you will please forget all that part. But this is a kind of confession because I own that I defrauded you out of your money and I had no right to do so. But I promise to repay it if you will be so generous as to accept a pound or two at a time after I go back to the hospital at Edinburgh in a few weeks. I hope you will try to for-give me too and forget all that happened. I had no right to deceive you as I did or to expect anything from you.

Yours truly,
WINIFRED GOFF.

A letter that explains much, and leaves so much more unexplained. I wrote her the briefest note in reply; a mere line to say that I should not think of accepting any money from her and she would please consider the matter closed. Not a reference to all her tortuous circumlocution. She was always an enigma and she can remain one to the end so far as I'm concerned.

And that, Ahrman, is positively the end of my adventure."

ENTR'ACTE (*continued*)

"DO you believe me?" was Mertoun's direct question.

Ahrman did not answer immediately. He was admiring the *décor* of the little room—buff-washed walls with panels of dark blue and silver—and possibly half-asleep too in the depths of the dark-blue leather chair. The wood fire had burned low. The air was filled with merry, floating shapes of smoke from the pipes, wreathing now high, now low, very fascinating to follow in their effortless flight. Ahrman thought of how a world-famed ballerina might one day watch that dream of graceful motion uplifting from her own cigarette, until she died from the ache of impossible achievement. The wonder of such motion was too exquisite to be quite unconscious. The smoke veil was composed then of millions of little living creatures, glorying in their art.

"Do you believe me?" Mertoun's voice had taken a sharper tone. He was a little hoarse from his narration. "Because if you don't——"

"I do believe you," Ahrman said.

"Do you mean it? You believe me! All of it! All of it!"

"Every word," said Ahrman. "I don't see why it shouldn't be faithful and true. But if I hadn't—what?"

"I should have gone out into the streets," said Mertoun. "I should have walked all night. I should have become a Flying Dutchman of a creature in the London streets—until I'd found somebody who would have listened and believed. It must be the most awful thing in the world, not to be believed . . . You did mean it?"

"Now you can't believe me—yes!"

Mertoun cried with a touch of drama: "My soul . . . I see it all!
You're humouring the lunatic."

"No, no! I swear I'm not."

"Thanks." Mertoun's look of relief was not assumed. He went
on: "You can't think what it means to me that the first man I met
should be you, and that *you* should believe me. Because probably
no other man in London would."

"I can think of several who would," said Ahrman.

"Men I know?"

"Sir Hubert Torry, for instance."

"Oh, the ghost man. I couldn't bear a professional spook-hunter.
I've always thought of them as being half in the clouds. This is
earthy, practical, real. You believe me. Well!"

"And what now?" said Ahrman.

"What now?

"What are you going to do about it? You can't mean this to be
the end." Ahrman chose his words carefully. "I mean . . . don't you
long to see the play out?"

"The play. Carrying on my analogy of leaving during the last
act. Well, of course I could always go back to the same theatre
another night if I were really keen to see how it all ended. But it
doesn't work out so neatly in actual fact. I've no excuse to go back
to the region. I hope Ingram and Joan will soon be in London."

"And meanwhile," said Ahrman, "your friend Barr and the
Roman ghost approach one another like blindfold gladiators in the
arena. . . . I say, there are some striking analogies in this story!"

Mertoun laughed, and checked himself. "No, I mustn't laugh
about it, or soon I shall come to look upon the whole thing as an
imaginative joke and hate myself for my flippancy. No, Ahrman,
no laughter. It was death to two men." He paused and then asked
searchingly: "Do these things . . . do they *happen*? I mean, in all
your life have you met anything like it before?"

Ahrman wrinkled his forehead. "Nothing quite so . . . so graphic,
perhaps; but when I was young down in Cornwall there was an
affair in a neighbouring village. A family of three was wiped out
by—something. It was always a profound mystery, and after this
long time I can't give you the details. There wasn't very much to

know. Then there was the Tarleton Case, which you'll remember, when Major Tarleton appealed to the police for protection against the family ghost; and the presence in his house of an utterly prosaic, thirteen-stone bobby certainly broke the spell because there was no more haunting. I know of a castle or two that the owners won't live in . . . but no, my reminiscences are slightly childish, I'm afraid. I can't cap your tale with a better one. I think it speaks well for England that it can still raise a decent ghost. . . . By the way, how's your business after all this neglect? Anything doing?"

Mertoun brightened. "As it happens, yes. I've got quite a good commission if I care to take it up. A letter came yesterday morning from John Lecky, the show producer—I used to be at school with him. He's putting on a big show in May and he wants me to find him a chair for his Venetian Lady; he says, the most beautiful chair in the world."

"How long does he give you to scour the world?"

"A week. But that's ample really. I know where the chair is—in Vienna. I rang up Lecky and told him it would cost him four hundred pounds, and he seemed quite disappointed that I hadn't said fourteen hundred. I can negotiate and have the chair sent; though, of course, it would be better to go myself."

"You'll go, I take it?"

"I would, like a shot, but . . . supposing Joan writes."

"Could she write anything that would make so much difference?"

"She might want me to go back there at once."

"And she might not," said Ahrman. "Young man, you're making too much of your part in this act. You're only a super. Go to Vienna at once; it'll do you good. Leave to-morrow morning."

"I may," was all Mertoun would concede. "I may hear from Joan to-morrow too."

They walked out into Whitehall, and Mertoun began feverishly to talk of other things, to emphasize, as it were, his normality.

Ahrman was anxious to get home, a craze which often begins to attack people after forty, so he took advantage of a suitable break in the conversation to say: "Well, now, how do you get home? We're going the wrong way for you, aren't we?"

"That's all right," Mertoun said; "I'm not in a hurry, and I can take a taxi. What about you?

"Oh, I can take a tram near here . . . put me down within five minutes of where I live. You must look me up again some time."

"Just one thing," said Mertoun quickly. "Thinking it over, was there anything more I could have done? Under the same circumstances, would another man have been more resourceful or effective, do you think? I can't help wondering. Actually I can't see anything else that I could have done, but that may be due to my own denseness."

"I shouldn't worry," said Ahrman. "No two men under the same set of circumstances would ever behave in exactly the same way, but at least you didn't seem to blunder. It seems gratuitous to bother over what you might have done. You might have made a most unholy mess of things up there if you'd been tactless—that leaps to the eye—so congratulate yourself that you're well out of it."

"It baffles me . . . how—if ever—I let Miss Goff down."

"You may never know. Forget it."

"I'll have to." Mertoun nodded. "So long, then. Good night."

"Good night." Ahrman added emphatically. "And you be sensible and go to Vienna. Business first. It's a good rule."

There was no letter from the North, and Mertoun left England next morning. The journey to Central Europe was no novelty to him, and he knew the Vienna to which he was travelling rapidly, the real Vienna, not the song-and-dance city of romantic legend thrust upon his eye by London's theatrical posters. It would be the same as ever, a grey city with tall grey buildings, swept by the icy winds of February and grindingly cold; the Prater dingy and bare, the river—blue Danube indeed!—black and sloppy with ice; the clanking trams, round and round the Ring in noisy monotony; people in streets and cafés with their grim, unhappy faces; swarms of beggars. As for the talked-of night-life . . . well, it paid them to work up a little tinselled gaiety for the tourists.

He took a *droschke* to the Bristol Hotel—not that he thought it romantic to ride in a *droschke*, but because he had set out to walk from the station, having little luggage to carry, and sudden rain had descended, and there was no taxi in sight—and after lunch considered the job in hand.

It might take him anything from twelve to forty-eight hours to get in touch with Wertheim, the elusive Jew with whom he wanted to trade. Wertheim's whole life was spent in "passing through" Vienna. Mertoun guessed that this deal would take him two or three days, and the sooner he took steps to catch Wertheim on the wing the better.

He was about to telephone when it occurred to him that he might walk round to the Jew's office which was on the Kärntner-strasse, not five minutes' walk from the hotel.

A clerk received him.

"I want to see Mr. Wertheim," Mertoun said in German. "When will he be here? I want the earliest possible appointment."

"But Mr. Wertheim is here now. What is your name, please?"

This was incredible luck. "Tell him, Mr. Mertoun from London. Can he spare me a quarter of an hour?"

The clerk returned quickly. "This way, Herr Merrto'n."

The prosperous little Jew, who always dressed very badly and never appeared to be working very hard, hauled himself out of an English saddle-bag chair.

"Vell, Mr. Merrto'n! You valk in alvays sudden, isn't it? You're lucky too, because I go to Italy in the morning for t'ree veeks. A little holiday, no. Vot you come for now?"

"I want that chair from the Elpenschloss," said Mertoun. "I saw in last week's *Connoisseur* that you'd acquired it. Where is it, and when can I have it? As usual I'm in a tearing hurry."

"T'at chair," said Wertheim, "she goes mit me to Italy to-morrow. The Count——"

"Oh, Tommy!" Mertoun interrupted with calm impatience. "How much is he giving you for it?"

The Jew began to murmur something in the fifty-thousands which proved that the complicated system of reducing practically worthless *kronen* to a recognizable monetary value was for the moment beyond even Hebrew technique.

"I'll give you three-fifty," said Mertoun, "in English notes. It's here—seven fifties—and you'd better pocket it. That's the best deal you've done this week."

"Na, na! But I couldn't t'ink——"

"Right-ho," said Mertoun, taking up the notes. "I'm not arguing. I can't be bothered. I'm going." He was half-out of the door.

"Coom you back——"

"What for?"

"As a goot coostomer——"

"Cut that out," said Mertoun. "How am I getting the chair to London?"

"I haf her here," said the Jew. "I put her on the train to Paris tomorrow morning, isn't it? She is in London Friday. You haf a little drink?"

A quarter of an hour later Mertoun was in the street again. Wertheim was reliable once he had made a bargain, and the chair would be duly delivered in London, quite safe and sound. And Mertoun realized that he had been in Vienna just over an hour and a half and all his business was done. Wasn't that just the contrariness of life all over? It might have taken him three or four days; he had counted on two.

The next thought that occurred to him was that the time was twenty-past two and the Trans-Continental express, the best train of the day, left for Paris at three. What had he to wait for in Vienna?

An hour later, leaning back in his corner seat, rolling along towards France, he laughed long, though silently, over this whole helter-skelter business. A room booked and unbooked, all in an hour. That hadn't worried them at the Bristol. Little Wertheim, so comic. . . . Mertoun had said at the end: "You know, you ought to come to England, Wertheim. It's incredible that a cosmopolitan like you has never seen London!"

The little Jew gave one emphatic jerk of his head. "Not never do I come to England so long as I live. My vife is in it."

Mertoun was back in London almost before he realized he had left it. The next morning there was a letter from Joan Hope. He called Ahrman on the 'phone directly after breakfast.

"That you, Ahrman. . . . Yes, I've been and come back. . . . Not impossible at all. . . . Will you have dinner with me to-night? . . .

Good. Meet me in the Criterion Grill at eight. . . . So long."

"You move quickly," said Ahrman that night when he looked up from the tricky task of choosing his soup.

"I did in this case." Mertoun sounded pleasantly assured. "I was in Vienna less than two hours. There wasn't anything to tempt me to stay, so I caught the afternoon train back. I got the chair, and I was notified that it had arrived at Dover this morning. And I've heard from Joan—Joan Hope."

"Oh yes? That business . . ."

"Have you thought of it since?"

Ahrman made a gesture of assent. "Quite a lot. . . . But is there anything to tell me? Anything to add to the loose end?"

"Not much," said Mertoun; "it was reassuring to get the letter, and yet I'm disappointed. Joan isn't coming back to London yet. Ingram won't come. You can guess how difficult it is to keep him in the same mind for two days running. It seems that Ingram is thoroughly roused by the recent appearance of the ghost. He has been taking his bicycle out at night and scouring the moorland roads in the hope of seeing Gracchus. Think of anyone wanting to! It's rather horrible for Joan, but she's so plucky she makes light of the whole thing. Still, it isn't good to think of her left behind in that disturbing neighbourhood. Ingram says that he won't leave until he has seen Gracchus."

"So Miss Hope has got hold of the complete story?"

"Evidently. I hope she isn't afraid. She wouldn't tell me if she were."

"Any local news? Did she mention your late host, or young Barr?"

"Oh yes. She said that the Colonel's disappearance was still a profound mystery. People were getting tired of discussing it in the village. She had been for a walk past the house and down to the beach—I wish she wouldn't do that kind of thing alone, it drives me frantic—but she hadn't seen anyone about the house. They say in the village that Charlie Barr never leaves the house now, and won't see anybody. He's got fear into his marrow, of course, and his way of facing the fact is to stand his ground doggedly and wait . . . as it were, come on now, do your worst! I couldn't do it myself, but people are built differently. Charlie's Yankee-bred, which may account. But I never was so sorry for a fellow in all my life. Honestly, Ahrman, if he'd asked me to stay on with him— barring my business obligations—I believe I would. He's never had the chance to make a friend since he came over, confined to that isolated place. He must be the loneliest man in England. And then there's Joan . . . well, as long as she's up there and I'm down here there's going to be about as much peace of mind for me as would lie on a threepenny bit. I've no right to feel it, but there it is."

"And on the whole," Ahrman continued, "your general impression is that you've got to get back into the theatre by hook or by crook."

"How could I?" said Mertoun, as frankly as a boy.

"You admit that you want to see the end?"

"If there's going to be an end. . . . I don't see how there can be. But I want Joan out of it, and I want Charlie's house made safe for him. It isn't my business, it's pure interference on my part, but I want those things."

"Danger to yourself?"

"That wouldn't worry me a bit. And in any case, it looks as though the danger were confined to Barrs."

"What about that shepherd?"

"Oh, Blaik. Well, I can only think that he interfered."

"Which you'd do yourself quite cheerfully for the sake of Miss Hope and——"

"Cut it out," said Mertoun, attending to the menu.

"When you told me your tale," said Ahrman suggestively, "you made the mistake of telling it to the most curious man in London; moreover, a man who has a holiday falling due to him towards the end of April. Mertoun, if nothing has happened before then, would you think it interference on my part to suggest that I go up there—fishing will do; there's always fishing in a place like that— and see for myself?"

Mertoun put down the card and thought a minute.

"If you go," he said, "I go. I can fish as well as you—which isn't saying much. Do you think we could?"

"It won't be before the end of April," Ahrman reminded him. "Several weeks."

"Things move slowly up there," said Mertoun. "There's nothing to prevent my going back for a holiday. I never thought of that. I could look Barr up, whether Joan is there or not. . . ." He thought for a few minutes. "It is a good idea, Ahrman; and you're a good fellow. I didn't think you'd have been interested to that extent; it isn't in your line."

"Lots of things you wouldn't believe," said Ahrman sagely; "they're all in my line . . . all in my line."

"But ghosts . . ." Mertoun murmured. "Time is having its natural effect and I can look at my impressions now with the detachment of a practical man. I was half-ill all the time I was at that place; half-ill, and badly taken by surprise. But of one thing I'm certain—I wasn't deceived. With these eyes I saw a ghost, and the dead victim of a ghost. I saw. . . ."

"The waiter!" Ahrman whispered warningly.

PART II

HAMLETH'S DIARY

THE DIARY OF HAMLETH GOFF

JANUARY 23. At the Strickan Light.

So here we are at the Strickan Light, me and Dad, and somebody else. And there's twelve weeks to go, all but one day, before we see the shore again. I bought this book in Thorlwick, a good, stout log; and very glad I am when I think of the long days and nights at sea, and yet not at sea. For I've been a few trips on tramp, trawler, and coaster and always you could see the waves cutting away from you and there'd be land on your bow maybe, changing-like from hill to plain or harbour or river mouth, and sometimes you'd have a run before the gale till you sighted port; but here on the Strickan it's always the same. The same waves pounding on the concrete, and away over there the black line of the coast, and between it and the open sea the Strickan Points, seven of them, like sharks' teeth rearing out of the rough water.

A man has a lot of time to think, even when he's cleaning the reflectors and cleaning and fuelling the four-wick burners and carrying paraffin fuel from the stores to the lantern-chamber; and I never was one that was fond of thinking for the sake of thinking; not unless I could write it down, that is. So when I bought this fine log-book and carried it home, Dad says, "What's that?" And I said, "It's to take to the Strickan with us, Dad." You see, we were going on duty on the night of the 22nd. I said: "I'm going to keep a log, Dad, only it's what they call a diary where I put down all my thoughts." And he growls and says: "There'll be no log kept on the Strickan, bar the Trinity House, and that'll be kept by me." So I said nothing and I had it my own way. And when we pulled out from Thorlwick on the 22nd, Father and me, I'd the book in my chest and a bottle of ink and pens and the works of William Shakespeare too.

But there was a lot happened before we pulled out of Thorlwick. I'd a letter from my sister Winifred, the same that's nursing Colonel Barr at his house called The Broch. It's a little thing she can do for the Colonel who always did so much for our family, and grateful we are to him too, though for us rough northern folk it's easier to be doing than to be saying! But she's been there, poor girl, from the time the Colonel fell down in a fit after his brother, Mr. Ian, was murdered on the cliffs that dark night. And there she vowed she'd stay, if there was to be any saving of the Colonel from the same fate.

But Winifred she knew that Dad and me were for the Strickan on the night of the 22nd, so she wrote to me and here's her letter:

DEAR HAMLETH,—

I must see you before you go to the Light. Come when you get this, and be in the Shrubbery of this house to-night between twelve and one. Don't let anybody see you, for it may mean life and death to Somebody. You mustn't fail me.

WINIFRED.

I said to Dad: "I've had a letter from Winifred. She wants to see me about—you know what. See here!"

So he read the letter and he said: "Rubbidge."

I said: "I'd better start if I'm going."

And he didn't stop me, because neither of us would dare to do contrary to what Winifred tells us.

It was dark as pitch when I got out of the motor-coach at Bullachtown, and I'd nine miles to walk. I know all the folk about that countryside, and I longed to look in at one or two farms and have a crack about old times and see some of the lads I used to work with before we went away to Thorlwick. But Winifred had said not to let anybody see me, so I set out without so much as a bit of cheer from the Fox and Shaw. It was a night too, the twentieth of January, raw and still and black, with the promise of nasty weather and not so much as a star. I'm a seaman and I've no liking for a night without a star.

So I got to the house where Colonel Barr lives; The Broch they call it, after that ugly bit of a ruin that hangs on the hill where they say there's a haunt. Anyway, there's no man would go near it when I was a lad, and I doubt they won't to-day either. It's been there hundreds and hundreds of years. Nobody saw me come to the house, but there was a light in two of the downstairs windows, where there's one big room, the library they call it. I didn't know what time it was, for I couldn't see my watch, but I knew Winifred wouldn't come out while there was anybody abroad in the house.

I waited among the thick shrubs by the gates, lying on my face and watching the lighted windows. After a long time they went dark, and then the night closed down and you could feel the midnight hush stealing on you, like when you're out with the haddie fleet at sea. I waited and waited, like she'd told me to. It was a long time. Then she came, all wrapped up in a black coat.

"Sssss!" she whispered. "Ham!"

"I'm here," I said, cracked-like, trying not to make a noise.

"Come after me," she said. "We've got to go indoors."

"We'll be seen!" I said.

"No," she said. "Not where I'm taking you."

She took me in by a little back door, and I'm used to moving softly, so she made me. We went up some stairs and I had to feel very careful for the treads, but there was carpet on them and it made it easy to walk light.

Then she opened what was just a cupboard in the thickness of the wall, and she whispered, "Get in there. Then we can talk."

"It's a cupboard," I said, stupid.

"Yes," she said, "and a thick one. Nobody's going to hear us. And I can keep an eye on his door."

"His door?" I said.

"Yes. That's it, where the light from the window falls," she said. "I never take my eye off his door."

I said, thick-like: "Would it come that way?"

"Yes," she said, "it would."

So I was dumb, because she knew better than I did, and she'd told me all about the curse of the Barr family from what she'd seen for herself while she was staying with our aunt at Adam's Cranny, and from what she'd put together while she was in that house.

"Be careful!" I said.

"Yes," she said, quite calm, "I am being."

"Has anything else happened?" I whispered.

"Bits of things," she said. "Enough to frighten me to death."

She pulled the cupboard door to on us, leaving just a crack for her to peer out at the Colonel's door.

"It might be by night or it might be by day," she explained. "I'm always watching."

"You wouldn't have much chance against that fiend," I said.

She shook a bit. "I'd face him!" she said. "And that's more than anyone did the night he grappled with Mr. Ian."

It was my turn to quake then, and I said: "You're a brave girl, Winifred, but if it's the Colonel he's set on taking next, then the Colonel he'll get. He'll wait patient-like. Very patient and watch-ful, in the dark, waiting for you to take your eyes off the Colonel's door; and then he'll come down quiet like the storm-clouds come, and very quick, like he came upon Mr. Ian. It's you watching the Colonel, Winifred, and him watching you; and I'm a seaman and I know what watching means. You're only a woman; and we know what he is. . . ."

"Then it's my wits against his," she said, very calm, "and that means the Colonel's got to be away from here."

"Will he go?" I said. "And to where?"

"He'll go," she said, "because he's docile like a child, and he'll do anything I tell him. He's strong enough too, with the help of me and a brawny young fellow like you, Ham. He'll go quiet too, in the middle of the night."

"So you mean you'll get him away and not tell anybody?" I said.

"I'll tell nobody," she said. "The fewer people know the better, and three of us is enough for the secret—you and me and Dad. Just his three humble friends. And when he's gone I'll go on guarding his door, but inside there'll be an empty room. I'll be easier in my mind if it's so."

"I'll give you credit for being a clever girl!" I said, for she always had a head on her, had Winifred, as Dad and I know. "But where's the Colonel going to, anyway?"

"To where not even that fiend can reach him," she said, as cool as you please. "To the lighthouse."

"To the Strickan Light!" I said, all of a gape. "Winifred, you've gone mad."

"Not a bit," she said. "I've got it all worked out. When is it you and Dad go out?"

"The night of the 22nd," I said.

"At what time?"

"Round about full tide," I said. "Say two a.m."

"That'll do fine," she said. "You'll bring the boat in here to the little bay, and Dad'll wait while you help me to get the Colonel aboard. You must get him a jersey and oilskins, and he'll step off at the Strickan as third man. Then the three you relieve can take the boat back to Thorlwick."

"Stop!" I said. "What about Tammas Bell?"

"Who's he?" she said.

"He's the third man," I told her; "he goes out with Dad and me."

"No, he doesn't," she said, "for you'll stop him. You'll find a way. And he'll keep his mouth shut, for he'll draw his money just the same when the twelve weeks is up, and there'll be five pounds of my savings for him too. If anybody asks any questions he can say a man from Burnfirth has changed duty with him. I'm leaving all that to you, Ham."

"I must say you've got it all thought out," I said, "but Dad'll never agree."

"Oh, yes he will," she said. "If he doesn't, you can tell him I'll come and see him and it'll be the worse for him. There's one that has the last word in our family, and that's the one they call Winifred."

She was right too.

Then she changed her tone suddenly, and she whispered: "I've something else to tell you too. There's a man staying here in the house. Captain Mertoun."

"What!" I said. "Not him that Douglas . . ."

"Yes," she said, "and he's like Douglas said he was, a brave man. He's a big, tall man with steady eyes, and I don't think he'd be afraid of anything . . . not even of the fiend himself. I've talked with him, and I'm hoping. Yes, I'm hoping, Ham. But I daren't say anything yet. I have to be so careful. I was nearly for telling him everything yesterday, but I caught myself in time. It'll have to be slow, but I believe I've got a champion sent by heaven."

"How did that man come to be here?" I asked, astonished.

"I sent for him," she said.

"You sent for him!" I said, so amazed that I forgot to whisper and she had to hush me. But by then I'd have believed anything that Winifred did, or was said to do.

"Yes," she said. "I wrote to him in the Colonel's name to come and do some work in the house. I'm keeping him here as long as I can. He doesn't know anything, of course. I can't tell you the whole story now because there isn't time. He's only been here two days."

"You're a wonder!" I said. "Now what is it you want me to do?"

"Listen carefully," she said, "because I shan't see you again till all's ready, and if you fail me it'll mean death for the Colonel as sure as the Strickan Light goes round. On the night of the 22nd you and Dad must land the boat in the bay. It's a good landing-place, for there's always a strip of shingle uncovered, at high tide, and there's caves. Then you must come up here to the house, to the little door at the side where we just came in. I'll meet you there, and we'll get the Colonel out and down to the boat. Don't forget the jersey and oilskins, and I'll bring the other things he needs. Tell Dad, Winifred says it's got to be! Do you understand? And you must settle tomorrow with Tammas Bell."

Well, that was her plan, and after talking it over a bit longer I left the house and walked back in the early morning to Bullach-town, where I got the motor-coach home in time to find Dad at his breakfast. So I told him all about it.

He swore he'd have nothing to do with it. He wouldn't touch a scheme like that with a forty-foot pole. It was as much as his job and mine and Tammas Bell's were worth. He'd be dismissed and

I'd be dismissed, and Tammas Bell too. No, he wouldn't be mixed up in a thing like that anyhow, not for fifty Winifreds.

So when he'd had his say I said: "Well, I'd better be getting round to see Tammas. There's no time to lose."

And he said: "I suppose you had. Eh, dear, that girl 'ull bring my grey hairs in sorrow to the tomb. Sharper than the serpent's tooth, as the prophet said."

"What prophet, Dad?" I said, innocent-like.

"Why, Habbakuk!" he says sharp. "And after the schooling you've had. . . . Well, you can still learn something from your poor old Dad."

So I went round to see Tammas Bell.

I never realized before, I may say now, how the path of evil-doing is made broad and easy. Mistress Bell met me at the door before ever I could open my mouth.

"Tammas is very bad with the bronchitis," she said. "He won't be able to go to the Strickan."

"Never mind," I said. "I'll get a man I know from Burnfirth to take his duty, and I'll see Tammas draws his pay just the same. Only tell him not to say too much about it, for we're not supposed to arrange these things among ourselves."

She was so relieved she nearly cried, and I knew both she and Tammas would keep their mouths closed. It was too easy, evil-doing. Hardly fair on a man. I thought, "We're fighting the devil, Winifred and me, and yet here's the devil helping us. Seems queer." But that didn't stop me, anyway.

January 24.

I went on writing last night until the dawn broke, and Dad came up to relieve me and put out the light. It was a foggy morning and we set the Daboll siren blowing. Then I went down to my breakfast with the Colonel, who was looking very well, and happy enough too. We'd made him into cook and that pleased him. He liked to be useful. He was well enough, though a bit dazed-like, and he didn't seem to find it odd that he should be on a lighthouse instead of in his own big house. After breakfast he helped me set up a big, new frame aerial we'd brought out, and we heard a man talking in Paris or one of those places. I don't know what he was talking about, but his voice sounded kind of cheering above the beat of the sea.

But I must tell how we got the Colonel out here in the dead of the night. It's mid-afternoon now and I've just come from the look-out. There's a big sea booming round the concrete, and tossing the spray clear to the platform. It's a grand sight, the sea in its power. Thousands of gulls are clinging to the rock, settling on the rails of the look-out, and whirling like snow-clouds round the beacon, or glittering like silver plumes where the light catches their wings. The Colonel was up there too, and he never tired of holding his arm for the creatures to swoop down on it with their little coral feet and stabbing nebs. He's like me, loving the sight of a wild bird. I was telling him how once I went with some lads to the Bass Rock to see the wildest birds in the world by thousands on their ledges where the foot of man can't climb and the hand of man can't destroy, and we saw there gulls that we couldn't name, and skuas and smews, and terns and razor-bills, and gannets and divers and petrels and grebes and auks and cormorants; but that was when I was working on the great cod-bank. So then I taught him how to set the lobster-pots and the nets, and later he drew in a fine codfish himself and I never saw anybody so proud. I said he'd be tired of eating fish after twelve weeks.

From the look-out I could see the shore, just the black line of it over the tumbling waves, and I wondered what Winifred was doing and what she would have to tell me when I saw her after all the weeks to come.

She let me into the house a bit before two in the morning.

"You've come!" she whispered, as though she'd been waiting all day and wondering, as I dare say she would. "Is Dad below at the bay?"

"He is," I said, "with the boat and the things for the Colonel."

"And what did he say?" she wanted to know.

"You may well ask," I said. "He says we'll be put in prison for this, the both of us. It's against the law, Winifred."

She laughed at that. "Much a Northumberland lad ever cared for the law," said she. And I suppose she's right. We were always a lawless lot, especially them of us that have lived so near the Border.

She took me up the stairs. There was a high old clock singing tick-tock, as loud as the smith strikes the anvil. We came to the Colonel's room and he was waiting, dressed.

"Good day, sir," I said, very respectful for the Barr family; "I've come to take you a little trip, circumstances excusing the early hour."

"Winifred says I'm to go with you," he said. "A good girl. I always mind what she says."

"That's right, sir," I said. "So do we all at home."

It seemed to me we were making a terrible noise, the three of us in that sleeping house. Fit to wake men deafer than I knew were sleeping there. Winifred was scared, for she kept glancing, glancing; and so slowly we went down the stairs it was like as if something was clogging our feet.

"Quick! Quick!" she kept whispering under her breath, for she couldn't help it; it was the Colonel who went so slow. It was bitter for him, I doubt, leaving his home in the dark of the night because a fiend was driving him out.

"Mr. Mertoun's room's the nearest," said Winifred. "If he should hear us and come! He sleeps badly at night, I know."

"What for?" I said.

"He's heard things!" she whispered, very low, so the Colonel shouldn't hear. At that, it wasn't so much as a whisper, for only her lips moved without any sound, but I read her meaning. "He asked the housemaid was there a ghost," she said later, as she slipped back to help me close the side-door. Then she slipped the key in her pocket, and we both breathed easily in the free, salty air, tasting the sea.

"Then he knows something already?" I said.

"Oh yes," she said, "and he's asked me to go for a walk, Ham! I'll have to be careful, but I think he's going to be our deliverance and the saviour of this house."

"You'll be able to go a walk," I said, "now the Colonel's safe away."

"Yes," she said, and the light of the open sky catching her eyes I saw them shine. "I had to put him off before. I was afraid of saying too much."

"But he knows there's Something in the house?" I said.

"Oh yes; he knows that."

"Does he know about how Mr. Ian was killed?" I said.

She shook her head, and we had to hurry back to the Colonel. We took our time over the walk to the sea. There was nothing to hinder us. The wind was fresh and the clouds rode high. Then we went down the cliff path to the bay, and there was Dad waiting and grumbling, with the boat drawn up on the shingle. But he greeted the Colonel and said it was a proud day for him to be carrying a Barr in his boat.

While the Colonel put on his jersey and oilskins, Winifred and I talked. There were tears glimmering in her eyes. I shook my fist at the land where the house stood. "Curse him!" I said. "Curse the evil fiend that's prowling there; him that's come from the vasty deep with black heart and murderous hand, the bad spirit of an honoured race. If I'd only been there the night Mr. Ian . . ."

"No, Ham," said Winifred. "Neither your strong hands nor my woman's wits are enough to contend with the powers of darkness. It'll take knowledge that we don't possess. But Mr. Mertoun . . ."

"Ah," I said. "He'll know what to do, Winifred."

"I'll test him first," she said; "test him hard and strong. And if he comes through I'll tell him all. But I must test him and try him. I'm waiting my time. It'll come."

She helped us to push off the boat, and doing so she grazed her arm against the gunwale so that the blood sprang dark on the whiteness from wrist to elbow. She wrapped her cloak round the bruise, and the last I saw of her as we pulled away she was standing upright under the cliffs, not even waving, just watching us out of sight. A brave woman, I say.

Well, we came to the Strickan at last and moored at the iron ladder. Joe and his mates were ready and waiting at the look-out. It didn't take ten minutes all told to change duty.

"Who's your new mate?" said Joe, looking at the Colonel.

"Name of Bates," I said. "From Burnfirth."

"What's happened to Tammas Bell?"

"Ill," I said. "Bronchitis bad."

The three of them dropped down into the boat with their chests and Joe's cat, and they rowed away on the flood into the dark. The three of us were left on the Strickan, and I went up to the lantern-chamber to take over the Light.

February 2.

The days go by and there's nothing to write. The Colonel is in good health, and Dad's old cat has given us three pretty kitlings. We've had little but foggy weather and the seas have run high. This morning the fog lifted and we saw a fine Norwegian steamer go by, too close for safety; but she hailed us and changed her course and came to no harm. The horn was sounding, but fog plays havoc with your sense of direction, as I well know. I was wrecked myself in a trawler off the Bell Rock when I was a lad of fifteen. The sea-fog was heavy that night and the horizon seemed full of clanging bells.

February 4.

I was dreaming last night. A boat came out of the fog and tied up at the foot of the ladder. Then I saw a man climbing up and I hailed him, but he didn't answer. When he came in sight I saw that he was dressed like the picture I once saw of a Roman soldier. I shouted, and he seemed to fall back into the sea. This makes me think of Winifred and wonder what is happening there. I should like to talk about these things to the Colonel, but Winifred said I must never do that. She thinks his memory is wiped clean of that horror, and what would happen if it were brought back to him? So I said nothing about my dream, not even to Dad, but I find my eyes turning to the ladder now and I strain my ears for a dipping oar. Am I a fool?

March 19.

This is the first time I woke to see the sunlight glittering on the green waves, and the white foam sparkling as it leaps around the rock. A bonny sight, but we daren't count on spring so early. The wind is bitter cold, and the gulls are screaming as they fly. Dad says the cod-fleet went by at dawn. Two nights ago there must have been a wreck up the coast, for the sea has been full of drifting spars. Some we lugged in for fuel. At least, we have plenty of tobacco. I have to go up now. There is so little to write. The Colonel is very well. Only four weeks and three days more.

April 23. At Adam's Cranny.

Last night I gave Winifred my diary to read and she said it was a poor thing. It was all scraps, she said, and if she'd have had a diary she'd have written something every day, no matter whether anything happened or not, if it was only thoughts. Then she gave it back to me and said I'd better tear out the pages and burn them, but I didn't. I've got some more to write about now.

I'm stopping at Adam's Cranny to give my uncle a hand in the fields, and Winifred's stopping here too to keep house for my aunt who's bedridden. The Colonel's at Thorlwick with Dad, but nobody knows that. We pulled away from the Strickan about ten o'clock on the morning of the 21st, and made harbour on a fine afternoon, and as I was restless and wanted to stretch my legs I said I'd pack a kit-bag and walk over to see Winifred, a matter of thirty miles or so. I set out at dawn the next day. It was good to see the familiar country again, bleak and bare as it was; for the spring comes late, and though the sky was blue and merry the wind was as fierce as a tiger's claws and combed the earth coldly through. There was not a green blade to see.

Up on the moor I sat down to rest, and presently I spied two men coming over the hill, not men of our country I saw at a glance. They carried rod, line, and creel, and wore yellow mackintoshes and little tweed hats with a neb at each end. When they saw me they said good morning.

"Good morning," I said, sitting still.

"You're a sailor?" said the older one, quite pleasant, stopping as though he wanted to talk.

"Not at the moment, sir," I said, very cool. "Yesterday I was a lighthouse keeper and to-morrow I'll be a farm-hand."

"A lighthouse-keeper!" You'd think he'd never heard of such an employment, the way he said it. "Not by any chance the keeper of the lighthouse we can see from here?"

I peeked up and looked east, and there sure enough across the

shoulder of the moor and across the grey billows of the North Sea
I saw the Strickan, like a wee silver pencil winking in the sun. But
I didn't say anything; I was thinking, and I thought to myself that
this might be some nosey official who'd got hold of the idea that
there'd been a man on the Strickan who'd no right to be there. So
I made up my mind I'd be stupid. When you're a countryman they
always expect you to be half-daft, so it's easy to mislead them.

"Is that the lighthouse you're from?" he said at last.

"It might be," said I. "There's nothing to tell one from another."

"But isn't that the one they call the Strickan Light?" he said.

"Is that what they call it?" I said. "The townsfolk have some rare
funny names for places, I know."

"What's your name?" he said, offering me his cigarette-case. I
took a cigarette, and scraped a match on my boot-sole and said,
"They call me Ham."

I thought he looked disappointed, and next minute he turned
to the other man and said, "I thought for the minute it might have
been ——" Then he looked back at me, and asked did I live in these
parts.

"Well, I do and I don't," I told him.

"But you know the district?" he went on.

"Oh, ay," I said, sounding as if I didn't know much.

"Then can you tell us," he said, "where we'll find a bit of fishing
farther afield? We're tired of the Spannet."

"Oh, you are?" I said. "Well, I was tired of the Spannet myself
before I was twelve. I could tell you a place or two where you'd get
what I call sport." And then I wondered if I'd said too much. It's
difficult to keep on being daft.

"Where's that?" they both asked.

So I told them a place or two, and they seemed pleased. "We'll
go out that way tomorrow, Mertoun," said the older man to the
other; and at that I pricked up my ears and kept my eyes down,
which is an easy thing to do and not noticeable.

"Well, good morning," they said.

"Good day," said I, and went on sitting by the side of the road
until they were out of sight.

Then I went on to the village, and slipped into the parlour of the Red Buck. This was what I'd come all the way for. I waited, and it was as quiet as you please in there, with the window a wee bit open and the sunbeams slipping through, and some pink hyacinths just breaking into bloom on the sill. She must have heard me, for presently she came running in and said, "Who on earth's that?" As if she didn't know.

I said: "It's me, Lily." And she said: "Oh, is it you, Ham?"

She was looking very pretty in a blue dress like the colour of her eyes.

She said: "Father'll be in soon. He's just stepped over to Doctor Mackie's to get something for his cough."

"I didn't come to see your father, Lily," I said, because I thought I'd better put that right before we went any further. "So Doctor Mackie's about again, is he?"

"Oh yes," she said. "Why, of course, he had his accident before you went away, didn't he, Ham? I'd quite forgotten. It seems a long time since you went away, and such a lot of things have happened."

"It seemed a long time to me too, shut up there on the Strickan," I said. "I thought about you often and often, Lily. Did you ever think about me?"

"Perhaps I did," she said. "But if you've just come back you won't have heard about the goings-on we've had here?"

"I haven't heard anything," I said.

"Haven't you seen your sister—her that was nurse to Colonel Barr at the big house?"

"Not a glimpse," I said. "I had a letter to say she was at Adam's Cranny. I'm going there to-night."

"Oh, you are out of things!" she said, laughing up at me. "Why, I suppose you won't even have heard that Colonel Barr's disappeared!"

"What!" I said, all amazed. "How do you mean—disappeared?"

"Nobody knows," she said, dropping her voice. "It was the Roman ghost took him."

"No!" I said. "Not him again?"

She nodded. "He's been about. He's been seen on the cliffs by a man that was staying at the big house, a man from London. On the cliffs, mind you, same as where Mr. Ian Barr was killed. There's nobody in the village'll go along that road now after dark; and I haven't told you the worst thing yet."

"What's that?"

"He's killed another man—James Blaik, the shepherd, that married the gipsy girl."

That was news to me. My brain went spinning, and I jumped up in my excitement.

"What, Lily!" I said. "The Roman soldier! James Blaik! I can't believe it. When did it happen?"

"Oh, it was something like nine or ten weeks ago," she said. "It made a lot of talk hereabouts. Some say it was James's own fault. He'd been using that nasty ruin up on the hill for a sheepfold at nights, and everybody knows it's not a canny place at all. They all said something would be happening to him, but when it came it came sudden. Two of the men found him on the moor in the early morning, dead, with a knife in his back. It was the Roman soldier's knife. And this man from London had seen the Roman soldier the night before, striding across the moors with a face like thunder and shaking a spear ten yards long. If the man from London hadn't fallen on his face he'd have been a dead man too."

"You don't say!" I said, staring at her. "But what happened then?"

"You may well ask," she said, leaning against the window beside me, and not stopping me when I put my arm around her waist. "It wasn't two days after when the ghost came again, and this time he spirited Colonel Barr away—clean out of his bedroom, before the eyes of them all, and he hasn't been seen or heard of from that day."

It took me a few minutes to clear up this tangle; I mean, to sort out the part about the spiriting away of the Colonel, of which I knew everything, from the part about the killing of James Blaik, of which I knew nothing. I felt guilty and queer, and I wished I'd been to see my sister first, so I'd have known a bit about these things.

"But haven't they searched for the Colonel?" I said.

"Oh, they've searched," said Lily meaningly. "And the very ones that searched were afraid to look too close. Mr. Barr came down here one night and said that all the men must turn out——"

"Mr. Barr?" I said.

"Yes. Mr. Charlie Barr, the young one. He's left all alone at the house now, and he's locked and bolted himself in. They say he won't stir out until he knows what's happened to his uncle. Terror-struck, I'd say. I expect he'll be the next to go."

"To go?" I said, rather stupid, for I could think of nothing but my part in "spiriting" away the Colonel.

"Why, yes," she said, opening her eyes. "The Roman'll get him for sure. They're laying odds in the bar it'll be before Whitsun."

I laid my hand suddenly across her mouth, and she laughed and bit me like a kitten.

"But what about this man from London?" I said. "Where is he now?" For I suspected that I'd just met him on the moor.

"He went away," Lily said, "and about a week ago he came with another man, a friend of his, to do some fishing. They're staying with Palmers at the Halfway Farm."

"He's not come, do you think," I said, "to get another look at the Roman ghost? After all, he's the only man that ever saw that monster and came back alive."

Lily shivered. "Worse for him," she said, "if he has. There's the mad doctor too—you remember him—he's crazy about the ghost. Goes out to look for it at nights on a bicycle. I've heard him sounding his bell as he went past here in the dark of a howling night, and I've dipped my head under the bedclothes so I shouldn't see anything. He's got a girl staying with him, the mad doctor has, a girl from London. There was some talk a few weeks ago about him and her going away from here for good, but they say now that he says he won't go until he's found the ghost and buried him and burned his ashes. But my granddad says the Roman was here before the mad doctor, and he'll be here when the mad doctor's dust and ashes himself. He says they may come and they may go, but this'll always be a haunted spot, and no denying it."

I wished now that I hadn't started her talking about these things, and I tried to get her away from it by asking her whether there was any cottage empty in the village, for Lord Twelvetrees' agent had promised me the next; and she said, yes, there was James Blaik's cottage.

"Molly Blaik," she said, "has gone away and taken the bairns with her. They do say she's gone back to the gipsies."

So I said nothing more, except that it was time I was going if I was to walk to Adam's Cranny.

It was past midday when I came to the farm, a bonny house on a steep hillside, white-painted, so you can see it glimmering many a mile away like a laughing face with blinking eyes where the sun catches the window-panes. All around there's nothing but the moorland for the sheep, criss-crossed with their little tracks, and yellow in summer with the wild pansies. I've stood up there on the "top," as we call it, and seen clear away to Thunder Crag, which is thirty-five miles to the westward as the crow flies but more than a hundred if you were to walk it, up hill and down dale.

Winifred was standing there, shading her eyes from the sun.

"Well, Ham!" was all she said.

"Well, Winifred!" said I.

I went into the house, and slung down my load, and stirred the peat-clods until the fire leapt out. It was very comfortable there. The men were away in the fields below the intakes.

"The Colonel?" she said at once.

"At Thorlwick," I said, "and as well as can be. But how long is he going to stay there, Winifred?" I was thinking about what I'd just heard that morning.

"He must stay there," she said at once. "You haven't said anything to anybody?"

"Not a word," I said, "but he can't stay there for ever."

"He'll stay there," she said, "as long as I say so."

She was paler and thinner than when I saw her last; different somehow, as though she'd seen and heard things the memory of which would never let her be; like witches that they say ride on men's backs, though you can't believe all you hear.

"What happened," I said, "afterwards?"

She knew what I meant. She drew in a long breath.

"Everything happened," she said, "just like I thought it would. Just like I thought, Hamleth, only far, far worse than I ever thought. It was like a nightmare . . . so stealthy. From the first it began . . . little things you'd hardly notice. Then bigger things. There was a picture slashed to ribbons in the night. I fetched him—Mr. Mertoun, I mean. I thought, he shall see it for himself. He shall face it, as I've got to face it, day and night. He failed me, Ham. It's no use telling you just how and why; perhaps you can guess. I blamed him at first, but I didn't afterwards, for I don't think he could help himself. The poison of that house had been breathed into his eyes and his brain. When I realized that, I longed for him to go before anything worse should happen, but he grew curious; he wanted to see things for himself. So he saw things. The stone in the cellar with the writing. It was there. Deeper and clearer. And then they had a sitting one night, with the mad doctor and some others and a medium to call up the spirits. They asked me to go down. I'd have died first! I crouched on the stairs, hardly daring to breathe, waiting to see where that devil would strike. He came—the Roman. He spoke to them, a terrible, shouting voice; and then there was a crash, and I rushed to the closed door, trembling so I could scarcely stand. The door flew open; it was all over. Nobody was hurt, but he'd thrown a knife and it was stuck in the wall above the mantel, high up out of reach. When that night was over I was not so frightened. I thought, he's done his worst. But I didn't dream what would happen. The awful thing, Ham, the awful thing . . . it came so suddenly . . ."

"I know," I said. "James Blaik."

She turned round to me with flames leaping in her eyes.

"You know! How can you know?"

"I went to the village," I said. "I heard everything."

"Who told you?"

"Lily," I said. "Lily at the Red Buck."

"What did she tell you?"

"That the fear of the Roman," I said, "has got the whole village in thrall. Why should the fiend kill Blaik?"

"I don't know!" she whispered, and hid her face in her shaking hands. "Ham! Ham! I was there when they brought the news . . ."

"And Mr. Mertoun," I said with horrified curiosity. "He saw . . ."

"He saw," she said very low, "what no man can see, and live. But he got away in time. He was saved."

"He's back again," I said bluntly.

She dropped her hands and stared at me. "What do you mean?"

"Didn't you know?" I said. "Lily told me that Mr. Mertoun and his friend had come up for some fishing. They're staying at Palmer's, over to Nunnwood, and what's more I've seen them. Two gentlemen met me on the moor and asked me could I tell them where there was some good fishing. They asked me about the Strickan too; it may have been a guilty conscience, but I didn't like it. I said as little as I could, and they went on, and I heard one call the other Mertoun . . . But go on telling me about the big house. How did they find out that the Colonel was gone?"

She wasn't paying any attention to what I was saying; I had to ask her again.

"They asked me what I'd done with him," she said with a weary look in her eyes. "Mr. Barr was frantic. He said: 'We must search the moor. We must get the police.' I stopped all that. I said: 'It's no use. The Roman has taken him.' Nobody could say anything after that."

I stood gaping at her for a minute as the whole story grew clear in my mind. Then I laughed as though I should never stop, till she caught me by the ears and made me stop.

"Laughing!" she said. "How can you? How can you?"

I was sorry then, for she'd been through it and I hadn't.

In the evening when the men were in the house she called me and said, "Come out into the yard. I want to say something to you." I'd seen all day that her thoughts were far away. It was raining, and we climbed into the loft and crushed in among the stuffy hay.

"To-morrow morning you're to start early," she said, "and you're to go to Palmers' and ask to see the gentlemen who are staying there. Tell them you know all the fishing places about here and you'll go with them and show them the best streams. Make them take you. If they offer you money, take it, or they'll suspect you; but if they don't want to engage a man, then say you'll go for nothing for the sake of the sport. Then listen to all they talk about, and find out why they're here. If they want to talk about ghosts, then talk about ghosts. If they ask you about the Roman, tell them all you know about the Roman and all you've ever heard. If they've come here hunting a ghost, Ham, we must make sure they don't go back without one."

I could see her eyes glinting at me in the dark.

"I'll do it," I said. "But if they begin asking me about the Strickan——"

"You're not to talk about the Strickan. And they mustn't know you're my brother."

I slid my feet over the slippery boards of the loft, and I heard a mouse go scuttering. "Hst!" I said. "The ghost! The ghost!"

She didn't laugh. "Ah!" she said. "The murdering fiend!"

And the way she said it made my blood run cold.

April 24.

In the first place they don't know anything about fishing. That Mr. Ahrman couldn't so much as whip a hook to gut. I took them up to the Lewan Beck which was swollen nearly to the level of the bank, with great eddies swirling round the roots of the bushes and deep, still pools sucking at the hollows. They knew enough to sink their bait, and there they sat, the two of them on the puddly grass. Bottom-fishing. They sat two hours and Mr. Mertoun landed a half-pounder. I never heard such a lot of talk about anything in my life. Well, I knew then that they weren't anglers and that that was just a blind. They'd come to our country for bigger game than trout, though they hadn't said a word yet to make me prick up my ears. I couldn't help bragging.

"You ought to come up here in the summer," I said, "and see the men whip a stream when it's clear, with a dry-fly. I favour a Red Spinner myself. I took out a three-pounder just where we're standing one night last summer. I've been after pike too. That's a tricky game. I knew a man play a pike all night, and then he got away. Strong, they are, and as savage as tigers. That's what I call sport. And it's grand too up here on a summer's evening, with a soft green sky over you, and the green fields smelling so sweetly and the water singing its song. That's the time to be catching fish."

Mr. Ahrman laughed. "We're beginners," he said. "I can imagine that proficiency brings its own reward."

I was tired of watching by then and thought I'd show them a

thing or two, so I baited a hook carefully and sank it just beside a tough, sunken root, and in a minute I took out a monster. As I was taking him off the pin Mr. Ahrman put down his rod, lit his pipe, and said: "I've been thinking, Mertoun, and I don't advise you to make any further attempt to see Barr."

I pretended to be having difficulty with my fish, and listened with all my ears.

Mr. Mertoun hesitated a moment, and then said: "I had seriously thought of forcing my way in to him, but if you think . . ."

"Don't do it. He evidently doesn't want to see anyone, so we'll respect his wishes."

"Yes . . . and one can understand it. He's unnerved. And yet, Ahrman, the least I could do was to call. I hate to think of him a prisoner in his own house."

"Perhaps it's the best thing he can do."

"To refuse to see anyone? Well, yes. But the sinister possibilities . . ."

Mr. Ahrman shrugged his shoulders, and asked me if we might move a little farther up the water. We went up, occasionally dropping our lines into a pool; but they weren't biting. Mr. Ahrman said to me: "I suppose you've lived around here all your life?"

"I don't live here at all," I said. "I'm living at a farm eight miles from here."

"Do you know a big house down by the sea called The Broch?" he said.

"You mean Colonel Barr's place," I said. "Yes, I know it."

"Colonel Barr doesn't live there now, does he?" he asked, as innocent as a calf.

"No," I said. "He was much respected."

"You don't mean he's dead?" he said.

"I wouldn't go so far as to say that," I said, "but he came to a bad end. All the Barrs do."

He looked at me curiously. "That's interesting," he said, and his eyes slid up to mine in a questing way and said as plain as could be, "Tell me more!"

That was where I hung back. "It's something I couldn't bring myself to speak about," I said. "Not if it was for gold and jewels."

"What about this young Mr. Barr who's living at The Broch?" went on Mr. Ahrman. "I suppose you know who I mean?"

"I know," I said, or rather mumbled.

"Well, he's a bit of a recluse, isn't he?"

"I wouldn't go so far as to say that," I said promptly. "I've never heard that he took more than a glass or two."

Mr. Mertoun gave a laugh like a dog yapping.

"Touché!" he said. That's French, and I know how to spell it. "I meant," said Mr. Ahrman, talking to me very sweet and gentle, as to a little child, "I meant that Mr. Barr shuts himself up in the house more than you'd expect in a strong young fellow. You'd almost think he was frightened of something."

"Well, I wouldn't say he wasn't," said I, pretending to be giving just a little away.

"Frightened of something?"

"Something that you can't touch with your hands nor see with your eyes," I said.

"Oh, come!" said Mr. Ahrman. "You don't mean ghosts?"

"And why not?" I said. "There's things been done hereabouts that'd turn a man's head about till he was looking down his backbone. There's been so many men slain on these moors both before Flodden and after that if their wraiths do walk it's a wonder there's a sprig of heather left for living men to tread. See the red stones in yon beck? They've been red for many a hundred years, and it's blood that set the stain in 'em."

Mr. Ahrman's jaw fell; and Mr. Mertoun said a piece out of Sir Walter Scott. " 'Scarcely Lord Marmion's ear could brook the minstrel's barbarous lay' " said he.

"That's true," I said, quite calm, "for the minstrel had been telling of the outlaws of the Border:

'How the fierce Thirwalls and Ridleys all,
Stout Willimondswick, and Hardriding Dick,
And Hughie o' Hawdon, and Will o' the Wall
Have set on Sir Anthony Featherstonehaugh,
And taken his life at the Dead Man Shaw.'

True as history, it all was."

Mr. Ahrman began to whistle something; and the other one said: "For cryin' out loud, Ahrman! We've caught a Diogenes."

"Him in the tub," I said.

When I got home at night I told all this to Winifred, word for word, and she was so mad with me she could hardly find words.

"You great stupid!" she said. "I sent you there to keep mum and to listen; and instead of that you've no more sense than to make a fool of yourself by showing off how much you know. You great, gaumless thing! You've done for yourself now . . . and me too. And perhaps the Colonel."

"No, I haven't," I said. "I'm going with them again, to-morrow."

"They've asked you?

"Yes," I said. "We're going to Nome Crag to see the caves."

That pacified her a bit. "Well, keep your mouth shut to-morrow," she said, "except when you're asked about ghosts, and then tell them as much as you think they ought to know. You see, they didn't come for the fishing after all."

About an hour later she came up to me with a letter, and it had Mr. Mertoun's name on it in printed capitals.

"Take this," she said, "and when Mr. Mertoun isn't looking, slip it in his creel."

"What for?" I said. "What is it?"

"You remember what I told you," she said; "that he'd seen something that nobody can see, and live? This is to warn him, but he mustn't know it's from me."

So I took the letter, and next morning before we started off from Palmer's place I slipped it in Mr. Mertoun's lunch-basket. This time it wasn't only the three of us; the mad doctor went with us, and a girl. She was a pretty girl; reminded me of a yellowhammer, just a bonny bit of mischief, and Mr. Mertoun was in love with her. Anybody could see that.

We set off to Nome Crag and I went first, carrying two cameras and the young lady's red mackintosh. It was a beautiful morning, and the whole earth was glittering in the sunshine and the birds singing fit to split their little throats. "Apr-rrrrril! Apr-rrrrril!" they were trilling away.

Mr. Mertoun and the young lady walked behind me, and I was

sorry for him, I was indeed, because he wanted to walk along staidly and talk to her, and tell her, I guess, how beautiful she looked, and she was just like that tricky yellowhammer, darting from side to side of the track and twirling on her toes, and even running up to me to ask me to sing a song with her, some nonsense about all the King's horses and all the King's men.

I thought to myself, "The matter with Mr. Mertoun is that he doesn't know how to manage women. I'd like to see my Lily leading me a dance like that!" You want to treat them rough; they like it. So after a while, when I was getting a bit sick of her, I said, "You'd better be getting back to your sweetheart, miss"; and she began to laugh, and ran back to Mr. Mertoun saying, "Did you hear that, Billy? He thinks you're my sweetheart!" So then Mr. Mertoun went very red, and then very pale, and I pitied him more than words can say—though I'd done him a good turn really, as I'll relate in due course.

Well, we got up to Nome Crag, and they talked about the view for about an hour before they thought of getting their lunch. I wanted to tell them the names of sixteen peaks you can see from there, but I remembered what Winifred said about showing off and I was as mum as a cold potato.

I didn't dare look at Mr. Mertoun while he unpacked his basket, but I knew he must have found Winifred's letter; and after lunch I overheard a bit. I was dipping the dishes in a spring, and Mr. Ahrman and Mr. Mertoun weren't three yards away, talking. The mad doctor and the girl were hunting for an echo in the caves.

Mr. Mertoun said: "I don't think it is from an illiterate person. I believe the printed capitals are meant to disguise the writing."

"Tell me again what it says," said Mr. Ahrman. "I can't read it without my other glasses."

"It says, 'DON'T GO NEAR THE BROCH AFTER DARK, FROM A FRIEND.' Does the broch mean the house or the ruin, or both? The capitals don't indicate. And who's my well-wisher?"

"No idea. Somebody who had access to the lunch-basket."

"That was hanging in Palmer's hall all night. Anybody might have come. Ahrman! I wonder—oh, but it couldn't!"

"Who are you thinking of?"

"I was wondering if it could be Charlie himself? If he had heard or seen anything . . ."

"I don't think it could be Barr."

"But he's shut up in that house, and he knows I'm here. He may have had some awful warning . . . or he may be planning something . . ."

"Something?"

"I mean, he may be getting on the track of the . . . of V. G., as Ingram calls him . . . Oh, never mind! Forget it!"

"And shall you heed the warning?"

Mr. Mertoun laughed. "My dear man, not on your life, if I want to go!"

I decided not to tell Winifred that bit, and a few minutes later the mad doctor came up with that pretty yellowhammer dancing beside him, and they all began to take each other's photographs. The girl ran up to me. "Come along, Mr. Guide!" she said. "You and I are going to be taken together, because I think you're fearfully good-looking—quite the best-looking man I ever saw. . . . Now, Uncle Peter! You're going to take this one." So she wound herself round my arm, and there we stood up together facing the mad doctor to have our photographs taken, and of course, as usual, I forgot to be cautious and that the mad doctor had known me ever since I was at school. He clicked the camera, and then, sure enough, he looked hard at me.

"Why, you went to school down in the village!" he said. "I know you quite well. Aren't you a Redburn?"

"No," I muttered, slinking away. He looked after me, puzzled.

"I'm certain I know that young fellow," I heard him say, "but I haven't seen him for years. Now what is his name?"

"His name's Ham," said Mr. Ahrman.

"No, no," said the mad doctor; "that's not it . . ."

"If we go a bit higher," I said, "there's a Lover's Leap. Some of the visitors fancy themselves at jumping across it."

They all decided they wanted to go, and it took their attention off me, for which I was very thankful; not that I minded, but I was the one that had to face Winifred.

So we went up to Lover's Leap, and Mr. Ahrman and the mad

doctor sat down to talk, and Mr. Mertoun and the young lady wandered away by themselves.

Now when I was a boy we used to go up there and play truant from church on a summer Sunday afternoon; and I remembered a little ghyll where we used to hide, a secret sort of place that nobody could find unless they knew it. So I thought now I'd like to have another look at that place, and sure enough there it was, just as we boys had left it, and hidden there I found a wooden ball and some bits of coloured glass and a broken whip. I sat down very snug, and pulled the thick, dead bracken across to hide me, and I was nearly asleep when I heard voices and Mr. Mertoun and the young lady came and sat down on two boulders just at the opening of the ghyll.

"I'm glad now that I didn't go back to London," she was saying. "I'm enjoying myself so much, Billy. I'd like to stay here for ever."

"All the same, Joan," he said, "it'll be better fun for us all when we do get back to town, and I'm thinking particularly of Ingram. This place is doing him no good."

"It's this ghost business," she said, and her voice sounded very worried. "I don't understand it in the least, but he keeps on saying that he won't go away until the ghost is laid, or discovered, or whatever it is you do to ghosts. That doesn't look to me a very hopeful outlook! How long are you staying, Billy?"

"I don't know; it depends on Ahrman. It's his holiday."

"Oh, he's on holiday, is he? Then I don't suppose you'll be here for long. Oh, Billy, I don't think I shall want to stop when you're gone. I say, couldn't you do something . . . a stunt . . ."

"What sort of a stunt?"

"Well, I mean, act up some sort of a shemozzle to make Uncle Peter think that this ghost is finished—exploded—what's the word? Oh, laid. Lay it, Billy, there's an angel."

Mr. Mertoun laughed and began to light a pipe, and I sat back and enjoyed myself, because I always like to hear conversations, and I don't tell all I hear either.

Presently she gave a little laugh, all about nothing so you'd think.

"What's the matter?" he said.

"Oh," she said, "I was just thinking what a pity it was to disappoint Mr.—Mr. Ham."

"Mr.—who?" he said.

"The nice guide," she said, "with the blue eyes. The one that thought you were my sweetheart, Billy." Her voice went very soft and alluring. I could guess the way she was looking at him.

"Now look here, Joan!" he said, horribly stern. "We had this over last night and I haven't altered one bit since then. I never meant you to know that I loved you. You wouldn't have known, but for . . ."

"Yes," she said, very breathless. "It was my fault. I simply dragged it out of you . . ."

"Well then, my dear, we're where we were before. You must forget it. In two or three years time you'll thank me——"

"Why shall I thank you?"

"When you meet—well, somebody else."

"I don't want to meet somebody else!"

"Now, Joan! We've been over all that."

She said suddenly, angry and yet hurt: "This is the first time in my life that I've been in love, and I think it's perfectly beastly. I told you I loved you! I do love you. And you won't believe me. I hate you, Billy, yes I do—no I don't—yes I do, I do!"

He said: "I know you love me, and I think it's perfectly adorable of you. You're the most wonderful girl that ever lived, and I shall say it to the end of my days. But I'll say again that you're not for me. I'm playing this hand straight, for your sake, Joan. I'm just twice your age. You don't understand what that means."

"I suppose it means that you've had heaps of girls before. Well, I don't mind."

"I wasn't thinking of that," he said, "but yes—it's true. I'm your first, Infant; you're my twentieth. But none of the others count now. When you're older you'll understand."

"And I suppose you think that I've got nineteen more to come before I make my mind up!" she said.

He gave a queer laugh. "Perhaps as many as nineteen; but keep them a little nearer to your own generation."

There was dead silence for a few minutes, and then she said

slowly: "So you won't marry me, Billy. All right. I shan't ask you again . . . But I'll see that some day you ask me, even if I have to wait ten, twenty, thirty years. Because I shan't change, and I don't think you will either. And I shan't give you the chance to forget me; I shall always be hanging around as they say in 'Bawston.' I mean it. I'm one of the new-Georgians, and we know what we want and we go right to it. I've met a lot of young men in the time I've been let loose. I didn't love any of them, but I love you and you make the rest look like ten cents."

"Go on," he said grimly. "This is jolly for me."

She flamed up. "You're afraid of me!" she flung at him. "Afraid to pick me up and carry me off. Oh, if you knew how women hated self-sacrificing men! And isn't it queer how men love to sacrifice themselves when it's someone else who has to suffer?"

"Shut up, Joan!" he said fiercely.

"I shan't shut up. I shall never shut up. You're a selfish beast. I wish I hadn't got my father's consent to marry you."

"Joan! What on earth are you talking about?"

She kept him waiting for a minute, and then she said: "Listen. I fell in love with you weeks and weeks ago, when you were staying at The Broch. That was when you fell in love with me, wasn't it? And you've been writing to me ever since. I waited until I knew that you did love me, and then I wrote to Poppa at 'Bawston.' I told him all about you, your war record, everything I could find out about you from people who knew you in London; and then I said to Poppa, 'I'm in love with this man. Can I marry him if he asks me?' And I got his answer yesterday morning. I'll tell you what he said. 'Dear Joan, thank heaven you've chosen a real man and not one of those young asses you used to play about with. Say yes when he asks you. He's lucky. So are you.' And on top of that you've let me down, Billy."

There was a long, long silence then; so long that I wondered what had happened, and whether I'd fallen asleep and the pair of them had gone away, so I pushed aside a bit of the bracken and peeped out. They were there. She had her face hidden in her hands and her shoulders were shaking. I thought at first she was laughing, being such a mischief, but in a minute I saw she was crying.

And I didn't know what she had to cry over either—women are queer!—for she'd wanted him all along, and now she'd got him, or as near as doesn't matter. He had both his arms round her and his face down on her golden hair. Soon she got up, tossed back her hair, and pushed him away.

"I'll never forgive you, Billy," she said in a choked kind of voice.

"That doesn't matter," he said. "Will you marry me?"

"No," she said. "I wanted to ten minutes ago; I don't want to now."

He jumped up and caught hold of her, hard, by the shoulders.

"We'll end this here and now," he said. "You'll marry me—by heaven you will, whether you want to or not! Turn round, and hold your head up. There's nothing to be frightened about."

"Frightened!" she said. "Billy—you beast!"

"You—what?" he said, horribly savage.

"You—darling! You darling!" she cried, and tipped herself right over backwards into his arms.

"Then you will?"

"Yes, yes, yes, yes, yes!" she said, and kissed her hand to him for every yes; and then just when he was beginning to realize it, she broke away and began running down the hill.

"Come on!" she called back. "It's past two o'clock. They'll think we're lost. Come on, Billy!"

He ran after her, and as soon as they were gone I crept out too and went down a quicker way and got back first. It had all been very interesting, and it was one of the things I wasn't going to tell Winifred.

When we got back in the evening to Palmer's place a little thing happened that I suppose I might have expected. It was just bad luck. Mr. Ahrman was paying me five shillings, which he did each day I went out with him, when the mad doctor suddenly stared at me and said: "I've got you now! Of course, you're one of the Goff boys that went away to Thorlwick."

I took no notice, but I felt my face go hot. Mr. Ahrman didn't seem to have noticed anything; he was turning over his change, looking for another shilling.

When I got back to the farm I realized that though I'd had a

very interesting day I hadn't much to tell Winifred, but as it turned
out all she wanted to know about was her letter; had Mr. Mertoun
got it?

"Yes," I said, "he's got it, and he doesn't know who sent it. I
heard him tell Mr. Ahrman so."

"That's good," she said. "Have they asked you to go out with
them again?

"No," I said.

She frowned. She was disappointed, and so was I.

April 26.

This morning early I went down our fields with a spade to
bank up the potatoes and I saw a man sitting under a wall in the
sun, smoking his pipe. When I got a bit closer I saw it was Mr.
Ahrman.

"Hullo!" he said. "So this is where you live?"

"It's my uncle's farm," I said. "I'm only stopping here to give a
hand. You've had a long walk over."

"That was nothing," he said. "I wanted to have a chat."

At that I went cold and then hot, wondering if I'd done anything, or rather if he'd found anything out. But I didn't see how he
could have done.

"It's a fine morning for once," I said. "The weather here's very
treacherous."

He looked, the same as I was looking, over the fields and the
valley to the hills on the other side. Being country-bred I could see
a faint green haze over everything which meant that already the
sun was kissing the sods to life, and though the air was too sharp
for growing weather it was sweet and strong and made you want
to leap stone walls and whistle loud. The river was like a green
ribbon coming out of the dead brown fells, and twisting, blowing, and winding its way to the green and purple sea. I knew just
how the sea would look on a morning like this, and I could almost
feel a boat pulling under me and dancing on the silver-tipped
waves.

I stood gazing, lost in a dream, with my elbows propped on the
spade; but Mr. Ahrman said: "I want you to help me, Hamleth; I

want you to do something for me." So he'd got hold of my name. I wondered who he'd been talking to.

"I might," I said.

What he said was, "I want to see a ghost." I'd been expecting something of the kind.

I looked at him. "There's plenty hereabouts," I said. "Ghosts of lords and ladies and soldiers and monks, you can have your pick. But common people like me don't walk when they're dead."

He held out his tobacco pouch. "Fill up," he said. "You're a clever young man. I like you."

"Is that it?" I said.

"Yes, Hamleth. But you weren't quite clever enough. If you'd been a bit more clever you'd have known how to be a bit more stupid. . . . And now about this ghost."

"What ghost?" I said with a sort of faraway look.

"I mean the Roman soldier that walks at night and kills Barrs . . . and others. I want to see him. I shan't be satisfied until I see him. Can you help me, Hamleth?"

"I can't," I said. "I haven't seen him myself."

"But other people have?"

"Mr. Mertoun saw him," I said; "and my sister Wi— and some people say that no one sees the Roman soldier and lives, so Mr. Mertoun had better watch out."

"Did you put the note in his basket?"

"Yes," I said, "but it was given me."

"How long have people here been afraid of the Roman?" he asked.

"I don't know," I said, "but when I was a little lad my grandfather told us that when he was a little lad his grandfather used to warn him that if he didn't behave in church he'd be given to the Roman soldier. That's a long while ago, a hundred years maybe, and they frighten naughty children with the same tale to-day."

"I want to see him," he said eagerly, "armour and all. Supposing I go out on the moor tonight, up by the cliffs—I know his haunts—what are my chances of a view? I'll take the risk."

"You won't see him," I said.

"What makes you say that?"

"You won't see him," I said.

"Now, Hamleth, you've got a reason for saying that. You know the ghostly habits!"

"I don't know about habits," I said, "but I know you won't see the Roman, not if you wait until the moon turns blue, and that's all I'll say."

"Hamleth," he said, suddenly wheedling, "why did you pretend not to recognize the Strickan when I asked you about it?"

"Because I thought it wasn't any of your business," I said.

He laughed. "Now whisper the answer softly . . . weren't you lucky to get Colonel Barr on and off the lighthouse without being caught? And how long are you going to keep him at Thorlwick?"

I thought I should have dropped. My knees went weak, and the sun went spinning all round the sky and everything seemed to turn upside down. I thought, "It'll be prison; as sure as fate I'm ruined and doomed."

"What are you talking about?" I said. "Colonel Barr, he disappeared. The Roman soldier took him out of his bed."

"That's one of the things he didn't do," said Mr. Ahrman calmly. "Winifred Goff took him out of his bed, helped by her brother Hamleth Goff and her father Ewan Goff, in the dead of the night, and hid him in the lighthouse and afterwards in a cottage at Thorlwick, and a very clever trick too. You've got brains, you Goffs."

"How did you find out?" I muttered, praying that it wasn't through me.

"Through an alliance," he said, "of common sense and imagination which is a most valuable part of my mental equipment."

"We're ruined," I groaned.

"Oh no!" he said coolly. "I congratulate you. No one knows but myself, and I shan't tell. The future disposal of the Colonel will be your funeral, or rather your sister's, because I imagine she's the controlling force. I suppose you did it because you were afraid for him?"

I nodded. "Winifred was," I said. "She thinks a powerful lot of the Colonel. She said if he was left at the house the Roman would surely get him."

"How long does she intend to keep him at Thorlwick?"

"She says, until the Roman soldier's quiet in his grave."

"Oh! Then she believes he can be laid?"

"She believes," I said, "that he can be bound hand and foot, but it'll have to be a man the like of which she's never seen who does it. She had hopes of . . . somebody, once, but he failed her." I'd nearly mentioned Mr. Mertoun's name, but I thought better not.

He looked at me then for quite a long time, and he looked down at the earth and then across to the river and the fells. Once he opened his mouth as though he were going to speak, but he caught my eye and looked away again, thinking better of it. Presently he got up, swung his stick, and prepared to go.

"Get on with your spuds," he said. "A healthy life. And thanks for an illuminating conversation."

I felt like a gull that's been driven right up against the glare of the Strickan Light. "That man," I said to myself, "has read every thought I ever kept hidden in me." And when I thought of what he might have read, I went so hot that I couldn't keep my foot on the spade.

After that the thought of Mr. Ahrman had a fascination for me. I couldn't keep my mind away from him while I was working. I made up my mind not to say a word to Winifred, because after all our secret was safe and she'd only have worried herself and tormented me.

April 28.

After that I couldn't rest until I'd seen him again. I wanted to know what he was doing with his time. The next morning after I'd met him in the field I got up early and made some excuse to be away all day. Then I walked the eight miles to Palmer's farm, climbed a wall, and sat down where I could keep my eye on the house and see who came and went. The morning crept by, but I didn't see Mr. Ahrman or Mr. Mertoun. I was afraid all the time that someone would come along and notice me, so soon after midday I got up and walked over to the village. There it was easy to loiter and while away the time without anyone wondering why you should be doing it. Lily came out to me and asked me a lot of questions, but somehow I wasn't near so interested in her as I was in waiting for Mr. Ahrman. Women seem to think you ought to be in love with them all the time, instead of on proper occasions when you haven't anything else on your mind. Somehow a man can't think of two things at once.

About five o'clock I saw him coming and he went straight into the Post Office. A few minutes later he came out with a letter and a big parcel. There's only one delivery—in the morning—and if people want their letters in an evening they have to go and fetch them.

When Mr. Ahrman came out I was standing just across the way, as if making up my mind whether I'd go into the Institute for a game of billiards.

"Oh! Is that you, Hamleth?" he said.

I jumped, as if he was the last person I expected to see.

"Oh, good afternoon, Mr. Ahrman," I said. "Have you got that big parcel to carry home?"

"Looks like it," he said.

"I'll take it up for you," I said. "It's on my way home."

So we started off to Palmer's, but I was very disappointed because he talked about nothing but farming and fishing and coal-mining and wireless.

However, when we got to the farm he said, "Come right in with it," and I took the parcel into the sitting-room where his things were and put it down on the table.

"Books," he said. "They're heavy things to carry. Thanks very much."

"That's all right," I said, looking round and wondering where Mr. Mertoun was.

"You've got eight miles to walk," he said. "You must have something before you start."

He fetched a pie out of the sideboard cupboard, and a bottle of something, and some cheese.

"Fall to it," he said; so I did, and he sat down and lit his pipe and looked right through me.

In a few minutes Mr. Mertoun walked in.

"Hullo, Ahrman!" he said. "I hope I haven't kept you waiting. We've been all day in search of some falls that Joan wanted to show me; she said, a most marvellous sight. Well, her bump of locality must be faulty because though we walked for miles and she swore we were going in the right direction, we never got to any falls. However we had a good enough day. When we got back we found that the Mother Shipton housekeeper had taken to her bed with spasms, so I didn't stay for supper as Joan said it would have to be boiled eggs and I couldn't think of anything worse. . . . Did you get down to the Post Office? Any letters?"

"Yes. There's your reply from Barr."

"Oh, good. What does he say?"

"Well, naturally I didn't open it. Shall I?"

"Yes, do," said Mr. Mertoun. "Read it while I'm having a wash."

He went upstairs, and I finished my supper very slowly and watched Mr. Ahrman out of the corner of my eye. He took the letter out of his pocket and slit the envelope, and then he unfolded the letter so carefully you'd think it was likely to fade away, and he read it and left it lying on his knee. I was so excited I could hardly remember to keep my eyes down, wondering what they were planning now.

Mr. Mertoun came down. "Well? What's the answer?"

"No good. Nothing doing."

"Oh."

"I'll read it while you unboot yourself. . . .' 'Dear Mr. Mertoun,' he says, 'it is good of you to write and offer me friendly help. I appreciate your motive, but I must emphatically state that under the circumstances I prefer solitude and a policy of non-interference on the part of my acquaintances. At the risk of being churlish let me say that I shall really resent any well-meant efforts on my behalf in this neighbourhood. I have no intention of going away, at least not for the present, and I would not think of having another séance or attempting any such form of provocation. The idea is repugnant to me. M'Coul tells me you left your note in person. He has the strictest orders to admit no one to the house in future. . . . Yours truly, Charles Barr.' That's definite enough, I think."

Mr. Mertoun frowned. "Of course I shan't approach him again

---

[1] Hamleth was afterwards permitted to copy the original of this letter, which accounts for his accuracy.

after this, but I'm sorry he's cut himself off from society. If the danger is imminent . . . well, the barred doors of The Broch won't keep it out, and personally I'd always prefer to fight for my life in the open air. At any rate we've done our best."

Mr. Ahrman put the letter back in the envelope and I thought it was time to go. I had quite enough for one day to tell Winifred.

April 29.

What a black and awful day! When I woke I thought from the darkness that it was still night, and then I heard the sluicing and the roaring and the gurgling of the rain and I knew what sort of a day it was going to be. As far as I could see from the window was a blowing, creeping mist, and when it lifted long enough for me to see the hillsides, there were the same cold mist-shapes trailing their ragged skirts over the rocks.

My uncle was in a terrible temper. He turned on me. Told me I'd been here a week, guzzling his food and swilling his drink, and hadn't done a hand's turn of work, always gadding off by myself. Of course that was true, but I managed to stand up for myself pretty well. Then I got my waterproofs and walked out in high dudgeon. I hadn't a place to go but the Red Buck, nine miles away, and I wasn't feeling in the mood for Lily, so I mooched about the moor and felt badly used.

Everything was sodden and cold, and the road was like a river. When I did come in sight of the village I stood still, not knowing quite what I should do, and just then I saw somebody who was actually enjoying the wetness and the wildness of the morning, somebody I didn't expect to see.

She was leaning against a stone wall, wrapped in an old blue shawl and her hair was flying; short, black hair round her gipsy face. She was laughing and talking to somebody, a baby as dark as herself, sitting up in a corner of the shawl and crowing when the rain beat in its little face.

Well, of course that was Molly Blaik. She'd always been as mad as a hare, running out in all weathers and liking it, being half a gipsy. Her father was one of the Cowens who had a big farm and were almost gentry. He was tall and fair and merry, and a champion at sports like throwing darts and wrestling at fairs. In the end he went to one fair too many for his family—his mother had a nose a yard long and was very much above herself—for he brought home a gipsy wife, a quiet little thing called Roasinda Luck, and the Cowens threw him out and he got work on a croft miles away from his home. He and Roasinda had six children, and five of them were Cowens and one was a Luck. The five eldest, little Cowens, were as good as gold with long yellow curls and cheeks like pink sugar, and they went to Sunday School and grew up respectable if not noteworthy. But the youngest, Molly, was a real little gipsy, a bad little black-faced thing like a wild-cat, always running away from home and biting her teachers. Her own father and mother wanted nothing but to be rid of her, and when she was fourteen they sent her into service on a farm, which she tried to set on fire because she wanted to see what a burning house looked like. After that she ran wild for a year or two, and when she was sixteen she married James Blaik, her father's shepherd—Cowen had come in for some of the family property by then—and the pair got on very well together, for they were both fond of fighting. She had three or four children, and she was just twenty-one when her husband was murdered on the moor. I always liked her and she liked me. We were of an age and used to go to school together. I've been beaten many a time for playing with Molly Cowen, as she was then.

"Hey, Molly!" I said when I caught sight of her in the rain. "I thought you were miles away from here."

She looked at me with her queer, twisty smile.

"I've come back," she said.

Her long black eyes dived into mine and held them fast. She always had a way of making you feel a good deal more than she told you.

Presently she straightened herself up and jerked the baby against her shoulder. "Come along with me," she said.

We went to her cottage, and she lifted the latch and slipped in, I following her. The room was in a terrible mess and more dismal than the rainy moor outside. The fire was made of twigs which only smouldered, for they were damp, and gave out no heat and a lot of yellow smoke. There was hardly any furniture and the table was heaped up with rubbish, rags and papers and green rushes for basket-plaiting. On the stone floor a dirty white dog and several half-dressed children rolled about together. It was worse than anything I'd expected, even from Molly.

She pushed a chair towards me with her knee.

"You can sit down, Hamleth," she said. "I shan't eat you, though I could do. I'm clemmed, and I've got no money."

"No money?" I stammered.

"Not a penny."

"But how long have you been here?" I said.

"Two days."

"But surely you haven't——"

"No," she said. "They gave me a stale loaf and a drink of beer at the Red Buck, and the children pinched two big swedes last night."

I dived into my pockets while she looked at me, greedy like a crow, but all I found was a shilling and a packet of Gold Flakes, so I gave her those and she tied them up in a corner of her shawl.

"Why did you come back to—this?" I said. "Weren't you better off where you were?"

She said sulkily: "I came back to get my rights. You won't tell?"

"I was always a friend of yours, Molly," I said, wondering what sort of a tale she had stored up in her black head.

"It's treasure," she said. "Gold and diamonds."

"Where?" I said.

"Buried deep." Her eyes went flitting from side to side. I didn't doubt her; the gipsies know queer things.

"Is it here?" I said. "Where we can find it?"

She nodded slyly.

"Who told you?"

"Blaik," she answered.

I was surprised. I thought she had overheard something among the gipsies.

"But he's dead!" I said stupidly.

"Ah," she said. "He wasn't quick enough. The Roman got him. But a gipsy woman's worth two of any *mullo* (ghost). I'll have the treasure."

"Where's the treasure, and all?" I said.

"In the Roman's castle," she said. "In the tower of the *mullo* on the hill."

"The haunted tower?"

She laughed. "Look here. Look what I'm going to tell you. Blaik came home that morning in such a state. Rubbing his hands and licking his lips. 'What's the matter now?' I said. 'We're going to be rich,' he said. 'Now you keep your mouth shut, Molly, or it'll come to naught.'—'What's that, then?' I said. 'Have you found some money?' He laughed in his teeth. 'Found a gold-mine,' he said. 'You wait, woman, and you'll see.'—'The *mullo*'s tower!' I said. 'Is it hidden there?' 'Hush, woman!' he said. . . . 'If it's the Roman's treasure,' I began, and he hushed me up and said he wasn't afraid of any *mullo*. He was like that was Blaik; asking for what came to him. I could have told him if he'd have listened that the Roman wouldn't stand by and see his treasure carried away, but he wouldn't listen, so it didn't surprise me when he died on the Roman's sword. I went away for a bit to think it over, but now I've come back for what's mine. I've learnt two fine spells, one for a *mullo* and one for a devil, and I can take the gold under his very nose. But I'm not strong in the arm, Hamleth; I'll want a man to dig."

Then I saw what she was after, and I came out in cold prickles from my head to my feet. I wasn't so sure about her fine spells as she seemed to be, and I doubted if any spell was strong enough for the Roman soldier.

"Will you come and dig for me, Hamleth?" she said.

"Not by myself, I won't," I said, as quick as lightning.

She gave a scoffing laugh. "A big fellow like you! If the digging wasn't too heavy for Blaik——"

"Ah," I said, "and look what happened to him!"

That quieted her for a minute, and then she muttered something about her spells.

"Your spells won't help me," I said. "I must have another man— two other men."

Her face grew black with anger. "Two other men! To steal my treasure!"

"They won't touch your treasure," I said. "You shall have it all.

But I won't come without two other men. It'll have to be at dead of the night too."

"Under the moon," she added. "The spells need the white of the moon. And do you swear I shall go away with my own treasure and nothing to stop me?"

"I haven't said I'll dig yet," I said. "I'll have to see two other men."

"If they rob the widow," she said wickedly, "they'll come to beg their bread, but if they rob the gipsy they'll rot in hell."

"I'll tell them," I said, and pushed away my chair, nearly choked with the wood-smoke.

When I got outside the cottage I began to run, and I never stopped until I came to Palmer's place.

"Can I see Mr. Ahrman?" I said.

They took me in, and he was in his sitting-room, standing at the window and staring out at the rain. The table was littered with books and papers and camera-films and drawing instruments that I didn't know the names of.

"You!" he said, turning round and catching sight of me.

"I've got something to tell you," I said, "when the door's shut."

"Ah!" he said, and he went over, and shut the door himself, first looking out to see there was nobody in the passage.

"Now tell me," he said. "You're a good man, Hamleth, and there might be something for you at the end of the story."

"Molly Blaik has come back," I blurted out.

His eyes flicked open, and there was a bit of glowing thread in each one like the filament in an electric torch. What I liked about Mr. Ahrman was that he never asked you to explain what you said to him; he always understood at once.

"What has she come for?" he said.

I dropped my voice. "She says that the Roman soldier you're so anxious to see keeps a treasure of gold buried deep in the ruin on the hill. Blaik found it. He told her so, and ordered her to keep her mouth shut. He said they were going to be rich. That night the Roman got him. Molly was afraid and ran away, but she's learnt some spells from the gipsies and now she's come back to get the treasure. She isn't frightened. She told me all this because she likes me. I was the only one in the village who'd say a good word for her when she was a little thing and the children plagued her because she was dark and naughty. She wants me to go with her at the white of the moon and dig for the treasure. I think there's something in it, Mr. Ahrman. Molly's very shrewd. Blaik must have found something, and nobody else ever went near the broch, not for years."

"Wait!" Mr. Ahrman sat down and lit his pipe. Then he gazed into the fire, thinking, for a long time.

"Of course she told you this in strictest secrecy?" he said at last.

"That's so," I said, "but I haven't finished. I told you she wanted me to promise to go with her to do the digging. She isn't strong in the arms and she thinks it may be deep. She says it must be at the white of the moon because of the spells. Well, I wasn't so sure about her spells—not if I know the Roman soldier—so I told her I wouldn't come, not without two other men. I was thinking of you and Mr. Mertoun. Molly's only fear was that she'd be robbed of the treasure, but I told her you'd want nothing for your trouble but the adventure. All the same, if there are diamonds I think you might pick up a few."

Mr. Ahrman laughed in his throat. "There won't be diamonds," he said. "I've a pretty good idea of what the Roman soldier's treasure may be, and it isn't diamonds. But of course the whole affair may be well worth Mrs. Blaik's while. Stout fellow, Hamleth!" His eyes sparkled, and he was so excited that he got up and walked about the room.

"You're not afraid," he said, "to tackle the broch?"

"Not with you, I'm not," I said.

He laughed. "Mertoun will be thrilled. He's out at present; down at Doctor Ingram's. He's just got engaged to Miss Hope, the girl who went with us to the Crag, so I don't see very much of him now. As a companion he's a fiasco. Are you engaged, Hamleth?"

"I'm going out with a young woman," I said, "but I don't let it worry me."

"Oh, you philosopher!" he said. "Now listen; when is the full moon?"

"Night of Friday," I said.

He rubbed his chin with his finger-tips. "I don't like this white of the moon business," he said; "the sort of job we're after is best done in the dark with an electric torch and a black cloth to screen it, don't you think so?"

"I do," I said, "but you don't know Molly. If she can't use her spells she won't come, and she's half gipsy and very vengeful. I wouldn't care to cross her."

"Or double-cross her!" laughed Mr. Ahrman. "Well, we'll have to fall in with her terms, I suppose. By the way, who owns the land? Whose property is this broch?"

"All the land about here," I said, "belongs to Lord Twelvetrees, but he's far away and I think we won't bother about that."

"I see," said Mr. Ahrman, "that you've got all the qualities of a law-breaker!"

"Pooh!" I said. "What Northumberland lad ever feared the law?"

"Well, we'll have to fear it up to a point," he said. "There's a law of treasure-trove, and we'd better be on the right side. Would your friend, Mrs. Blaik, turn nasty if I were to bring a couple of strong fellows along to help with the heavy work? I can promise her they'll not be after her treasure. And if the Roman does show himself it'll make the fight all the merrier."

"A fight!" I said. "Ho-ho!"

Just at that moment Mr. Mertoun walked in and heard what I said.

"A fight?" he said. "What fight? Ahrman, you villain, what on earth are you hatching?"

Mr. Ahrman told him.

"By Jove!" he said. "It promises to be a circus. I've always longed to see the inside of the broch . . . and at midnight, with the prospect of heaven knows what eerie and horrible manifestations! Anything may happen. I foresee grimness unspeakable. But look here, Joan mustn't know, because if she does she'll insist on coming. She doesn't realize the horrid seriousness of the situation."

"Nobody must know——" Mr. Ahrman was beginning, when Mr. Mertoun took him up. "But Ingram, don't you think he'll feel left out of it if we don't take him? You know how tireless he's been in his search, and after all, the greater part of what we know about the apparition we got from him. What about it?"

"I don't think Molly Blaik would mind the mad doctor being there," I said. "He was always good to her."

Mr. Ahrman shrugged his shoulders. "What a crowd!" he said. "But it can't be helped. Ingram is fond of night roving; Joan won't notice anything. . . . Well, Hamleth, will you see Mrs. Blaik and tell her she's to meet us at the broch at . . . let me see . . . 2 a.m. the day after to-morrow; no, Saturday, isn't it? . . . Saturday at two in the morning. How can we be sure of her?"

"I'll see to her," I said. "I'll bring her."

"And spades, Hamleth."

"I'll bring two," I said, "and Molly will have one. I'll have to tell her you think there's money in it for her. She won't come else, and she may give us away."

"There'll be money," he said. "Is she in poor circumstances?"

"Starving," I said.

"Take her this." He took a pound note out of his wallet, and something else which he folded and gave to me. "For you," he said. "You're my liaison officer, Hamleth." That's French and I know how to spell it. When I got outside there was a five-pound note. I liked Mr. Ahrman better than any gentleman I ever met.

After that I went down to the Red Buck and got round Lily to give me some dinner. She was very glad to see me after such a long time.

After dinner I went back to Molly Blaik and told her that Mr. Ahrman and I were going to get her treasure out for her, but it was against the law and if she told anybody or played any tricks on us we'd go free but she'd go to prison for the rest of her life. Then I gave her five shillings, because I knew she'd never had a whole pound in her life, and if she got one she'd very likely get merry drunk and brag to the whole village where the money came from.

It was late in the afternoon now, and as I was coming away I saw Mr. Mertoun standing on the step of the Post Office. He stopped me.

"So you're Winifred Goff's brother!" he said.

I nodded.

"Where is she?" he said. "I should like to see her again some day."

"She's at my uncle's farm," I said. "It's a long way from here."

"I want to ask her," he said, "about a letter she once wrote me . . . something she said. Shall you be seeing her?"

I thought it was no good pretending not, for he would find out from Mr. Ahrman that I was staying at Adam's Cranny, so I said that I was going there now.

"Then will you take her a message?" he said. "Tell her that I don't know how I failed her, but I didn't mean to; that if she means I might have helped her to defend Colonel Barr from the fate which actually overtook him, then it's a matter which causes me the bitterest regret and I hope she will believe that I did my best under very difficult circumstances. . . . Can you remember that?"

"I'll remember," I said.

It was clear that Mr. Ahrman had kept his word to me, and not even Mr. Mertoun knew what had really happened to the Colonel.

I went to the Institute then and played billiards, because I wasn't anxious to go home until my uncle had gone to bed.

Walking over the moor was grand in the night, because the rain had cleared the sky and the stars were blazing round the moon as she climbed. The farm looked like a black huddle on the hillside, and the wet roof glittered under the moon. I slipped in and went up to Winifred's room.

"Oh, Ham, you bad boy!" she said. "Where have you been?"

"You may well ask," I said. "I've been doing your work."

I sat down on the end of the bed and looked as hungry and cold as I could.

"What do you think of this?" I said. "Molly Blaik is back, and Mr. Ahrman has made up his mind to see the Roman, and there's a buried treasure in the broch—the ruin I mean, not the big house, and we're going with spades at dead of night to fetch it away, and Mr. Mertoun says will you please to forgive him for failing you because he hopes he'll have better luck next time. What do you think of that?"

Her colour came and went in her face, and her eyes were big and bright where the moonlight caught them.

"Oh, Ham!" she said. "What will they find? Tell them . . . tell them all you dare!"

"I daren't tell them a word," I said, "but you don't need to tell that Mr. Ahrman anything. He can read what's in me. Him and me understand each other."

"No, Ham?"

"He knows what I daren't say."

"Ham! I'm nearly frightened."

"You needn't be," I said. "Not if you knew Mr. Ahrman."

"And Mr. Mertoun?"

"He doesn't know anything, but he thinks there'll be some fighting at the broch."

"Oh, God!" she said. "I hope not. That fiend must have the strength of ten!"

"I hope there's fighting," I said. "Winifred, it's funny none of us ever set foot in the broch. Fright, I suppose. I wonder what we'll find there? Mr. Ahrman spoke as if he sort of knew."

"I nearly think I know too," she said.

"Gold and diamonds?" I said quickly.

"Not that," said Winifred. "No. Forget what I said. Are you really going to the broch?"

"Of course!" I said. "What have I been wasting my time telling you?"

"When?" she whispered.

"Not to-morrow night," I said, "but the night after, at two o'clock in the morning."

"Mr. Ahrman is a very determined man," she said; and then we both gave a shiver and a start as we heard a board creak in the house, which shows what a pitch we'd worked ourselves to.

"It may be Uncle," she said. "Get to bed quickly, and we'll talk in the morning."

So I pulled off my boots and tiptoed to my room under the tiles, and here I sit now writing because I can't sleep. And don't want to either.

May 2. At nine o'clock in the evening.

So this is the last time I shall write in my diary because I'm tired of it, but Winifred says I must finish what I began, so all that remains to tell is the doings that happened at the broch this morning before it was daylight.

I went to bed last night with the rest of the family at nine o'clock, but when the house was quiet I was quickly out again and rummaging in the dark of the barn for the two spades I'd hidden there, holding the old sheep-dog cur by the neck for fear he'd bark with excitement and give me away. Then I stepped out over the moor with a spade over each shoulder, just like a ghost myself in the starry night. I hoped somebody might see me and take me for a spirit, and then I suddenly came to my senses and thought of all the ghosts of the dead who might be watching me now, pointing their clayey fingers and shaking their clammy rags as they slid and writhed through the heather, the Border ghosts and the Scottish ghosts and the English ghosts and the Roman ghosts too with their short, sharp swords, and it was all I could do not to throw down the spades and run for my life. In the end I got to Molly's cottage and knocked three times on the door. There wasn't any need for me to knock three times, except that they do in books. "Come in!" she said, and when I went in she was sitting in the corner with only a candle lit and the fire a heap of white wood ashes.

"Are you ready?" I said.

"I've been ready for hours," she said.

"Fetch another spade," I said.

"It's here." Then I saw it lying on the floor at her feet. She pushed back her short black hair with both hands and held it up close against her head. I thought she looked like a witch.

"If it's gold," she said, "I'll buy a living-waggon and go on the road. And I'm having it all, except perhaps two pieces for you, Ham. If those friends of yours try to take any I'll claw them till they howl like dogs. You don't know what I can do!"

"They'll not take your gold," I said; and we started out, but when we met the others Molly started to scream and make a terrible shindy. That was because there were six of them, Mr. Ahrman, Mr. Mertoun, the mad doctor, and three others. One of them I'd seen somewhere before, though I couldn't just mind his face. Luckily we were in the middle of the moor and there was nobody to hear Molly yelling with rage. She thought all six of them had come to do her out of her treasure, and it was all we could do to make her believe that they'd only come to dig. So in the end there were eight of us, and we went up to the ruin in twos and threes, as stealthy as weasels.

I went just behind Mr. Ahrman and Mr. Mertoun, carrying the spades.

"You're so thorough, Ahrman," Mr. Mertoun was saying. "Of course I commend the virtue, but I've hardly seen you to speak to for two days. Wednesday you go dashing off to Heaviburgh, or farther still—I don't know—and come back in a car at midnight; at two o'clock in the morning you leave the house again complete with ulster and shooting-stick . . . yes, I saw you, though you thought you were very clever! Back some time after dawn; Thursday morning a car drives up to fetch Mr. Ahrman; off you go; back last night at supper-time, not to talk or be decently sociable but to spend the whole night writing letters. You are the limit! I thought you'd given up business for the duration of this trip?"

"The trouble is," said Mr. Ahrman, "that business won't give me up. Yes, I have been busy the last two days. But why discuss it now? Heavens, man! Get yourself into the mood for treasure-hunting, can't you?"

"I don't give a damn for the treasure," Mr. Mertoun said, "but I'd give my ears to see the Roman soldier. . . . By Jove, Ahrman, look there!"

"What is it?"

"The cliff-edge, and the beam from the lighthouse. Just as it was on the night when I saw him, but then there was winter in the air and to-night I can smell the earthy scents of spring. I wonder if that makes any difference. The moon's rising too. Curse that gipsy woman and her spells, if they're keeping him away! I could almost believe . . . I say, we're getting close." We were on the slope of the hill and the ruin crouched above us like a black beast. Mr. Mertoun stopped and looked down below, and there lay the Barrs' big house, all in darkness and sharp against the sky.

"Look!" said Mr. Mertoun. "Poor old Charlie's prison. All I'm out for is the satisfaction of telling him that he's free at last. I'd

like to have told him what we're after to-night, but it wouldn't do.
It might raise his hopes, only to end in something worse for him.
If he were with us to-night I'd be feeling a good deal more scared
than I actually am."

"That's what I told you," said Mr. Ahrman, "when you suggested bringing him."

"But in spite of his letter," Mr. Mertoun said, "I shall make
another attempt to see him to-morrow."

"To-morrow!" Mr. Ahrman's voice made my hair stand on end,
the way he said that simple word. "Wait and see what to-night
brings."

"We're in for it," I thought. "There'll be dead men on the heath
before morning."

They all had electric torches but Molly and me, and when we
got to the top of the hill those little lights danced out and around
like corpse-lights in a graveyard, flashing on the old grey stones
and the tallest nettles I ever saw. Witch-nettles, Molly said they
were. She was shivering like with ague, and I saw her fingers were
crossed and she was saying her spells already.

"Don't!" I said. "Save them up, or they'll be no good when he
comes."

"They're good spells," she muttered.

"They'll have lost their power," I said, but she went on hugging
herself and muttering, and the moon slowly climbed up the sky,
paling out the stars and making the blackness blacker and the whiteness bright like silver. I could hear the roar of the sea beyond, and
the wind hooting along the shore and rustling through the heath.

"Come in! Come in!" said Mr. Ahrman, taking the lead. "Don't
hang back. There's nothing here but . . . well, nothing. Look for
yourselves."

"Civilization!" said Mr. Mertoun. "Step right back into the
lost ages. The nettles that Adam planted, that stung Eve's white
shoulder."

We were inside the round tower, and it was like being at the
bottom of a pit. The entrance was all broken down and gaped
open, and we had to climb over the fallen stones to go in. The walls
were crumbled too in places, but when they were whole they must

have stood thirty feet high. In the chinks, under the flash of the torches we could see the tight-curled roots of ferns, and a hazel-bush was sprouting from a gaping, earthy crack. It must have been full twenty feet across the floor of the place, not that any one of us could see the floor, if it was paved or just bare earth, for the weeds and nettles that covered it were like giants, and the dead growth of hundreds of years had made a tangled carpet underfoot.

The torches went flashing round and my head began to swim with the strangeness of it all. This was the place that as boys we'd dared one another to go to, and not one of us had ever dared. You see, it wasn't only our own fears, it was the tales our grandfathers told. I glanced at Molly and she looked ready to fly, although she'd got seven men with her.

Suddenly Mr. Mertoun said: "Do you remember that night at the Club, Ahrman? When you . . . when I——"

"When you smashed the wireless?" Mr. Ahrman said.

"Since you put it so tactfully—yes. The fellow who spoke was describing an excavation. He said that they dug and discovered a heap of relics of the Celtic age, ornaments and weapons and such things, so it's a fact that they do exist. It really looks as though this place had never received the attentions of the antiquarians. Has there ever been any digging here?" he added, looking at me.

"Digging!" I said. "Digging, did you say? There's never been but two pair of feet set down in this place since the day them that built it left it, and one was Jamesie Blaik's, and the other belonged to the devil himself, the one that kills, the one that Mr. Ahrman calls the Roman soldier."

Molly overheard me, and she let out a queer sort of moan, and even the men who'd come to dig, who were handling the spades I'd brought and flashing their torches, didn't seem to like it. Then Molly began to talk a lot of gibberish like nothing I'd ever heard in my life, and the sound of it in that evil place, with the high walls and the cold moon sneaking above, was enough to set anybody's hair on end.

"We must get to work," said Mr. Ahrman. "You two men take two of the spades, and you the other, Hamleth. We others can hold the torches for you."

"Where do we begin, sir?" one of the men said.

"Ah, wait a minute . . ."

But just then Molly interrupted. If they'd known her as well as I do, they'd have known that Molly Blaik would never keep herself quiet long, especially if she thought she wasn't getting her rights. I think in the back of her mind was the idea that this was her affair and Mr. Ahrman was taking too much on himself in giving orders. So she said: "Wait a minute. I'll tell you where to dig."

Mr. Ahrman looked round at her, puzzled, I suppose wondering if she really did know anything.

"Last night," she said, "I had a dream, and Blaik came to me all dressed in black and he said that nobody was to touch his treasure but me. And he showed me this place, with the nettles and the boulders and all, and he said that I was to dig . . . there!" Her finger shot out and pointed to a place.

"Oh, come!" said Mr. Ahrman. "We can't dig on the evidence of a dream. We must sound the ground."

"You'll dig where I say," said Molly, "or I'll scream till I wake the big house and the village too. They can hear me two miles away when I scream."

Mr. Ahrman tried to pacify her, but it was no good and she screamed. Two miles away! They must have heard in South Shields and all down the Tyne. But one scream was enough, and Mr. Ahrman gave in and told the men to dig.

So they dug, and I dug, and I was so excited I could feel in my bones I was going to turn something up in a minute, gold or diamonds or dead men's bones; but the minutes went by and we didn't find anything. Molly had told us wrong; if there was a place this wasn't it.

"Go on!" she kept saying greedily, "Go on!"

Mr. Ahrman looked annoyed, standing there smoking his pipe. He never said a word.

After a bit I said: "It's no good, Molly. The treasure isn't here. I've got it down to solid rock." And in a minute the other two men agreed with me. So Molly saw it wasn't any good, and as she was greedy to get the treasure she said: "Stop then, and try somewhere else."

Mr. Ahrman turned away and began walking round the walls, striking them and beating the weeds and nettles, and at last he came to a place where there weren't any weeds and nettles, and there he stood still, looking down. Then he called: "Mertoun!"

Mr. Mertoun went over to him, and I went too, because I pretended to myself that I'd heard him call Hamleth.

"Do you remember," Mr. Ahrman was saying, "that in the edifying discourse to which you referred a few minutes ago, we learned—unless I'm very much mistaken—that the relics discovered by our friend who spoke on the radio were found in an underground chamber, below the level of the broch. Well, why not here? And since you ask me so nicely, what do you think of this for the place?"

As I said before, where he was standing there was no undergrowth, only a lot of big, scattered stones, fallen from the broken wall above.

"Supposing," said Ahrman, "there was the entrance to an underground cache, under the stones?"

Mr. Mertoun went down on his knees and rolled a couple of the big stones over.

"Look!" he said excitedly.

"What?"

"These stones I've just moved . . . the grass was green *underneath* them!"

"And what does that mean, Sherlock?"

"I don't know!"

"It means," said Mr. Ahrman, "that they've been moved from their original position, and recently. Quite right, friend, and I moved them."

"You? I didn't see you."

"I moved them on Wednesday night," said Mr. Ahrman, "when you saw me go out at two o'clock in the morning. But don't tell anybody."

Mr. Mertoun was dumbfounded. So was I.

"What!" Mr. Mertoun said. "You came here on Wednesday night, alone?"

"Sure."

"But . . . good lord!"

"I had an automatic."

"Why did you do it?"

"Wanted to have a look round by myself before the circus came."

"You might have brought me!"

"A look round by myself, I said. . . . Somebody's coming."

It was me moving in the shadow that hid me, so when I knew I was seen I came out into the ring of torchlight.

"Are we going to dig here, Mr. Ahrman?" I said.

"We are," he said. "Here—give me your spade, and you get one from the other men. Mertoun, call the others and tell them I want all these stones rolled away to the other side, every one, well out of the way."

So they did that and it took quite a while, but when it was done the bare ground was revealed, and the round white beams of the torches drew together and they all poured down their circle of blazing white light on one place, where the earth had been loosened and trampled down.

"Now, Hamleth!" said Mr. Ahrman; and he and I put our spades to it with one great heave of earth.

Down . . . down . . . not two feet, and my spade struck something hard, and I gave a kind of shout that must have sounded queer, as if I were being strangled. So we turned all the earth away, and it wasn't an underground chamber, it was a box; a blackened box made of I don't know what—wood or steel—with iron bands. When we had it free it must have been four feet by two, a great hulking thing.

"Smash it open!" said Mr. Ahrman, and I did. The first thing that we saw was a flash of scarlet, and evil it looked, winking up at the white light of the torches. I wouldn't have touched it for a hundred pounds, but Mr. Ahrman stooped down and lifted it up, and there it was, stained and draggled and tattered, the tunic of a Roman soldier.

Molly gave a little cry and fell down all in a heap. She never said another word about treasure. I found myself holding my head with both hands. It was all there—the battered breast-plate, the sandals, the helmet. . . .

Mr. Mertoun's face was as white as a sheet.

"It is! It is!" he gasped. "The twisted neck-guard, bent from a blow. I saw it that night . . ."

"What is all this? Who are you?" a voice cracked out.

We all whirled round, and in the broken doorway there stood a man, a furiously angry man with bare head and unshaven chin, a pistol in one hand and a torch in the other.

"Charlie!" cried Mr. Mertoun.

"Who's that? . . . Oh, Mertoun, it's you! You gave me a nasty turn. I saw lights moving up here, and I couldn't imagine what on earth was happening."

"So you came up to see? By Jove, Charlie, I admire your pluck."

"Of course I came to see. I was ready to shoot too. But what are you doing? Why, there are dozens of you!"

Mr. Ahrman stepped forward. "Mr. Barr, I believe? Well, we're trespassing, Mr. Barr, but I believe this isn't your land? No? That's good; it spares us a profound apology. And we've just made the discovery of a lifetime."

"What's that?"

Mr. Ahrman held up a scarlet rag and a battered helmet of tarnished brass.

"Those? You never found them here? . . . But, by Jupiter, they must be at least fifteen hundred years old!"

The mad doctor and I were still kneeling by the smashed box, and suddenly he pushed his hand down into it. "There's something else here," he whispered to me. "Ah!" He shouted it. Everybody turned to see.

The mad doctor was holding up something that I couldn't account for; it looked like a veil of grey gauze, but he shook it in front of his own puzzled eyes, and what do you think fell out of its folds? Why, the stub-end of a fat, pale-brown cigarette.

"Not quite so old as that!" I heard Mr. Ahrman's voice ring out, and suddenly all the men in the enclosure seemed to rush together and there was a crash and a thud, and a torch whizzed through the air like a comet and narrowly missed the mad doctor's head.

I slipped away into the shadows until I heard what I was waiting to hear . . . his voice again.

"Charles Barr," he said, "I am Inspector Ahrman of New Scotland Yard, and I have with me the district Superintendent of Police and two constables. I hold a warrant for your arrest on a charge of murdering Ian Barr and James Blaik, and I warn you that anything you say may be used as evidence against you."

I didn't wait to hear another word; afterwards I was sorry for anything I might have missed, but at the time I was in a hurry to get home.

I ran nearly all of that nine miles. When I got to the farm dawn had broken and its pink fingers were trailing through the eastern sky. The farm was just waking, and Winifred stood watching for me at the yard gate.

I ran right up to her and looked her in the face.

I said to her: "They've got that devil."

"Who have?" she said.

"The police," I said.

"Thank God," was all she said. And then she began to cry.

Here ends the diary of Hamleth Goff.

PART III

AHRMAN'S REPORT

I

THE trial of Charles Barr, *alias* Chippy Barron, *alias* Doctor Gladius, lasted for eight days and occupied the headlines of both London and New York newspapers; though the greater sensation was probably apparent in New York, where Doctor Gladius, the psycho-analyst, had conducted his fashionable practice. The prosecution brought many witnesses across the Atlantic to identify the accused and to give evidence of the nature of his activities in the States. Among them, curiously enough, was a Texas Ranger called Phillips who held a nine-year-old warrant for the arrest of one Chippy Barron on a charge of robbery and murder at Galveston, Texas, in 1922. Phillips had long ago given up hope of ever discovering his man and was emphatic in his identification of the accused. He even went so far as to talk loudly of extradition so that Texas might have the honour of dispatching its own miscreant, but this was out of the question.

The New York witnesses included men and women well known in business and society, so well known that for their own sakes their names were suppressed to the newspaper-reading public.

Doctor Gladius had practised in New York for about four years, from 1926 to 1930. He had been all the rage in his day, a society craze. His luxurious apartment on Riverside Drive had contained silver-framed photographs of his distinguished clients; his limousine was a gift from the van B—— family, which was among the first ten of New York's four hundred. The income of Doctor Gladius at the height of his fame was estimated at something like twenty-five thousand dollars, and where it went to nobody knew, except that when he finally disappeared from Riverside Drive he left behind him nothing but debts, and had he remained he would have found himself in a very tight position indeed. Doctor Gladius, in fact, got away while the going was good.

II

The full story of his career emerged like the picture on a jig-saw puzzle.

His father, Roland Barr, was an Englishman; his mother came from Milwaukee and had Indian blood; in fact, her father was said to be a full-blooded Sioux. I say, said to be, for this was not proved. The son, Charles Barr, was brought up, as you might say, all over the place, his father having independent means and a roving disposition. His education was comprehensive, if unconventional, and at eighteen he had half a dozen completely different handwritings of which he was master, and, what is noteworthy, three different voices. Displaying this last trick of his, he would stand behind a screen and carry on a conversation between three men, so flawlessly that even a critical listener could not catch him tripping. As a young man he left home to go on the stage. His father died; his mother married again; Charles Barr was no more, and a certain Chippy Barron appeared in Galveston, Texas, in a Stetson hat, with his pockets full of money.

Mr. Barron made a good living in—or I should say, out of—Galveston, until some years later when he went too far. He broke into a ranch-house some few miles out of town on the night after a big deal in stock had taken place, opened a safe containing several thousand dollars in bills, was surprised and recognized by two occupants of the house, fought, shot and mortally wounded one of them, and escaped, never to be seen again—not as Chippy Barron, anyway.

I don't think he was ever cut out for burglary or violence. His brain was better than his hands, and he realized it. He was capable of subtler methods, capable of commercializing his wits and talents.

A few years went by; and Doctor Gladius dawned upon New York. The years had doubtless been spent in preparation for that dawning. To outward appearance his profession was harmless enough and even praiseworthy. He undertook to cure all the neuroses and phobias induced by the hot-speed living of a hectic city. At a price, of course. He had the sense to know that cheapness is never fashionable, and that a twenty-dollar fee for a consultation would ensure him the very best clients and plenty of them. Further treatments might run you into the hundreds or possibly thousands of dollars. Stories came out and ran round the town. A Jewish banker's wife, worn out with maintaining her position as the best-dressed woman on Long Island, became a victim of persecution mania. A guilty conscience, probably. Doctor Gladius held her fat hand and cured her in six visits. He charged her a thousand dollars, and she continued her visits from time to time at the same rate of fee, and sent all her friends.

The breaking of Miss Victorine M——'s engagement "by mutual consent" caused a nine days' wonder. Miss M——, having eaten nothing during this period, was taken by her mother and two chauffeurs to Doctor Gladius's exquisite reception-room, where she confessed that she had been jilted in favour of an English peer's daughter, just over on a visit. She emerged an hour later strangely radiant, and left next day for Europe, where three months afterwards she was married to a Balkan prince. She then confessed that Doctor Gladius had prophesied this pleasant eventuality, but withheld details. For the next six weeks the apartment on Riverside Drive was besieged by society buds, all clamouring for Balkan princes. They didn't get them, though they paid in hundreds of dollars and confessed to having been thrilled by the processes of the consulting-room. Hundreds of business men were rejuvenated and vowed that, queerly enough, their businesses looked up from the day they went to Doctor Gladius; hundreds of society women were restored from their boredom, languor, and neurasthenia to plunge again into the whirl of social triumphs.

What was the secret of it all? Of course it was hypnotism at its most subtle and powerful. Literal hypnotism with no frills. On that point a great deal of the evidence at the trial turned. Of course the great point of the defence was to deny *in toto* that the accused had ever practised, in fact had any knowledge whatever of, hypnotism. Was incapable of hypnotizing a rabbit; had never tried to hypnotize so much as a rabbit, and would have no notion as to how to go about the process did he so desire. What did he do with his clients? Held their hands, gazed into their eyes, and crooned in a monotonous, soothing voice about pleasant, vague matters. The room was just right. Silver walls and ceiling; indirect lighting, amber and subdued; a black carpet; a bowl of white orchids fresh each day, in and out of season; great chairs, soft as sinking into a cloud; a ball of crystal held in the silver hands of a classic statuette. Simple applied psychology, said the defence. Ha ha, said the prosecution; gazed into their eyes, did he? Call Mr. Meakin of Des Moines, Iowa. And Mr. Meakin admitted that he had once run a School of Necromancy—what a title!—and taught heaven knows what queer arts, chiefly to actors who wished to tour the States under the title of Professor Knebiolski or The Western Wizard. He identified the accused as one of his most proficient pupils between the years 1924 and '26. Accused had afterwards gone to New York and practised under the name of Doctor Gladius. Was accused capable of hypnotism? Capable! Why that fellow could have hypnotized a deaf-and-dumb cow-puncher two hundred miles away so that he couldn't get down off his horse until he was released from the control.

Defence tried hard to discredit this witness and stuck to its former position; in fact, Barr's line throughout was total and absolute denial of all the charges brought against him.

As I said some time ago, though Doctor Gladius was minting money he was spending a good deal more than he made; in fact, his position promised to be nasty. It was also rumoured that the new District Attorney of New York County had an eye on such practices as his own; not that he was in any way suspect, but all the same he had to consider the future.

Barr had always been interested in his English father's family history and was well up in its details. He confided to one of his clients, an elderly man-about-town, that his father's family, consisting of three bachelor uncles, owned an estate in England and a fortune of several million dollars. He was the only child of his father and therefore heir-presumptive to this richness, though the bachelor uncles were quite unaware of his existence and therefore capable of leaving the lot to charity. What ought Barr—or rather, Doctor Gladius—to do? The elderly man-about-town client thought that under the circumstances he personally would write. So Charlie Barr wrote, just a nice, simple, friendly letter from a long-lost nephew, and back came a very cordial and gratifying answer from the three elderly Barrs in England suggesting that their brother's son whom they had never seen should come over on a visit. Charlie declined. The idea didn't appeal to him. A few months later he was informed of the death of his Uncle Bourdon, the eldest of the three bachelors. "Uncle Bourdon is dead," a letter informed him. "You will some day be heir to our house and estate. Won't you come over and make your home here?"

"It'll be a long time to wait!" thought Doctor Gladius. "They may live twenty years yet." And I suppose at once came the horrid thought—need they?

So he realized his dwindling funds, buried Doctor Gladius in a single night, and slipped away to England to see for himself. Being an opportunist he had no plans, and at first the outlook in that desolate spot would seem bad—until he stumbled upon the legend of the Roman ghost and saw how it could be worked up into a monstrous fraud. It was so essentially the material most suitable for his peculiar talents.

He would begin cautiously, gently reviving the legend, keeping it alive, inducing people to talk, with understanding of a village's powers of repetition and exaggeration.

Then the spirit in the house. First, things moved out of place, with infinite caution and patient persistence until somebody begins to notice and the servants talk and it gets to the ears of the masters. Easy then to become more daring, run downstairs one night and pop a hat from the hall into a kitchen saucepan. The poltergeist has arrived. And later still a convenient thunderstorm gives him the opportunity to play that trick with the marmalade and convince everybody of supernatural activities. Meanwhile he is the dutiful nephew, keeping himself to himself on the pretext of having much writing to do, amusing himself with frequent holidays. Being canny—as the local people say—with their money, his uncles had put him upon an allowance which they considered sufficient for a young man; hence more grounds for resentment when he thought of the fortune which was piling up and which he might never touch until he was too old to enjoy it.

The stone. That was a clever touch. One day he confesses to having heard the legend of the stone, and would like to see for himself. His old uncles take him down to the cellar; the stone is uncovered. Why, what is this? The inscription is legible, with the aid of a magnifying-glass! (He had been careful not to overdo it. A sharp penknife and some earth rubbed well in.) In the credulity of poor Ingram, the doctor, he finds an unconscious ally, and he trades on the fact.

The haunted broch is his greatest find; an inviolable sanctuary. His next step is to buy the Roman dress and armour, easily obtained from a theatrical costumier in Edinburgh. (The tradesman was found by the prosecution and remembered the sale, but was unable to remember the purchaser well enough to identify him with the accused, or to identify positively the armour which was found buried in the broch, so this evidence was not entirely satisfactory. Here again Barr, through his Counsel, denied all knowledge of the costume.)

As the foggy winter nights come on, Charlie probably tries out his masquerade, a scarf of grey gauze obscuring his features. No one sees him stalking the moors. A born gambler, he has to stake everything sooner or later, so he resolves to plunge at once. A struggle on the cliff, and all is over with Uncle Ian. Complete success. The sandal-print has incriminated not a man but a ghost. One step nearer the fortune, and now he must be prepared for another long wait before tackling Uncle Germain, ill upstairs with a nurse in attendance.

Well, of course, as everyone knows by now, that nurse was the snag. Nobody got within twenty yards of Colonel Barr, and the nephew fumed in vain. He couldn't protest too much. The Colonel was saved from his brother's fate by the pig-headed devotion of his nurse.

Charlie's undoing was the coming of two not very clever people to the house, Winifred Goff, the nurse, and Mertoun, the "glorified auctioneer," as he called himself; at least I'll take back the "not very clever" with regard to the nurse. She may not have been an intellectual, but she was one of the cleverest women I ever came across in my career, and as a strategist I class her with Hannibal. More of her in due course.

Charlie's fraud was a masterpiece, a superb piece of acting from beginning to end. He had himself well in hand, he never hurried, he never went too far. I can't see that he made a single error, unless you account the insulting of my own intelligence, which he couldn't have been expected to foresee.

Of course there were unfortunate happenings upon which he hadn't counted, the chief of which was the obstinate temerity of the shepherd Blaik. Blaik was probably only the second man within a hundred years who set foot among the nettles of the eerie ruin on the hill; the first was Charlie himself. It was a nasty situation for Charlie. Even if Blaik should not discover the secret cache with its hidden trappings, the fact that one villager could visit the broch unscathed would end in the quashing of that superstition and the entry of many other people. And it was much too early for Gracchus to disappear altogether!

It is pretty certain now, however, that Blaik was inquisitive and made the discovery which Barr dreaded. Being shrewder than most of his class, the shepherd didn't run to the village crying, "Look what I've found!" Instead of that he waylaid Charlie and tried to make a bargain, but Charlie had had experience and knew that the only way to deal with a blackmailer is to silence him. Blaik told his wife that he'd found a gold-mine. He went out that night in the darkness to meet Charlie Barr, and instead he met the Roman ghost. He had overrated his own shrewdness. Though he didn't know it, that was Barr's last crime. His luck—if you can use the word luck in connection with the hitherto uninterrupted success of a clever villain—was already on the wane. The disappearance of his uncle, Colonel Germain Barr, left him in the dark without a plan. He waited for something to break, and he waited just a little too long.

As I said, the trial lasted eight days; Barr was found guilty on all charges, and condemned to death. His Counsel tried to get him to appeal on the grounds of insanity, which would have had a good chance of proof. Barr scorned the very idea.

III

The two most interesting witnesses were Mertoun and Miss Goff. Mertoun's evidence covered most of the ground of the story which he told me at the National Progress Club one night in February. I have that story now in manuscript, and I have made several notes upon it which may be of interest to those who have followed the narrative without completely understanding the implications of the various incidents.

To begin with the arrival of Mertoun at The Broch, in itself an unwelcome interference with Barr's plans; but understanding it to be his uncle's wish he could not complain. He would make the best of the visitor for a day or two, and of course nothing out of the ordinary should happen while Mertoun was in the house. What kind of man would Mertoun be? He proved to be affable, and later, credulous. Barr, accustomed to summing up men, took the measure of this one almost on sight.

Mertoun complained that on his first entry into the house he was conscious of peculiar mental distress, as though something were wrong. I account for this by the fact that though he emphatically denies the suggestion, he was acutely sensitive to atmosphere. There was something wrong with the house; had been for months, and Mertoun sensed it.

Barr, of course, hoped to get rid of him soon; within a couple of days. Miss Goff, dexterously weaving her plot—the plot and counter-plot at this point are very intriguing to the observer of the game—Miss Goff had planned otherwise. She invented the job of cataloguing the library, and Barr couldn't protest or show any desire to interfere with his uncle's plans, being so solicitous for the old man's health as he must always appear to be.

Mertoun stayed; and Mertoun had already got the creeps and

learned that there was a ghost story connected with the house. He took the story to Charlie, and Charlie realized that the surface of the lake was stirred and he must be very careful. Now notice how cleverly he encouraged Mertoun's suspicions with frankness and good humour, leading the other man on, preparing him for anything. Inwardly I'm sure he cursed the obstinacy of Mertoun, who would not let the subject alone. The ghost had a fascination for the visitor, and at last Barr decided to impress Mertoun and with the same stroke revive the village rumours of a malignant doom for the Barr family. A brilliant stroke. The slashing of the family portrait. Mertoun fell for it as the salmon for the hook.

Now for an important point, the hypnotizing of Mertoun. This was literally carried out, and accounts for his periodical fits of illness. It was good practice for Barr and he had an easy subject. Barr had my friend so completely under a spell that he could influence all his thoughts and actions. And yet when in one of their talks Mertoun mentions hypnotism, notice how neatly Barr discredits it. The cleverness of all that man's lying was that it contained a little truth. The hypnotic influence was of course most apparent on the night of the séance when Barr made it impossible for Mertoun to remove the Roman sword from the wall. More of that later.

The dices were certainly loaded against Barr from the time that Mertoun entered the house. Instead of being able to let Gracchus sleep for a fortnight he found himself compelled to build up a tremendous structure of deception to meet the demands of circumstance. Mertoun's chance visit to Doctor Ingram, a firm believer in all spirits, including that of the Roman soldier, led to the emergence of the whole of the ghost story. Mertoun was thrilled and came home full of it. Notice Barr's composure even after this revealing visit to Ingram. Events have compelled him to talk about the ghost, and since he is so compelled he will do it frankly. No display of anger or resentment. It is a masterpiece of self-control, and yet in one sentence of that ensuing conversation in the library Barr did reveal himself when he said, "I might have guessed you couldn't come to this cursed place without getting an inkling." That whole scene, with Charlie's dramatic outbursts, was a marvellous piece of acting.

That night he went to the cellar and worked on the stone for Mertoun's edification. He knew the story would go round the village, which was all to the good. Just another instance of how he turned everything to his own ends, including the discovery of the Society of Antiquaries.

Then the séance. His first impulse was to refuse flatly. During the night he saw the thing in another light; the light of a marvellous opportunity. A séance presented no difficulties to him; he was on his own ground, a master of his profession, and a match for any hired medium. So he proved to be. The tricks were easy and never overdone. The wretched medium was in the grip of a personality of tremendous power. The voice of Gracchus, the crashes, the hurling of the sword, were nothing to a man of Barr's accomplishments. Mertoun, you remember, tried to withdraw the sword and couldn't; Barr did it with ease, tossed it into a drawer, and during the night came down to retrieve it and hide it in a suitable place.

But during all this time Barr had his bad moments. He was not made of iron, and the strain of constant alertness, the planning of perfect detail, had their effect on him. He was not fooling children, after all, but intelligent men, and one slip would have finished it all. Mertoun sometimes found him depressed and morose. On the morning after the séance, Mertoun says, he was "haggard, chilled, and tight-lipped."

Now the Blaik affair. Mertoun administered the first shock, and a shock it was. A man, a shepherd, was using the haunted broch as a sheepfold, defying the superstition upon which Barr depended for his protection. But see how subtly Barr spread the prophecies that Blaik would come to a bad end. He was never too badly shaken to think six moves ahead; not that he had any thought at the time of removing Blaik, but he must prepare for eventualities. I imagine that he watched Blaik carefully, slipping up to the ruin at the first opportunity to find out if his secret was safe. It wasn't. Blaik had been nosing about, and Blaik was waiting for this very visit. He thought he had Barr on toast. How much for the secret? Go away, Barr told him, and don't tell anyone, and to-morrow night I'll meet you with a hundred pounds.

The hour was well chosen, the place, and the night. Mertoun was out somewhere. The moor was dark, foggy, and utterly deserted, and the Gracchus story was rife. Barr slipped out, dressed in the Roman's armour, tied the gauze veil across his face, and waited for the shepherd. It only took a minute. He rose, stretched himself, and made off up the heathery hill to the broch, stripped off the trappings, and was back in his own study in a quarter of an hour without anyone having seen him go out or come in.

Later he deemed it wise to go down to the library for a friendly chat with the visitor whose time was—fortunately—growing short. Another day would see the end of this wretched Mertoun.

Oh, this thrice-wretched Mertoun! Think of it . . . picture the scene. Mertoun all agog. What is he saying? "I've seen him. I've seen the Roman ghost!" And crash on the floor went the cigarette-case from Barr's nerveless hands; the first time he ever lost himself. Seen him! Mertoun had seen him. Where? And doing what?

Mertoun told the details, and Barr, cursing the lighthouse and the fool that invented such things, asked if the face had been recognizable. Oh no, it was a satisfyingly ghostly face. A face of smoke. Well and good. And the incident passed over. I believe that all these lucky escapes induced the idea in Barr that he could never fail. And yet the scene on the moor when Blaik's body was found, and the subsequent inquest, meant two or three days of maddening suspense and strain for the murderer, now becoming more and more entangled in the meshes of his own plot. His dismay was real enough; he wasn't acting all the time. I am thinking of the occasion when he and Mertoun met Ingram and Joan Hope, and Barr, as savage as a pestered animal, explained himself: "You see, I'm all in." So he was, and Mertoun merely misunderstood the reason for it.

The result of the inquest restored all Barr's confidence. The reaction was intoxicating; that was why he made up his mind to break down the opposition and get at his uncle—who you will recall had actually been out of the house a fortnight! This was a crucial moment, and I suppose that had not Miss Goff already taken her daring step nothing could have saved Colonel Barr. Charlie's *real* shock when he found the empty room and realized its significance required no histrionic aid. It was the first definite move in the game that had not been engineered by himself, and I can see him asking himself in a horrified way, what did it mean? No, there was no acting now—except the perfectly marvellous acting of the nurse. She was overwhelmed at the disappearance; she was speechless, terror-stricken, appalled—all in rapid succession. She thoroughly deceived Mertoun, and if she didn't deceive Barr she baffled his understanding. And then she crowned her little scene with the obvious explanation. Gracchus has taken him! What could Barr reply to that? Barr, who had openly credited the Roman soldier with far more mysterious and sinister deeds than the abduction of an elderly man under the noses of his household.

There was no reply. Barr must clear these people out of the house, and think. So the nurse went, and Mertoun went; and how many hours of fruitless thought were put into the problem of that disappearance can only be conjectured, never known. But I have gone beyond the scope of Mertoun as an eye-witness.

IV

Now for Miss Goff. This is the key to the whole position; as the reader has probably guessed long ago, Miss Goff *knew* from the beginning. And yet when I say knew, I make a stronger suggestion than was actually the case. Miss Goff knew merely by the evidence of her own wits, without having the slightest proof that would make her suspicion into an established fact. Miss Goff knew with a woman's utter unreasonableness, scorning logic and evidence, flying straight to the point indicated by her own intuitions, and sticking there.

She was primitive at heart, country born and bred, in spite of the veneer of her hospital training. She worshipped the Barr family; she hated Charlie at sight for a fortune hunter. She didn't believe in ghosts, much less the Roman one, and what she said in her heart was . . . so feminine that any woman will understand . . . "I hate him. Therefore he murdered his uncle and will murder his other uncle if he can. But he shan't."

The logic is marvellous!

She was a brave woman, fearless for her own safety, though she can't have realized until she got into the house what a difficult and dangerous job she had undertaken and what a clever villain she had pitted herself against. Because she outwitted him in the end I say she was a natural, born strategist. She came to The Broch immediately after the death of Ian Barr, scarcely daring to admit to herself that she knew how and why that death had been accomplished. The countryside was ringing with the story of the Roman ghost, a terror by night. "There is no Roman ghost," Winifred Goff told herself, quietly moving about the house. "Charlie Barr is the Roman ghost." She told it to herself again and again until she was convinced, though frightened of the conviction. She knew that she stood alone and was utterly without evidence. Many people asked at the trial, why didn't she confide her suspicions to someone? The answer was, partly that she was reserved and secretive by disposition, and partly that her own ignorance gave her an unholy dread of incurring grim penalties for slander and libel. It is not in any case prudent to bring a terrible accusation for which you have no proof against your neighbour; in Miss Goff's case there were other complications. She played a waiting game, and dared to put a ban on her patient's room. Later she learned the strong points of her position; how Charlie's very culpability made it impossible for him to defy her. One night, however, she woke in a panic, realizing how careless she had been. While she was in her room the Colonel was unguarded, and of course it would be during those night hours that the "ghost" would strike. The dreaded event would take place, and again she would be without proof for her intuitions. Next morning she moved her belongings into the tiny dressing-room which opened off her patient's room, and there in future she slept with the door and one eye open, and the Colonel's door bolted on the inside. She also took the precaution of greatly exaggerating the Colonel's illness; it was sufficient excuse for all this watchfulness.

She found the discarded letter to Mertoun in a blotter at a time when she was feeling particularly discouraged and afraid after weeks of anxious watching. As she said in her evidence, nothing had happened during those weeks. She had no complaint about Barr's behaviour, beyond the inexplicable feeling that he was only

waiting for her to relax her vigilance before adding another tragedy to the family record. She wondered how long this state of
affairs could last; how long she could keep up the pretence that the
Colonel was very ill indeed; what would happen if she were suddenly dismissed. All these forebodings, together with lack of sleep
and recreation, had reduced her to despair when she came across
that letter and thought it must have fallen straight from heaven.
She was convinced that Mertoun, her brother's hero, would save
the situation. Everyone knows how she arranged for his arrival,
was dismayed to find that he only intended to stay a couple of
days, and promptly invented an excuse for a stay of a fortnight.
Her first steps in conspiracy were so successful that she grew bold.
The removal of the Colonel by night to the lighthouse was a mag-
nificent step, planned and carried out by her, without a hitch. Once
he was out of danger and she had only an empty room to guard,
half her anxiety was gone, and the longer she could keep up the
deception the greater chance of his ultimate safety.

Well, there was Mertoun, and from Mertoun she expected great
things. She didn't know him well; her story was one that could not
be poured into a stranger's ear. He would probably have laughed
and left the house thinking her mad, or else warned Charlie Barr
that the nurse was dangerous. Her idea was that the story must
gradually dawn upon Mertoun—as in fact it did—and that as it
dawned his intelligence would, like hers, reject the idea of a ghost,
and aided by her suggestions come round to her own way of thinking. So she would gain a powerful ally who would not be ignorant
of the proper steps to take. She had not counted upon Barr's hypnotic power over Mertoun, or Mertoun's own readiness to accept
the supernatural. When she knew, she scorned him, which was
rather ruthless of her. Of course she was terribly disappointed, but
I don't think Mertoun was altogether to blame. Others may think
as they will.

Miss Goff was right in supposing that Mertoun's knowledge of
the ghost story would result in a few confirmatory parlour tricks by
Mr. Barr. She had by now become uncannily clever at foreseeing her
enemy's moves. But they were such deft moves; no clumsy mistake
for her to pounce upon. From then on, she and Charlie played a

kind of chess game, very exhilarating, I'm sure; and Miss Goff grew more and more daring in her finesse, until on the night that the Colonel's disappearance was discovered she brought out her trumps and took the first game of the rubber. No—the second, wasn't it? Yes; for Barr won the first, Miss Goff the second, and I the third. That's right. And as Miss Goff and I were playing together . . .

I learned that on a certain night not long after Mertoun's arrival Miss Goff, awake in her bed, heard stealthy footsteps—Charlie going downstairs. She guessed he was gone to set some scene, so when ten minutes later she heard him as stealthily return she gave him half an hour and slipped down to see what he had been up to. The slashed picture.

She thought, "I'll show this to Mertoun. It will open his eyes. Ghosts don't cut up canvas!"

She fetched Mertoun, and Mertoun showed her quite clearly that he was by now Charlie's victim instead of her ally. That was what she meant by saying that he had failed her in her test. After that, of course, she had no hopes from him. She went on bravely playing the game alone.

She even grew so bold as to throw defiant snippets of talk at Barr. After taking up the papers, for instance, to get the approval of the non-existent patient, she flung out at Barr, "Who knows from whose hand it will come?"

This was a deliberate challenge, and I consider that she was taking unnecessary risk in daring so much. Also after the séance— during which she had sat on the stairs, wondering how far Barr would dare to go—when Mertoun told her wonderingly that Gracchus had paid a visit; "Oh yes," she said coolly; "I thought he would." What did Barr make of these things?

Which brings us to the question of whether he ever suspected her of knowing more than she should. Personally I'm sure he didn't. He made the great mistake of underrating her intelligence. He disliked her and thought her stupid and purposely enigmatic; that was all. He did make one attempt to prejudice Mertoun against her—just a precautionary measure—when he cried impulsively on one occasion: "Mertoun, I don't trust that woman."

The killing of Blaik broke Miss Goff down; to her it was very dreadful, and all her fears were revived. It was as well that she then decided to get away. She could do nothing more. All that remained was to allow the discovery of the Colonel's empty room, and she decided that the next time Barr asked for admission he should have it. She would leave Fate to make the occasion and to direct her words. So the discovery was made and Miss Goff put up her wonderful bluff, with that simple argument which admitted of no discussion. Gracchus is out to destroy the Barrs; you have proved that for yourself; therefore he has taken the Colonel . . . and you can't question either that or the existence of Gracchus without getting yourself into a very nasty position, Mr. Charles Barr!

And with that she left the house.

With regard to her brother, young Hamleth, a lazy young rogue but likeable. He was the one person to whom Winifred had confided her secret suspicions. Even the father believed in the ghost story. Hamleth believed Winifred, simply because she said it was so, but he also possessed a strong vein of superstition which complicated his ideas on the subject. All the same, Barr was always "that fiend" in their secret conversations, and they both longed to see him brought to book. Thence their willingness to assist my inquisitive delvings into the subject of the "haunt" without having any idea of my official position. I suppose they thought me a Mertoun minus the Mertoun failings—which I haven't admitted to be failings at all. Well, I'm glad I didn't disappoint them.

Miss Goff in the witness-box was the coolest person I ever saw. Hamleth, of course, was not called. I never saw him after, and I hope he was properly grateful for the work I put in when suppressing the lighthouse story from the evidence in the case. It was my own case, luckily, and in the end I managed to work Thorlwick hard without any mention of the Strickan; which was a good thing for both Hamleth and his father. They had undoubtedly prevented murder, though they might have paid a heavy penalty for their ingenuity. The story of the Colonel's escape had no real bearing on the case, which was to prove the charges against Barr, and the incident was barely mentioned.

V

Now for my own part in the affair. How did I come into it at all? We must go back to the very beginning, when Mertoun first told me his unusual story in the Club. That story as told to me is probably still fresh in your mind. Just how did it strike you? Perhaps no two people alike.

When I was a very young man in the Metropolitan Police Force one of the things I was taught was to reject anything which insulted my intelligence.

I'm not going to say that a ghost story insults my intelligence; for that would be as bad as stating that supernatural phenomena are a farce, and I should have a hundred letters in the morning from a hundred estimable people telling me that though apparently a man I am really no better than a low form of pond life.

No. But what insults my intelligence is a ghost who hangs about and commits double murder. It can't be. I've met them before. So almost at the first I had to discredit that very plausible-sounding ghost—I was disappointed at having to do it—and to substitute the age-old question, *cui bono?*

Charlie Barr, everybody shouts. How easy. Well, let me say at once that I didn't jump straight on Charlie. Why should I? What was the matter with the Colonel, for instance, or even Ingram, or the man-servant M'Coul as a suspect?

First I concentrated on Ingram, as he seemed such a likely subject with his unbalanced mentality. It was the kind of thing that would appeal to a man like Ingram, to project himself into the personality of a legendary ghost, to dress up in the fantastic trappings of a Roman soldier and stride about the moors on dark nights, mad with power, until he actually came to believe himself a reincarnation of Gracchus. Brain-storms might account for the murders, completely forgotten after they were committed. I never thought him a conscious murderer. What washed Ingram out finally was the fact that he couldn't have been in the house and produced the phenomena, and since in any case there was no criminal intent on Ingram's part there was no question of an accomplice in the house.

I went to Somerset House to see how the Barr money was left. Ian Barr's will was produced. He had left over six hundred thousand, to his brother Germain Barr during Germain's lifetime, and afterwards to his nephew Charles Barr, of New York. I next turned my attention to old Germain, the shadowy Colonel Barr who played such a passive part in the story. I wondered if that passivity were part of the plot, whether seclusion in his room on the grounds of illness were a neat alibi for the Roman soldier. In that case, of course, the nurse would have to be an accomplice, and possibly the man M'Coul also.

Motive? The Colonel already had the house and all the money. Could it simply be abnormal greed and megalomania that had caused him to wipe out his brother, and was he now trying to get rid of the interloping nephew? It didn't seem to me a strong enough motive, though the means and opportunity were all right. I may say here, that whoever the murderer was it was plain from the first that the shepherd Blaik had been killed because he knew something he shouldn't. What that was I didn't attempt to guess at this stage.

If the Colonel were guilty, when and why had he staged his own disappearance? The motive for that baffled me. It was not as though any hint of discovery threatened him. There was no suspicion as far as I could see.

Could the man M'Coul alone be the malignant spirit of the Barr family? Fraud on such a grand scale seemed too much for a servant. There was lively imagination behind these crimes. Meanwhile I thought it would be interesting to know a little more about the American nephew and his past history, and a few cablegrams sped between my office and the Detective Bureau of the New York Police Department. What I asked for in the first case was information about a young man who wrote books on psychology and had probably practised recently in New York as a psycho-analyst— name, Charles Barr.

Answer came back that there was no such person known. I then asked if any such person of different name could be traced, who had left for England in the autumn of '29 or spring of '30. The answer was that Doctor Gladius fulfilled the conditions, age thirty-seven, tall, medium build, dark, scholarly appearance; had written two books privately published; practised as psycho-analyst on Riverside Drive; antecedents unknown; left New York to avoid bankruptcy during winter of '29-'30; said to have gone to join wealthy relatives in England. Suspected of doubtful practices, necromancy and hypnotism, by District Attorney, but no case made out.

Well, if that wasn't our friend Charles I was ready to eat my hat; and it was all very suggestive too. Hypnotism and necromancy were words lush with suggestion in this case. Again I cabled to New York for fullest details of the activities of "Doctor Gladius," and I received a comprehensive reply.

This was quite enough to send me north for a little fishing, while hiding the real purpose of the expedition from my companion, Mertoun. Charles Barr appeared to have had ample motive for descending upon his somewhat miserly old uncles, and means and opportunity for relieving them of their fortune before he was legitimately entitled to it. All that, of course, didn't make him the villain, but he was well worth watching.

By now I had a manuscript of Mertoun's story as he told it to me and as you have read it for yourselves. I read it carefully again, in the light of young Barr's presumed criminality, and at once light fell on what had been inexplicable. To a man capable of "hypnotism and necromancy"—oh, those marvellous words from across the sea—a masquerade on the lines of the Roman ghost would present no difficulties. It was easy to see also how Mertoun had been taken in. The more I read, the more I marvelled at the consummate artistry of Barr, the amazing skill of his plot. He never hurried his part or overplayed it. But this wasn't convicting him of the murders, or identifying him with the Roman ghost, which was practically the same thing. I should need something more tangible.

One of the first problems I set myself to solve was, what had actually happened to the Colonel? Where had he gone to? That disappearance had come as a real shock to Charlie. It was definitely *not* part of his plan. One piece of knowledge I shared with this simulator of ghostly visitants, and that was that the Roman was not to blame. Beyond that, like Charles, I was flummoxed. Two alternatives emerged from nights of thinking: either the Colonel had gone of his own accord, tired of his imprisonment, suspecting that some evil threatened him; or else the enigmatic Miss Goff had staged the affair. In any case, she would be an accessory to the escape.

I favoured the idea that it was all her doing; the Colonel had recently had a stroke, he would not be capable of much individual effort. Now what had she done with him?

She must have got him to some place not too far away, and she must have had outside help. But what help can a country nurse call upon, having neither money nor influence? Her own people. She had told Mertoun how they were all indebted to the Colonel. But who were Miss Goff's people, and where did they hide themselves?

I couldn't come to any definite conclusion until I made copious inquiries about Miss Goff and discovered that her father and brother were lighthouse-keepers, lived at Thorlwick, and had taken up occupation of the Strickan Light on the night of January 22nd. It would not take two strong men more than three-quarters of an hour to row to the lighthouse from the cove at the foot of the cliffs just beyond The Broch.

I went to Thorlwick and made cautious inquiries. The Goffs, father and son, had gone to take up duty at the proper time. The third man, Bell, had been ill and unable to go. Nobody seemed to know who had actually gone as third man. I went to see Bell on the pretence of getting him interested in a new kind of insurance. I led him round to his recent incapacity for work, but he was a mum fellow and I learned nothing. I then went on to discover the three men who had vacated the lighthouse for the Goffs' occupation. From them I learned, circuitously and with much expenditure of tobacco, that three men had relieved them and the third was an unknown man, said to be from Burnfirth. I left it at that, satisfied as to what had happened to the Colonel. Then came that interesting meeting with young Hamleth by the moorside. I thought I'd caught a Goff, though he deceived me for a day or two, and when I knew I was right I sprang the whole thing on him to his consternation.

Now for the closing scenes. I had two problems in my mind,

temporarily shelved but ready for future pondering. Where did Barr keep his stage-properties? And what was it that Blaik knew?

I came to two wrong conclusions. First, that Barr's cache was in his own study under lock and key; and second, that Blaik had seen the masquerader in full rig sneaking away from the house to make an appearance on the moor and impress Mertoun, had followed curiously, and met his end. Obviously death was the only answer to anyone who accosted the Roman ghost.

These theories may have been stupid, but for a long time they satisfied me.

I wanted to get my hands on that Roman costume, to examine it, and see if the neck-guard were twisted in the way that Mertoun had described. My only idea was for me and Mertoun to get access to the house, for Mertoun to engage Barr, and for me to make a bold attempt at a reconnaissance. Afterwards I was prepared if necessary to take my life in my hands and burgle the study, complete with outfit. I can't tell you in detail what an outfit I had with me, packed among my holiday luggage; but there was an up-to-date set of burglars' tools—red lamp, electric torch, rubber gloves, three cameras, enlarging apparatus, and stacks of chemicals. Mertoun would have swooned at the knowledge.

Mertoun was eager enough to see Barr, and if I hadn't discouraged him would have forced his way in and spoilt the whole thing. I could see I should have to work very slowly to get the man's confidence. Mertoun then wrote a letter, and when the answer came I waylaid it—Hamleth Goff has described this incident—and took care that no hands but mine should touch it. I hoped to get the impressions of two fingers and a thumb, but when I took the paper upstairs and dusted it I was disappointed. Even the fold had taken no impression. It was rough, matt paper and the fingers that used it had been perfectly dry.

I then went in for direct methods. I found the father of Gwennie, the housemaid at The Broch, a crude, grasping-eyed farmer—or rather crofter, for he worked the few acres unaided, and kept about a score of fowls and a vicious sow.

I said to him in the blunt way he understood: "Can your girl Gwennie keep her mouth shut?"

He said that Gwennie could do it as well as most people if the inducement were of the right kind. His actual words wouldn't bear reproduction, being both dialectical and objurgatory.

I said: "I want to see Gwennie next time she's home. If she agrees to do what I ask she shall have a pound in advance and so shall you. If she completes the job and *keeps her mouth shut*—that's the main thing—there's another pound each for you. What about it?"

He said: "Give us my pound now." I did. He said that Gwennie would be home for an hour or two the following evening, and she'd do whatever I wanted, and he'd see that she was as mum as the grave, and what about him taking care of Gwennie's pound too? I wouldn't agree to that.

The next night I went up and saw Gwennie. What I wanted was the glass from Barr's bathroom, after he'd used it for his teeth in the morning. Gwennie saw nothing queer in a request that was worth four pounds. She brought the glass the very next day—"and I gave it an extra good polish too!" she said proudly. I controlled a desire to flay her and pointed out—as I may say I had pointed out on the first occasion when the prospect of the reward had prevented her from listening to a word I was saying—that the glass must be in its original soiled condition, and that she must let it dry and wrap it with the utmost tenderness in a piece of tissue-paper or a duster.

She did it at last and got her money; so did the father. I left them scrapping over the division, not accepting equality of terms for the labour involved.

I got enlarged photographs of three perfect prints, thumb and two fingers of the right hand, and imperfect ones from the left hand, blurred I feared by Gwennie. But it was quite as good as I could hope for.

I then seriously applied myself to a plan for discovering the Roman's outfit.

It has been asked me, why, if Barr was so wary, did he not suspect the return of Mertoun with a stranger and take the precaution of destroying the evidences?

Partly because he had no real grounds for suspecting Mertoun and me. Again because the clothes were valuable to him and he would require them in the future, if and when the Colonel came back. This is the strongest reason; he would have to be at bay before he destroyed his stock-in-trade, and far from being at bay he wasn't even threatened, so far as he knew. Besides, it isn't an easy matter to get rid of a brass helmet and cuirass. Try it.

The return of Molly Blaik was a nasty twirl of Fortune's wheel for Charlie. As soon as Hamleth brought me the story of the "buried treasure in the broch," and how Blaik had held the secret of a "gold-mine" I saw light in the darkness, and suspected that the shepherd's "gold-mine" was actually a blackmailed goose that might be induced to lay golden eggs.

I wondered then how I could have been so criminally blind to the significance of a haunted tower in which no one would dream of setting foot. That would be a far better and more convenient cache— not to say dressing-room—than a study in the house. And of course Blaik had blundered in and found the actor's properties. . . .

That afternoon I went over to Heaviburgh, saw the Superintendent of Police, revived the evidence of the Blaik and Barr murders, and told him what I was on the track of. Was he ready to stand by?

He thought I was quite mad—with the north-country man's supreme contempt for London nit-wits—and told me in plain language that the Heaviburgh police could very well look after their own duties without any interference from long-eared London detectives. After that he said that when I'd found some decent evidence to put before him he might be persuaded to give me a hearing; and he condescended to tell me where the Chief Constable of the county lived.

That night when I thought Mertoun was asleep I armed myself with torch, automatic, pocket camera, digging tools, a suitcase full of stuff, and set out alone for the broch. I guessed that there wouldn't be much spadework; the things would have to be easily accessible. I screened my torch and had a good survey of the ground, finally seeing how easy it would be to remove a few stones, apparently naturally scattered, and make a shallow trough underneath. Some of the larger stones resisted me; I left them alone and concentrated on those which came readily. To a scrutinizing eye it was possible to see that these had been handled and overturned before.

At last I uncovered a patch of newly turned earth, trampled down. A few spadefuls uncovered the box which was made of oak, and I forced the lock with a jemmy and thrilled to behold my spoils. The helmet was my best find, for when I powdered it I saw perfect prints at the two sides, just where the wearer would grip it to lift it from his head. I took flashlight photographs there and then—and these, let me say at this point, I developed directly I got back to the farm, enlarged them, and found them identical with the prints on the tooth-glass.

I also took photographs of the helmet, back and front, showing the twisted neckguard, and of the breast-plate and sandals. I guessed the use for the veil, which I did not disturb, thereby missing Hamleth's own ridiculous discovery of the cigarette-stub caught in the clinging meshes of the gauze. Doubtless Charlie smoked during his long waits scores of cigarettes, and I consider that little accident of a stub which he thought he had tossed away a piece of sheer bad luck. But you try smoking with a gauze veil slipped down over your chest and you'll see how easily it could happen.

When I'd got my photographs and seen all I wanted I replaced everything with the utmost care and returned home. I knew I couldn't have been seen from the house because of the way I'd screened my lights. When we came afterwards in force, I let them play about like a school of glow-worms to their hearts' content. I knew it would fetch our man.

The next day I got a car and went off to the Chief Constable; we also got through to the Heaviburgh police, and obtained the magistrate's warrant; and I chose two men as well as the Superintendent to see the evidence and help me make the arrest.

The remainder of the story you know; Hamleth described it well. Barr went berserk when he knew he was captured, and we had all our work to get him away.

He got the best Counsel in England, Sir Ernest Boydell-Baynes, and sat like a statue throughout his trial. When sentence of death was pronounced he smiled. One of those stoics that you can't explain by ordinary standards, and a great scoundrel. To what do I ascribe his downfall? Not to any slips he made. Small circumstances, tiny chances, began to turn against him; some may like to say that it was right asserting itself at last against triumphant wrong.

However, speaking superficially, I do consider that it was the roughest luck on Barr that Mertoun should have had me for a friend and confidant. He might have told his story to any one of fifty other men who would have shrugged shoulders, said, "By Jove, old man, what an experience!" and forgotten all about it in twenty-four hours.

But fortunately for society these things do sometimes work out for the best, and I am convinced that some chance happenings are not chance happenings. . . .

It may be of interest to know that Mertoun and Miss Hope will be married this year when she comes of age. I think Mertoun has forgiven me for the shocking surprise I sprang upon him that night—it took him days to realize the truth—but I couldn't possibly have taken him into my confidence. His innocence was such a foil to my investigations. However, he has forgiven me, because I am invited to the wedding.

Ingram returned to London and was carried off by his friend, Joan's father, to Boston, where I have heard he is well on the way to complete recovery.

Colonel Barr returned with the utmost calm to his house and took up occupation again as though nothing had happened, with Miss Goff installed as housekeeper. As far as we know, he never discussed the story with anybody and didn't appear particularly interested in it. I have heard that he deeply resented the "laying" of the ghost which for a century had given distinction to his family record. I have no idea how he will leave his money, but I think not to the Society for Psychical Research. Mertoun called on him in the autumn—sheer curiosity to see the man for himself—and was dismayed to find the library in its old confusion. He didn't dare to show his disappointment, much less to ask for his cheque!

THE END

NEW AND FORTHCOMING TITLES FROM VALANCOURT BOOKS

R. C. Ashby (Ruby Ferguson)	He Arrived at Dusk
Frank Baker	The Birds
Walter Baxter	Look Down in Mercy
Charles Beaumont	The Hunger and Other Stories
David Benedictus	The Fourth of June
Paul Binding	Harmonica's Bridegroom
John Blackburn	A Scent of New-Mown Hay
	Broken Boy
	Blue Octavo
	The Flame and the Wind
	Nothing But the Night
	Bury Him Darkly
	The Household Traitors
	Our Lady of Pain
	The Face of the Lion
	The Cyclops Goblet
	A Beastly Business
Thomas Blackburn	The Feast of the Wolf
John Braine	Room at the Top
	The Vodi
Basil Copper	The Great White Space
	Necropolis
Hunter Davies	Body Charge
Jennifer Dawson	The Ha-Ha
Barry England	Figures in a Landscape
Ronald Fraser	Flower Phantoms
Stephen Gilbert	The Landslide
	Bombardier
	Monkeyface
	The Burnaby Experiments
	Ratman's Notebooks
Martyn Goff	The Plaster Fabric
	The Youngest Director
	Indecent Assault
Stephen Gregory	The Cormorant
Thomas Hinde	Mr. Nicholas
	The Day the Call Came

JOHN WAIN	Hurry on Down
	The Smaller Sky
HUGH WALPOLE	The Killer and the Slain
KEITH WATERHOUSE	There is a Happy Land
	Billy Liar
COLIN WILSON	Ritual in the Dark
	Man Without a Shadow
	The World of Violence
	The Philosopher's Stone
	The God of the Labyrinth

Selected Eighteenth and Nineteenth Century Classics

ANONYMOUS	Teleny
	The Sins of the Cities of the Plain
GRANT ALLEN	Miss Cayley's Adventures
JOANNA BAILLIE	Six Gothic Dramas
EATON STANNARD BARRETT	The Heroine
WILLIAM BECKFORD	Azemia
MARY ELIZABETH BRADDON	Thou Art the Man
JOHN BUCHAN	Sir Quixote of the Moors
HALL CAINE	The Manxman
MARIE CORELLI	The Sorrows of Satan
	Ziska
BARON CORVO	Stories Toto Told Me
	Hubert's Arthur
GABRIELE D'ANNUNZIO	The Intruder (L'innocente)
ARTHUR CONAN DOYLE	Round the Red Lamp
BARON DE LA MOTTE FOUQUÉ	The Magic Ring
H. RIDER HAGGARD	Nada the Lily
SHERIDAN LE FANU	Carmilla
M. G. LEWIS	The Monk
EDWARD BULWER LYTTON	Eugene Aram
FLORENCE MARRYAT	The Blood of the Vampire
RICHARD MARSH	The Beetle
BERTRAM MITFORD	Renshaw Fanning's Quest
JOHN MOORE	Zeluco
OUIDA	Under Two Flags
WALTER PATER	Marius the Epicurean
BRAM STOKER	The Lady of the Shroud

Lightning Source UK Ltd.
Milton Keynes UK
UKOW02f0055100315

247581UK00004B/266/P